Gangsta Luvin'

She Fell In Love With A Philly Goon

Slayed By:
Reds Johnson

This is a work of fiction. Names, characters, places, and incidents either are the product of the author's imagination or are used fictitiously, and any resemblance to actual persons, living or dead, business establishments, events, or locales are entirely coincidental.

Wahida Clark Presents Publishing
60 Evergreen Place
Suite 904A
East Orange, New Jersey 07018
1(866) 910-6920
www.wclarkpublishing.com

Library of Congress Cataloging-In-Publication Data:

Gangsta Luvin'
ISBN 978-1-947732-82-7 paperback
978-1-947732-83-4 ebook
978-1-947732-84-1 Hardback

LCCN: 2012450975
1. Gangsta 2. Love 3. Relationship 4. Family 5. Abuse 6. Sickness 7. Secrets 8. Friendships 9. Drama 10 Street life

Cover design and layout by Nuance Art, LLC
Book design by www.artdiggs.com
Printed in United States

Acknowledgements

Shout out to **God!** I had no idea I would get the opportunity to have this book, a book that was supposed to be self-published, published under Wahida Clark Presents. Lord, you continue to see the best in me. I've had so many ups and downs with my career. There have been so many times that I wanted to give up, but you continued to see me through. I'm forever grateful, thankful, and just so accepting of the blessings I've blocked for so long. All glory goes to you. 🖤

Shout out to my mother! My ridah, my mans one hunnid grand! My Light Bright. My right hand. My Bonnie, No Clyde! **Maria Ward**. Without you I don't know where I would be. Your FAITH in me kept me afloat. You are so beautiful and amazing, Mommie. I'm forever grateful to be blessed with a walking angel as a mother. Just like God, you saw the best in me even when I didn't see it in myself. You always told me, "Baby, your time is coming. Just pray and wait on it." I never had one hundred percent faith in it, but I kept going and never gave up. You told me that you had dreams of my career taking off, and me blowing up. You said one day I would no longer cry tears of pain, but tears of joy. Mommie, I love you, and no matter what direction my career goes, I will forever be grateful to have someone like you in my corner.

You stay ridin' with me through thick and thin. There's nothing no one could ever say that would make me doubt you in any way. I love the woman you were because you showed strength, you had hope and you had faith, and I love the woman you are now because you show courage! I love the woman you raised me to be, and I thank you for never giving up on me. Even though, at times, I gave you every reason to! There have been so many times I wanted to stop writing and give up on life, especially during my darkest days, but you always kept your foot on my neck, and I understand why. Your words were, "If you give up, they win, but if you keep going, you win." Mommie, your words of wisdom, motivation and inspiration will always be with me.

Thank you for EVERYTHING! Giving me life, love, care, strength, courage, nurturing, and the list goes on. But most of all, thank you for being my best friend, and thank you for being such a wonderful mother. Thank you for passing down the passion for writing, and the will to keep pushing even when I didn't want to. I love you, beautiful. Always and forever Queen Maria 💜 And to the readers, make sure yawl go purchase my mother's memoir *Truth Be Told: The Hidden Secrets!* It'll change your life!

LaQueisha Malone: Queen, thank you so much for being a wonderful mentor and friend. There are a lot of things that I would've never known when it comes to the literary world if it wasn't for you. I truly appreciate you sharing your knowledge with me. Everyone needs someone like you in their personal life and when it comes to their career. You are super positive, informative and your guidance can help so many succeed. Get yawl a LaQueisha, just not mine, lol. I love you! 💜

To the Queen of Street Lit, **Wahida Clark:** THANK YOU! For many years, I fought hard to get your attention. The moment I read Thug Matrimony I just knew I had to reach out to you. I did, and you responded. I remember back in 2012 I entered the Wahida Clark contest that Cash Money Content hosted. I won, and I couldn't believe it. I was going to get the chance to meet you in NYC, but the only problem was I didn't have a ride. I was crushed, and I cried for days. I went into a deep depression because I felt like I had missed my chance to meet you and show you my work. Even after, I still reached out to you from time to time. You responded each time and we always had small conversation.

I ended up winning another one of your contests, and once again I couldn't accept it. This time I didn't have a fax machine, lol. The struggle was real! I felt hopeless once again because it seemed as if my breakthrough was always stopped by the smallest things. Now, nine years later I am signed to you. I fought so hard for this; no one knows my struggle, and I'm not ashamed to share it because look where I'm at now! I didn't care if I bugged you. I wanted you to see my drive, determination, and hunger for success. Regardless of what happens, I'm so very thankful for the opportunity to have my name attached to yours.

Shout out to my Big Sister **Renae Johnson Aka Nae Nae**. I love you sis and thank you for all the love and support you've been showing me since our mother went to Party In Paradise. Your love and support means the world to me and it has helped me get through some of my darkest days. Last, but definitely not least.

My **Light bright**, my **babyzaddy/husband, Rayshon Farmer** aka **Blockboy** aka **Askari** aka **King of Philly Street-Lit.** Lol! You gon' crack up when you read this. But anyway, it's been such a tough road for us. The many ups and downs, trials & tribulations only made us stronger. Since 2015 we've been rockin' wit' each other, and here it is five years later and we still rockin' wit' one another. The continuous love, care and support you show and give means a lot. Thank you for being a shoulder whenever I need one to lean on and an ear whenever I need someone to talk to. Like I said before, what's understood definitely doesn't need to be explained. I got you, and you got us. We gon' continue to pray, grind and build this empire and make our umis proud. King and Queen status. I love you, forever and a day, Babyboy. To all the readers, make sure yawl go 1-click the *Blood Of A Boss* & *Shadows Of The Game* series! You won't regret it and that's a promise. 🤍

#IAmRedsJohnson

#ISlayBooks

To My Care Bears *Readers*

Everyone refers to me as the ratchet author because of my titles and covers. However, this book is very different from what I normally write. It takes place in an urban setting with urban families and urban language, but it touches base on a much deeper situation. I wanted to warn you all before you indulge in the pages of this book; it's not like what I normally write. What I mean by that is the crazy sex and fighting that normally goes on in my books, but it is indeed a page turner. I put my soul, blood, sweat, and tears in this book and I've never been prouder of myself!

Happy reading

Prologue

When Yoshi screamed into the phone and told him what was going on with his niece, Kick Down didn't say a word in response. Anger and frustration filled his body as his cellphone dropped to the floor of his girlfriend's apartment. Without saying a word, he grabbed his keys off the kitchen table.

"Baby, where you going?" she called out.

Kick Down didn't respond. He opened the front door with force, causing it to slam against the wall and put a decent size hole in it. He hopped off the porch and ran to the driver's side of his work van. He barely closed the door before he started it up and peeled off.

Bang! Bang!

Bang!

"I'ma kill that nigga! I swear I'ma kill him!" Kick Down screamed as he punched the steering wheel.

***

Onyae watched her mother pull her cell phone away from her ear without saying another word. When Onyae heard her mother say her uncle's name on the phone she knew all hell was about to break loose. She watched as her mother

1

walked out of the walk-in closet and hurried to put on some sneakers. Yoshi grabbed her metal bat just like the one Onyae had in her room.

"Let's go!" she yelled.

Onyae ran behind her mother. She had no time to put on any shoes, but she did have time to grab the metal bat that she kept behind her bedroom door. All she was worried about now was getting to NiNi's house because their uncle was about to set shit off, and NiNi's stepfather was closer to death than he would have liked to be.

She ran out of the house behind her mother and they hopped in her car. Yoshi started the car, put it in reverse and pulled out of the driveway so violently that Onyae's head jerked back. The drive from Yoshi's house to her sister's house was about three minutes away, and Kick Down lived about the same distance. Just as she suspected, by the time she pulled up, Kick Down was hopping out of his work van

Yoshi put her car in park and hopped out with Onyae right on her tail. Onyae was scared because the look in her uncle Kick Down's eyes looked like a lost soul. No words were said as they watched Kick Down run up the walkway and do what gave him his nickname back in the day.

Bang! Bang!

Bang!

Kick Down reared back and gave Neosha's door three hard kicks before it flew off the hinges. The way NiNi's house was set up, the basement was right there as soon as one opened the main door to the house. Kick Down slung the basement door open and ran down the stairs looking for Damon because, from the looks of his last visit, that was his favorite spot.

NiNi heard the bang, ran to her closet and got inside. She knew that Damon had gotten angry again and was coming after her. Fear seeped through her pores as tears rolled down her face, and her bladder grew weak. NiNi was now sitting in a puddle of piss, but she didn't care; her heart was thumping and jumping damn near out her chest. She covered her ears with her hands and closed her eyes as she rocked back and forth like a scared child.

***

Damon jumped out of the bed and ran out of his bedroom. He didn't even make it down the hall before Kick Down was coming around the corner into the hallway. Damon saw the glare, the anger, and the look of a madman in Kick Down's eyes. Damon didn't get a word out before Kick Down attacked him.

Whap! Whap!
Smack!

Chapter 1

It was the beginning of February and the sun was out, but the weather was cold. The grass and the leaves that scarcely clung to the trees were a mixture of green and yellow. It was 12:00pm on a Sunday afternoon, and NiNi had just walked back into the house after taking her daily morning walk. It gave her time to think and get away from the madness that was going on in her household.

At nineteen years young, NiNi Alexander felt like she had experienced every hardship that life offered. Day after day she battled demons within the walls of the home she shared with her ill mother.

She had a beautiful home that consisted of electric blue and black colors in the kitchen, and a stainless-steel sink, stove and refrigerator. The countertops were blue and black marble, and the floor had blue tiles. The dining room's crème and electric blue color scheme coordinated with the kitchen and housed a wooden table with matching chairs in the center of the room.

There was wall to wall carpet in the living room, and a Tilman Rossa plush blue sectional furniture set. But the entertainment center was indeed the center of attention, and not to mention her mother's beautiful plants that sat in each corner of the living room. Her home was amazing on the outside and inside, but the secrets the walls kept were horrific.

She walked through the kitchen and into the living room where she saw her mother, Neosha, sitting on the couch.

"Hey Mom, how are you feeling today?" NiNi took a seat on the empty space next to her mother.

"Oh, I'm just fine, my love. How are you? How was your walk?" she asked through a cracked voice.

Before NiNi answered, she got up and went back into the kitchen, looked into the fridge and got a bottle of water. She then grabbed her mother's pills off the table and walked back into the living room.

"Here Mom, take a sip. Make sure you take your pill at one on the dot. No sooner and no later," she explained.

Her mother took the water and drunk a generous amount; the next time she spoke her voice was clear as day.

"Girl, look at you. Always making sure your mother is well taken care of," Neosha said as she rubbed NiNi's chubby face causing a smile to appear.

"It's my job. You took care of me and now that I'm old enough, it's my turn to take care of you."

Neosha nodded her head and then turned her attention back on the Channel Ten News. That was her daily routine since she'd been sick. She would wake up, get herself together, make a cup of coffee, and sit down in the living room to watch the news along with her soap operas and favorite movies. NiNi leaned back and sunk deep into the couch. She wasn't really watching the TV; it was more like it was watching her.

"Have you talked to Auntie or Unc lately?" NiNi asked.

"I keep in touch here and there wit' Yoshi, but not so much Kick Down. Baby, Mommy don't have the strength or energy to do much, but you know when I do get it, I'm as normal as ever. I don't claim a damn thing, but I can't deny that this sickness has me completely out of it. It's as if I'm a different person at times. Some days I'm fussin' and cussin' up a storm, cookin' dinner, and havin' a good ol' time just like the old days. But then, there's days where I'm an empty shell. Can barely get out of bed, eat, and all I do is sleep," Neosha responded without looking back at NiNi.

Thoughts were running through her mind a mile a minute. NiNi glanced over at her mother and sorrow formed in her eyes. In September of last year, she found out that her mother was diagnosed with cancer. From what her doctor explained, it wouldn't have been as worse as it was if her previous doctors would have run the correct tests and caught it beforehand. She hated that her mother was sick, and she wished that she could do more for her, but she couldn't. The only thing that NiNi was thankful for was that her stepfather, Damon, was paying her mother's medical bills. Damon and Neosha weren't officially married, but he'd been around for so long that they were married by common law so Neosha felt like it was no rush to put a stamp on something that she'd already granted official years ago. NiNi She took care of her mother while he worked, and when he came home, she made it her business to leave. If she wasn't able to, she would spend all day in her room.

The vibration of her phone grabbed her attention. She sat up and reached inside of her pocket to remove it; she looked at the text message that appeared across the screen.

Onyae: *Girl, I dead got drunk as fuck last night. Shit crazy, but anyway I'm on my way to ya crib so be ready.*

NiNi: *Lmao you always doin' somethin', but okay.*

NiNi and her twenty-year-old cousin, Onyae, were thick as thieves so when she saw her text, she grew excited.

Onyae: *That's me! Is that fuck nigga there? If so, I'm not comin' in. I might not feel good, but I'll beat that niggas ass today.*

NiNi: *Yea, he's here, but don't worry. I'll be out there waiting for you. I don't need you beating no one's ass today, lol.*

Onyae: *A'ight. Xoxo.*

NiNi: *Oxox.*

She smiled when she got finished responding to Onyae's text message. Any sort of communication with Onyae brought sunshine to NiNi's cloudy days. They always made sure to end their conversation with hugs and kisses, kisses and hugs. It was a sign of love, care, and loyalty for the girls. They knew that regardless of any situation, they both had each other's backs. NiNi knew her cousin didn't play when it came to her, so she had to hurry and tell her mother that she was leaving. That way, Onyae and Damon wouldn't run into one another. Onyae couldn't stand Damon, but NiNi couldn't blame her because she couldn't stand him either.

"Mom, Onyae is on her way so I'll be leaving in a few."

Neosha looked her way and proceeded to stand up but NiNi stopped her.

"Oh girl, I'm not handicapped. I just wanted to get up and give you a hug and a kiss," she said as she shooed at NiNi.

NiNi laughed, bent down and gave her mother a kiss on the cheek. She wrapped her arms around her neck and gave her a tight squeeze.

"You wearin' that outside?" A deep voice boomed from behind NiNi, and it sent nervous chills up her spine.

NiNi stood up and turned around to find Damon standing there with a beer in his hand and eyeing her so hard she felt like she was standing there in the nude. He was mysterious, just like his sign, a Scorpio. His tall, slim, six- foot-five frame stood in the walkway of the living room. He wore a pair of old black jeans that had paint splashed on them in different areas, a pair of brown moccasins, and a dingy white shirt. His toasted almond skin complexion, black and grey dreadlocks and different colored eyes gave him an exotic look. He looked at NiNi for what seemed like an eternity, waiting for an answer and she finally gave him one

"What's wrong with what I'm wearing? Nothin'! And besides, I buy my own clothes. So, you have no say over what I wear, and when I wear it." She rolled her eyes and stormed past him.

Neosha watched her daughter and shook her head. The tension that appeared every time those two were in the same room was overwhelming for her. She couldn't understand why NiNi disliked Damon the way she did. She assumed that it was because her father was no longer in her life, but she couldn't keep using that as an excuse.

"Don't worry about her, sweetie, she'll come around," Damon said as he walked over and pecked Neosha on the lips before taking a seat in his recliner.

She adjusted her robe before speaking. "You've been saying that for ten years; she is now nineteen years old and nothing has changed. I tell you that girl can be a piece of work sometimes. Just like her father."

Damon nodded his head and took a long sip of his beer before letting out a mean belch.

Uurrpppppp!

"You're right, baby, but don't worry about it. Things will get better," he said with confidence.

Neosha left the situation alone. She picked up the remote control and turned to TV ONE which was playing another one of her favorite shows What's Happening.

***

NiNi was sitting outside on the porch when she saw Onyae walking up with sunglasses on. Her hair was up in a messy bun, so NiNi could already imagine what type of night she had, and she could hear her smacking on her gum before she even reached her house.

"You and that damn gum." NiNi laughed.

"Don't come for me, chick." She paused and blew a bubble before popping it. "Anyway, wassup with you; how my aunt doin'? And, bitch, you lookin' real cute today!" Onyae complimented her cousin.

NiNi didn't have much on; she wore a pair of black skinny legged jeans, with a hot pink spaghetti strapped shirt, and a pair of hot pink baby doll shoes. Unlike Onyae, who had on a pair of dark blue, acid washed, skinny legged jeans, a baby blue tank top that showed her stomach, and a pair of black sandals with rhinestones on the middle strap.

NiNi chuckled as she stepped off the porch; they walked through the driveway and began down the street. She waited until they reached the corner before responding.

"Ain't shit up with me, but my mom is doing good. To be honest, I'm praying that one day we go to the doctors and they tell us the cancer is gone completely. Wassup with you tho', chick?"

"Same shit different day, and I feel you, and you know me and God ain't too cool, but I'm prayin' for my auntie too. Feels me?"

NiNi looked at Onyae and shook her head as she tried to contain her laughter.

"Girl, you ain't got no shame. God is shaking His head at ya crazy ass."

"Shit, I don't blame Him, but ooh, let me tell you what happened and how my crazy ass got drunk last night." Onyae's phone went off. She looked at it and texted whomever it was back before continuing her story.

"You know Dawkins and them be cookin' that seafood and shit, so I went to pick some up on the South Side and it was this big ass barbeque. Girllll, you know my ass wasn't passing up no food, so I stayed." She smacked on her gum some more. "Next thing I know, the bottles started flowing and my ass got fuucckkkeed up."

NiNi started laughing as she listened to her story, Onyae was always so overly dramatic, especially when she told a story; this time was no different.

"You stupid as hell girl, but let's stop at Coastal's right quick so I can get me something to eat. I did my morning walk and didn't get a chance to eat anything cas' I was checking on Mommy and then you texted me," she said.

"Cool, I need to get me something to drink anyway." Sshe agreed.

"I think you had enough to drink," NiNi joked as she held the door open for her.

They both walked into the store and Onyae headed straight to the freezer in the back, opened it, grabbed an Arizona Mango Iced Tea and opened it.

"You buy first," said one of the workers.

NiNi looked back to see Onyae taking an Arizona to the head. She shook her head when she finally stopped and burped loudly.

Uurrrrrrp!

"Stop trippin'. I do this all the time. Hell, boss man, don't mind," she yelled.

"Girl, get up here and pay for that." NiNi laughed.

Onyae rolled her eyes and took her precious time walking to the front. She made sure to take a few sips with each step just to get at the worker. When she finally made it to the counter, she reached in her bag and pulled out fifty cents.

"Here, cas' it's only half a can left, so technically I only owe yawl fifty cents."

NiNi burst out into laughter. She looked at the worker who didn't find anything funny and laughed even louder because she knew that Onyae was serious.

"Yawl crazy; anyway, I'd like to make an order please," NiNi said.

The male worker took out a slip of paper, a pen, and he nodded at her.

"Give me a cheeseburger on Kaiser..."

NiNi gave them her order and then went to the chip aisle. Onyae was right behind her.

"So, what we doing tonight?" Onyae asked.

"It's Sunday, ain't really shit to do, but I'm stayin' at ya crib tonight," she responded.

Just then the girls' conversation was interrupted by laughter. They looked around the aisle and saw a group of guys standing there clowning around.

"Ooh hell yea, fresh meat," Onyae sang.

NiNi raised an eyebrow at her cousin as she pushed up her breasts and put her hand between her legs and smelled it.

"Had to make sure a bitch was fresh."

"You are such a hoe."

"I am not a hoe, I just like dick, now excuse me." Onyae left NiNi standing there as she went over to approach the guy of her flavor.

He had the skin complexion of freshly brewed coffee, with a hint of creamer; he looked to be a mere five-foot-ten. He had long hair which was in a neat bun on the top of his head, his hairline and his Sunni beard were shaped up nicely. Rocking a white T-shirt, a pair of black, knee length shorts with pockets on each side, and a crisp pair of white Jordans, he looked good enough to eat.

NiNi chuckled at her cousin's realness. She grabbed her chips and then proceeded to walk back to the counter to pay for her things. Her plans were put to a halt when her eyes connected with the guy that stood out to her the most. When she looked at him everything around her seemed to be invisible. She didn't know why, but at that moment, he was the only thing that mattered to her. His honey-colored skin tone and broad shoulders looked delicious. He was a teddy bear, standing at five-foot-eleven with a low-cut fade and a Sunni beard that looked so sexy with his goatee. His brown eyes seemed to look right through her, and for the first time in her nineteen years of living, NiNi blushed.

"Yo, let me get a dutch," he said.

She watched his every move, not caring if he noticed her or not. He had her hypnotized and he hadn't even said one word to her.

"NiNi, NiNi, girl I know ya ass hear me calling you!" Onyae's loudmouth could be heard throughout the small store.

"What?" NiNi answered with base in her voice because her cousin scared her.

"I've been calling you for the last five minutes. What the hell got ya attention," she asked.

Onyae looked at the guy who NiNi was staring at. He winked at NiNi and then left out of the store.

"Mhmmm, he's a cutie. I see why you were stuck on Mars. You should've gotten his number cas' ya ass needs to get laid," she said.

NiNi gave her the side eye before she finally went up and paid for her things. She gathered her bag and followed Onyae out of the store and took a quick glance around to see if she saw the guy, but she didn't.

"I'm so damn tired. I had a long ass day. Let's go to my house now so I can take a lil cat nap," Onyae insisted.

NiNi didn't answer. She was too busy thinking about the guy who damn near took her breath away. It took them ten minutes to get to Onyae's house. She lived in what they called the 'New Houses' located down the street in the back of the Dollar Store. They were around the corner from NiNi's house. Between the talking and NiNi's thinking, it slowed them down.

"Moommmm, where you at, boo!" Onyae yelled.

On their way into Onyae's room the bathroom door swung open.

"I'ma need for you to stop being all loud and fuckin' dramatic!" Yoshi responded, but she was just as loud as her daughter.

"Stop trippin', and who you gettin' all dolled up for?"

Onyae took a detour, walked into the bathroom, sat on the countertop and grabbed her mother's phone as she began to go through it.

"I got a date in a few and get out of my damn phone with ya nosey ass."

She swatted at her hand like Onyae was a child that had just touched a hot stove.

"Dang, he must be someone special since you ain't givin' me the tea about him and I can't go through ya phone. Let me find out somebody tryna wife you up on the low." Onyae folded her arms as a smirk appeared across her face.

Yoshi batted her eyes like a high school girl as she continued to put the finishing touches on her hair. Onyae eyed her mother suspiciously. She had never seen her act this way over any guy she'd dated in the past.

"What's his name?" she finally asked.

Ahem.

Yoshi cleared her throat before responding. "Khalif, and before you go to asking any questions, I already got all the information I need on him. I've been dating him for almost a year now. He's not like the rest, which is why I didn't discuss him with you like the others."

Onyae was surprised that her mother was defending the guy she was dating. They always had girl talk about the guys they'd both dealt with, but as she could see, this time was much different.

"When do I get to meet him?"

Once she realized how serious her mother was about the guy, Onyae's questions became dry and uninterested. It had been the two of them for so many years and now it felt like she was losing her best friend. Yoshi gave herself a once over in the mirror before turning her attention over to her daughter. She took a few steps so that she was standing in front of her and placed her hands on both sides of her heart shaped face.

"Tonight, and I know that you will like him."

She kept her hands on Onyae's face to see if her expression changed but it didn't. A part of her wanted to cradle her daughter and tell her that it would continue to just be the two of them, but she knew that would be a false statement. Yoshi was forty-one years old and she felt like it was time for her to love again.

"Come on now, don't get salty on me," Yoshi said, trying to force a smile upon her daughter's face.

NiNi stood in the hallway looking at her cousin. She knew exactly how she felt without her having to say anything. The relationship that she had with her mother was the same type of relationship Onyae had with hers.

"I'm Gucci, Mom," she finally spoke as she removed her mother's hands from her face and slid down off the countertop.

She walked out of the bathroom and headed straight for her bedroom. Yoshi looked at NiNi for comfort.

"She'll come around, Auntie. Don't worry; I'll talk to her." NiNi gave her an assuring smile.

"Thanks baby, I appreciate it. But on another note, how is your mother doing?"

NiNi swallowed hard at the mention of her mother. "She's doing well, thank God." Not wanting to discuss her mother's condition any further, she quickly ended the conversation before it could get started. "Well, let me go in here and talk to her. I hope you enjoy your date tonight."

She turned to her right and walked into Onyae's room and closed the door. She looked over at Onyae who had kicked off her shoes and was lying on her stomach on her queen-sized bed with her phone in her hand, scrolling through what she assumed was Facebook. NiNi took off her shoes and sat down beside her.

"Are you okay?" she asked, pulling out her sandwich; she unwrapped it before taking a bite.

Onyae looked away from her phone and back at her.

"I'm straight, you know," she answered.

NiNi was starving but hearing the hurt in her cousin's voice made her lose her appetite so she wrapped her food back up and placed it back in the bag. She crossed her legs on the bed and faced her.

"Onyae, I know how you feel, but look how happy ya mom seems. Don't you want her to be happy?"

Onyae sat up on the bed and folded her arms in a pouting manner as she looked at NiNi.

"I don't care what she does. She can be with whoever she wanna be with. I don't care."

It was clear to NiNi that Onyae was trying to convince herself that she didn't care because NiNi wasn't buying it one bit. Although they were cousins, they were also best friends, and the relationships they had with their mothers were priceless.

"Girl bye; I mean seriously, who do you think you're talking to? Boo Boo the fool?"

NiNi waved her hand at Onyae as if to say, 'get out of here with that'. Realizing that NiNi wasn't buying it, she finally gave in and revealed how she really felt.

"It's been us, just us, for years. Since my dad walked out on us, it's just been me and her. I ain't feelin' how she thinks she can just up and get another dude like Dad ain't burn us enough."

"So, you want her to be lonely for the rest of her life?" NiNi didn't need an answer because the way Onyae looked at her said it all. "You can't do that, and you know you can't. Now what if the shoe was on the other foot and you got in a serious relationship and your mother felt the way you do?"

When NiNi hit her with that, Onyae went from pouting to understanding in a matter of seconds. She didn't want to seem like she wasn't happy for her mother, but she was indeed hurt.

"What should I do?" she asked.

"Give him a chance, but if he fucks it up, then you be upset," NiNi answered.

NiNi was giving Onyae the same talk that she wished someone had given her back when it was time for her mother to pick her stepfather.

"You right, sis, and thank you. I know I can be a spoiled little brat at times, but you always help me see the bigger picture." She leaned over and hugged NiNi as tight as she could.

"I can't breathe." NiNi laughed as she tried to pull Onyae's arms from around her neck.

"Ooh, my bad," Onyae said as she let go of her. "But seriously, thank you. You always there for me no matter what."

NiNi didn't respond; all she did was give her a simple nod. In NiNi's eyes, she should've been thanking Onyae because if it wasn't for her she wouldn't have been alive at that very moment. Suicide attempts and NiNi knew each other all too well, and it was Onyae that saved her each time.

Chapter 2

"Onyyaaaaeeeee. Onyyaaaeeee. NiiNiiiiiii." Yoshi called out.

Both Onyae and NiNi jumped up out of their sleep. Onyae grabbed the metal bat that sat behind her door and NiNi whipped the blade out that she kept in her bra. They both ran out the room and followed her screams. They were startled once they got to the kitchen and saw a handsome man standing there with Yoshi.

"Damn. I mean excuse my language, but I would hate to get on your bad side, Yoshi. You have some major back up here I see," he joked.

Onyae nodded. "You better know it."

Yoshi couldn't help but to laugh at them. They still had sleep in their eyes, but they were ready for war.

"I'm sorry. I didn't mean to scare yawl. I just wanted to introduce yawl to someone special. Onyae, NiNi, this is Khalif, and Khalif, this is my daughter, Onyae, and my niece, NiNi."

Thirty-nine years young; he was the true definition of tall, dark, and handsome. Khalif was six -foot- five, and his creamy milk chocolate skin looked good enough to have for dessert. He had on a simple outfit: a white tee, a pair of dark blue jeans, and some all-white Air Nike's, but he still looked like a million bucks. His dreads were neatly done and pulled back into a ponytail, letting them fall to his back and his goatee was trimmed nicely.

Khalif took a step forward and held out his hand to Onyae. She hesitated for a moment until NiNi nudged her and she placed her hand in his. He gave her a small peck.

"It's so nice to finally meet you. Ya mother has told me so much about you, and I look forward to having dinner with you both so that you can get to know me."

Onyae pulled away and folded her arms across her chest while eyeing Khalif. He did the same thing with NiNi, taking her hand into his and kissing it. NiNi wasn't too fond of him kissing her. It was nothing against him, but she had her reasons.

"Well, it's 9:30 ladies, so I'm about to head out. I'll be back in the morning. If you need me call my cell, and his number is on the fridge as well." Yoshi explained as she kissed both of the girls on their cheeks.

"You be safe with my mom, you hear? Don't think this bat is the only thing I got because I keeps me a blade too," Onyae said to Khalif.

He looked at here and smiled as he reached into his pocket, pulled out his wallet, took out two cards and handed his wallet over to her.

"I took out my license and one of my black cards for tonight. But my ID is in there along with my social, credit cards, insurance card and anything else with my information on it. You can keep that until I drop your mother off in the morning." He winked at her as he held out his arm so that Yoshi could cuff her arm into his.

NiNi's mouth dropped open as she looked at Onyae who looked down at the wallet in her hand.

"I love you mamas, and goodnight," Yoshi called out before walking out of the door.

Onyae looked at NiNi who looked back at her. "Did he just give me his wallet? Like with all of his information in it? This dude dead ass crazy."

"Looks like he's just as serious as your mom," NiNi stated.

"I guess you right, but I'm not gon' get all excited cas' this all could be a front. I'm not buyin' it one bit," she said.

NiNi rolled her eyes, turned around and walked back into the bedroom. Onyae shrugged her shoulders and followed her.

"Let's go down to Coastal's. I know it's packed cas' it's almost ten o'clock," she said as she began to get undressed.

"I don't know why you like going down there when it gets late knowing all those dudes be there. That shit ain't even the move," NiNi told her.

Onyae scanned the many body washes that sat on her dresser. After a few seconds, she finally picked up the Strawberries and Cream Olay body wash.

"Duh, that's the whole point," she answered.

"Bitch, now you know I don't like being around a whole bunch of gu—

"Stop trippin'. You know I ain't gon' let nobody hurt you," Onyae said cutting her off.

She walked out of the room and headed into the bathroom. NiNi stripped out of her clothes and stood in front of the floor length mirror. Admiring every love handle on her four-foot-eleven frame, she could still see the semi fresh bite marks on her titties from the night before. And her thoughts traveled back there.

Hmmm, you like that, baby? I know you do.

NiNi erased the memory out of her mind and began looking in the closet where she kept the majority of the clothes that her aunt bought her. She knew it would be a bit chilly outside, so she settled for a pair of black leggings, a grey tank top and her black hoodie. After she was finished getting out her outfit, she walked out of the room and went into the bathroom to freshen up. When she got in there, Onyae was in the shower so she took the sink. She turned on the hot water, wet her wash rag and lathered it up real good with body wash.

"You know I got ol' boy's number from earlier, right," Onyae said.

"Don't I know it." NiNi giggled.

Clap! Clap! Clap!
Clap! Clap!

NiNi swung her head around towards the shower and burst into laughter. Onyae had no chill; she was a spontaneous Sagittarius so NiNi never knew what to expect from her.

"Girl, I can't with you!" she squealed.

"You hear that; that's them muhfuckin' clappers, girl. I tell you I'm throwing this ass in a circle tonight."

Onyae turned the shower off and pulled the curtain back. She snatched her towel off the shower rod and wrapped it around her. NiNi looked at her cousin through the bathroom mirror.

"So, are you okay now?"

NiNi could see that Onyae's attitude did a complete 180.

"I'm on some chills, but I ain't gon' front and act like I'm not still feelin' a way."

NiNi didn't feel the need to respond. She left the subject alone and finished washing up. After she was finished, she grabbed a towel off the back of the bathroom door and wrapped it around her. While Onyae was applying her make-up, NiNi reached over and grabbed a tube of eye liner. She applied two coats under each eye before capping it and putting it back in Onyae's make-up caboodle. Once both of the girls were satisfied with their slay, they left out of the bathroom and went back into the bedroom to get dressed. Onyae rubbed her body down with baby oil and NiNi rubbed her body down with cocoa butter baby oil gel. Onyae put on a pair of yellow thongs with a matching bra. She put on her black yoga pants, matching shirt and hoodie from Victoria's Secret PINK clothing line. She then sat on the bed and put on a pair of socks.

"Pass me my shoes, babe," Onyae said to NiNi.

NiNi had just finished putting on her leggings and shirt. She walked by the closet and picked up Onyae's black

Giuseppe Zanotti leather bucked sneakers, walked back over and passed them to her.

"Here chick."

Onyae was finished getting dressed and she stood up to admire herself in her floor length mirror. She was a five-foot-two true beauty. Her golden skin tone looked rich. Her thighs had the right amount of thickness with the body measurements 34-24-36; Onyae was definitely easy on the eyes. She wasn't at all bad looking in the face. Her almond-shaped eyes, pudgy cheeks, and cleft chin gave her a childlike look. She had big brown, doe shaped eyes and when she smiled, she showed all thirty-two teeth. She wasn't the least bit ashamed of her big gums and small teeth.

"I'm like, yeah, she's fine. Wonder when she'll be mine. She walk past, like press rewind. To see that ass one more time. Yassss baby yassss." Onyae dipped low as she jammed to the Fetty Wap song she was singing.

NiNi laughed as she finished getting dressed. She put on her hoodie and silver Giuseppe Zanotti low-tops. She appreciated the fact that her cousin kept her in nothing but the best considering she couldn't afford it on her own because she wasn't working. NiNi put her all into caring for her mother, and as a result, she stopped her life. She combed her neck length hair before giving herself a once over. Her Hershey's cocoa skin and dreamy eyes were ravishing. With the measurements 44-40-53 of course she had a tummy, but that only added to the voluptuousness of her body. Her four-foot-eleven build carried her thick thighs and juicy booty with pride.

Slap!

Both girls gave each other a high five because of how fly they were looking. Onyae grabbed her house keys off her dresser and looked at NiNi.

"You ready?"

"You already know, let's go," she responded.

NiNi walked out of the room first, and Onyae cut her bedroom light out before she left out. As they walked through the dining room and the kitchen, Onyae stuck a piece of gum in her mouth, and offered NiNi a piece.

"You stay eatin' some damn gum." NiNi laughed as she took the gum out of Onyae's hand and stuck it in her mouth.

"Girl, you know I gotta have my gum, but I also can't have my breath hummin' in front of no cute ass niggas."

NiNi walked out of the house as Onyae made sure the house was locked. She and NiN's houses were similar, but Onyae's two-story house with a wraparound porch was more lavish. Not to mention the beautiful inside. Emperador Café Marble floors in the kitchen and wine barrel wood in the living room gave the home a luxurious décor. A Safavieh's Adirondack collection black rug adorned each bedroom. Their house was so elegant; NiNi loved being there more than she liked being at her own home.

Chapter 3

After Onyae was sure that the house was secure, they walked down the two steps of her porch, and then down the driveway. Onyae put one hand in her pocket as she browsed through her phone with her other hand.

"Who you textin'?" NiNi wanted to know.

"Ol' boy from earlier; his name is Gutta. I wanna make sure he gon' come scoop me."

NiNi frowned. She had no clue they were going to be going anywhere other than the store. She wasn't too fond of being alone with guys, especially guys she didn't know.

"What do you mean come scoop you? I thought we was just gon' hang out outside of the store. You said nothing about going anywhere with anyone. That's that bullshit I be talkin' about," NiNi snapped.

Onyae sighed loudly and rolled her eyes to the heavens.

"NiNi please! Relax, girl. You know that I got you regardless. So, stop actin' like I'm puttin' you in harm's way."

NiNi shook her head but didn't respond as she continued to walk ahead of Onyae. The way Onyae came at her made her feel some type of way, and before things got out of hand, she chose to ignore her and the situation. Onyae felt bad for the way she came at NiNi. She started jogging to catch up with her.

"Yo hold up," she said, placing her hand on NiNi's shoulder to stop her.

NiNi stopped but didn't look back.

"What?"

Onyae took a deep breath before speaking. "I'm sorry. I didn't mean to come at you like that. I just want you to live ya life and have fun. I'm tired of you letting your past get in the way of everything."

Tears welled up in NiNi's eyes because no matter how much she confided in her cousin, she just simply didn't understand. She took her hand and wiped her eyes before speaking.

"Let's just go, okay?"

Onyae didn't press the issue much more. They continued to walk in silence until they arrived at their destination minutes later.

"*Aahhhh!*" Onyae squealed when she saw Gutta.

She ran over with her arms in the air, jumping into his arms as if they had been in an ongoing relationship. NiNi laughed a little as she surveyed the crowd to see if she saw the handsome guy from earlier. When she didn't, she became disappointed, but she didn't show it. NiNi walked past a few guys and she could feel them staring at her which immediately made her uncomfortable.

Please don't say shit to me, she thought.

NiNi finally got over by Onyae and her boo. She stood near them with her arms folded, mean mugging everyone. Her attitude was on one thousand.

"You lookin' good as fuck tonight," Gutta said to Onyae, wrapping his arms around her waist and giving her ass a gentle squeeze.

Onyae smacked her lips in a bougie manner and batted her eyes.

"I'm always lookin' good as fuck. I'm def not new to this fly shit. I'm true to this."

Gutta nodded his head. "Ard, ard. So, yawl ready to get ghost or nah?"

NiNi's stomach was in knots. Onyae nodded her way. "You ready to go, boo?"

"They all goin' with us?" NiNi asked with an attitude while pointing at the crowd before her.

Gutta chuckled. "A few of them, but don't worry, ma. We all fam over here."

NiNi's look let Gutta know that she was hesitant which caused him to look at Onyae.

"Shawty ard? I mean they gon' be at my crib, but they not ridin' wit' us if that's what she worried about."

Onyae nodded yes. She was well aware of how NiNi felt, but she wasn't going to keep discussing it. She wanted her to have an enjoyable time like she did whenever they stepped out, and that was what she set out to make sure happened.

"Cool, then let's dip out," Gutta said. Walking over to the passenger side door of his white Toyota Tundra, he opened the door for Onyae, and then opened the back door for NiNi.

She got inside and NiNi followed. Gutta ran around the side of his truck and hopped into the driver's side. He started it up, put it in reverse and honked his horn as he backed up. They drove in silence for a while until NiNi texted Onyae.

NiNi: *What happened to the guy that was with him?*

Onyae: *What guy?*

NiNi: *The guy from earlier. The one with the beard and low cut.*

Onyae didn't respond to NiNi's last text but she smirked because she was happy that NiNi was finally crushing on someone. It had been a rough couple of years for her and all she wanted was for her to be happy and to have some fun.

"Ayo where ol' boy from earlier?" Onyae asked.

Gutta glanced over at her. "Ol' boy? I was wit' mad niggas earlier. You gotta be more specific, ma."

Onyae rolled her eyes, but she had to chuckle a little because she liked that thug shit. "I'm talkin' about ol' boy with the Sunni beard."

Gutta had to turn on his overhead light so that she could see the frown that appeared on his face. "You do realize that half of my crew got a fuckin Sunni beard, don't you?"

"Don't get smart, nigga!"

NiNi was getting aggravated by all the back and forth so she finally spoke up. "The guy that had the white T-shirt on; he had a low haircut, and he bought a dutch in the store today."

Gutta made an O gesture with his mouth because he finally figured out who she was talking about. He turned off his overhead light and leaned in his seat as he drove before speaking again.

"Oh, ard. That's my big-headed cousin, Rayshon. Why?"

"What you mean why? My cousin tryna holla!"

"Onyae!" NiNi yelled as she reached over the seat and smacked her in the head.

She didn't like how she put her on blast like that. Neither one of them knew if he would even be interested and they didn't know if he was single. The last thing NiNi needed was to be turned down.

"You like my cousin?"

"I don't know him to be liking him." NiNi gave more attitude than needed.

Gutta waved her off because he knew when a girl was feeling a guy. He fished out his cellphone and scrolled through his recent contact history before pressing the call button. The phone rang a few times before the person on the other end picked up. Gutta put the phone on speaker as he spoke.

"What's good, bruh? What ya nut ass doin?"

There was rattling in the background followed by a voice that flowed so smoothly.

"Wassup bruh? I'm out takin' care of some business," he responded.

"Come through my crib when you get finished; somebody wanna see you." Gutta looked back at NiNi and chuckled.

She was so embarrassed, but the cat was out of the bag now so there was nothing that she could do; however, she appreciated Gutta's bluntness. It made the situation less awkward for her.

"Who?" he asked.

"You'll see when you get to my crib. Don't worry, shawty A1. So just hit me then, ya heard?"

"Ard one."

Click.

"I set it up. When he get to my crib it's up to yawl two to take it from there, ard?" Gutta asked, and then glanced back at NiNi.

Before she responded, he sent a text to one of his homeboys to tell them there was a change of plans and not to come over. He didn't want to make NiNi anymore uncomfortable than she already was and having a house full of niggas over would've done just that.

"A'ight," NiNi responded nonchalantly.

Gutta giving her the green light on her looks made her nervous all over again. She didn't know the first thing about dealing with a guy, but she knew that she was very attracted to Rayshon. Her stomach was in knots and her heart was beating a mile a minute. The only thing she could do was take a deep breath, lay her head back on the seat, and relax. Soon after that, NiNi drifted off to sleep.

Moments later, NiNi was awaken by Onyae tapping her.

"NiNi, girl, wake up. We here, and this nigga house look like it could be fly as fuck on the inside! Get yo ass up so you can see this shit," Onyae said as she tapped and shook NiNi's thigh continuously.

All Gutta could do was laugh. If it was any other female, he would have looked at them as a gold digger, but he could tell that Onyae was different. She was vibrant, outspoken, and down to earth. Her personality was raw as fuck, and if one didn't know her, they wouldn't be too fond of how blunt she was, but he respected the fact that she spoke her mind, and he could tell that right off the bat.

NiNi sat up, yawned and stretched. She didn't realize she had dozed off, but she was glad to finally be at their destination because the ride seemed to have taken forever. She got out of the truck and looked around. Although, she had only been to Philly a few times she could tell that's where she was. Gutta's house was a basic kind of lavish on the outside, but the area was nice so she could see why Onyae assumed that it was nice on the inside.

"Ard, yawl can come out now. A nigga tired of standin' out here," Gutta said to them.

He had already unlocked the door and opened it, but he had been standing there for the last couple of minutes holding the screen door and waiting for both Onyae and NiNi to get finished talking.

"Be patient nigga, we comin', "Onyae told him.

"Word nigga, chill out," NiNi added.

"Yo, Gutta!"

They all turned their heads simultaneously to see a light-skinned pretty boy run up towards Gutta out of breath.

"Fuck wrong wit' ya nut ass callin' my name all crazy?" Gutta asked with a screwed-up face.

"My bad, but I been waitin' to see ya truck pull up. These niggas over there round our block on Diamond Street settin' up shop. I had my strap, but them niggas cars deep. It was me and Lenny against all them niggas," the pretty boy explained.

"You came all the way from North Philly to watch my crib until I came home? Lil nigga, you could've called me to tell me that shit." Gutta frowned.

"I ain't want you or Rayshon to trip. So, I came up here personally."

Gutta shook his head and looked over at Onyae and NiNi who were still standing by his truck. He didn't want to handle business in front of the ladies, but he really had no choice. He had to do something to get the boy, who was known as Ron Ron, to get the fuck away and get back to work.

"Man, tell them niggas that's our block. Tell all them niggas that Gutta said I'ma light that block up if I catch 'em on it. Word to mother," he said seriously.

"Ard. I'm on it, Gutta," Ron Ron said, and turned to run back to his car.

"Zammmmnnnn! Everything good?" Onyae asked.

"Yea, now get yawl asses up here," he said.

They both laughed as they walked away from Gutta's truck, and walked up the five steps that led to his door and walked in. They entered a mini area, an enclosed porch which seemed to be where they could kick off their shoes and hang up their coats.

"How many bedrooms this is?" Onyae asked.

"Three, why? You tryna move in?" Gutta laughed.

"Shit, I might, but nah, I just wanted to know," Onyae responded.

"I heard, but anyway, yawl welcome to take a house tour if yawl want. It ain't much, but a nigga worked hard for it," he told them.

Both NiNi and Onyae could see stairs straight ahead. They knew that was the upstairs; at the moment, neither one of them was going up there. They glanced to the left and saw the living room which they both fell in love with. It was huge, and it had wall to wall hardwood floors. Gutta had a 50-inch flat screen TV that sat on a wooden stand. A shelf inside held his DVD player, PS3, PS4, and Xbox One gaming systems.

To their surprise he had bright colors in his living room. Orange, white, tan, and chocolate brown. He had a single three-seater couch along with a love seat and ottoman that sat diagonal from the couch. A big, colorful rug that matched the décor was laid in the center of the floor.

"This is nice. Fareal," NiNi complimented as she touched the couch to see how soft it was.

This was the first house they had been in that didn't contain a coffee table in the center of the living room, but it was no big deal to the ladies.

"Thanks ma," Gutta said. He walked past them, through the dining room, and into the kitchen which was right off his living room.

Gutta had a wide-open spaced dining room that held a mini wooden dining room table with chairs that sat on the outside of his open kitchen. A counter with cabinets on the other side separated his kitchen from his dining room. Everything seemed to be newly furnished or maybe Gutta was just that neat.

"This shit is nice, fareal. I know you got a nice ass backyard," Onyae said.

"Thanks, and yea I do. I might have a lil get together soon, and you'll be able to see it then," he responded.

Onyae liked the sound of that because in so little words she could tell that Gutta planned on keeping her around and that was just what she wanted.

"Yawl hungry? Want anything to eat? I don't really cook unless I need to, but yawl welcome to eat anything yawl want. If it ain't nothin' fast in here for yawl to cook, then feel free to take somethin' out. It's late so I can take yawl home tomorrow, you good wit' that?" Gutta asked while looking in NiNi's direction.

"My name is NiNi for the record, and yea that's cool. I'll sleep on the couch," she said.

"Nah, you ain't gotta do that. I got two extra bedrooms upstairs. My cousin got some of his stuff in one of them cas' he be stayin' the night here, but you more than welcome to stay in either one. You ain't gotta sleep on the damn couch."

"Okay," NiNi responded.

She stood there still looking around with her eyes when Onyae nudged her.

"You good, love?" Onyae asked.

"Yea, I am. I know you wanna take him upstairs and get busy so do you." She laughed.

"Oh, well of course, but I wanted to make sure you was good before I did that. You know a bitch ain't grimy. If you not good, then I'm not good!"

"I'm good, girl. Now, get outta my face, and don't be tryna come talk to me in the morning cas' I don't wanna smell no early morning dick breath!"

Gutta spit out his juice and burst out laughing.

"Yo, yawl two funny as hell."

"That's my bitch! Expect us to get down like this every time you around us," Onyae said.

Onyae saw that NiNi was starting to come around and that made her happy. She knew it was only a matter of time before NiNi would relax and be herself. She needed her to understand that she wasn't home so there was no need to clam up and be distant.

"I like real. So, I don't mind it at all. We ain't gotta go upstairs right now tho. We can sit down here, chill, and watch a movie," Gutta said.

"We can do that next time, but tonight I wanna fuck and I know you do too. Don't try to impress me with the small talk. Don't woo me in wit the fake shit. Woo me in wit ya realness, and we gon' be down for one another forevaaaa!" Onyae said in her best Cardi B voice.

NiNi was cracking up as she sat down and picked up the remote control and turned the TV on.

"I def ain't about the fake shit, ma, but I feel you. I just ain't wanna be too upfront about it; especially around ya cousin cas' I can tell she ain't like that," Gutta replied.

"My cousin is quiet until she gets to know you a bit, but she knows how I am. She knew I was feelin' you the day I approached you, now wassup?" Onyae asked with her hands on her hips.

"Say no more." Gutta gulped down the last of his juice and put his glass in the sink. "You sure you good, ma?"

Gutta looked at NiNi when he entered the living room.

"Bruh, I'm sure."

"Ard. My cousin got a key. So, don't be alarmed if you hear someone just walk in, and he the only nigga who got a key," Gutta assured her.

"I'm glad you clarified that, but yawl can go on now. I'm tryna watch TV," she said.

"Ooh, well excuse me." Onyae playfully rolled her eyes.

"Girl, you know I don't get to do this often," NiNi stated.

"I know, boo. I'm just playin'."

Gutta walked past Onyae and walked over by the stairs.

"You just gon' stand there?" he asked.

"Ooh, I was waitin' for my damn invitation, nigga," she shot back.

"Girl, if you don't get ya fine ass over here."

Onyae giggled and followed Gutta upstairs. He led her to the middle bedroom and opened the door. Gutta's room was nice and spotless. He had two mirrored, walk-in closets, and a flat screen TV that hung over the dresser. It sat directly in front of the wall that separated the closets. A huge Queen-sized bed covered in a grey and white comforter set, white curtains draped over the windows, and another dresser with a mirror connected to it, sat alongside the opposite wall.

"It's nice in here," Onyae complimented as she removed her black hoodie and shirt right after.

"Thanks ma," Gutta said with his back turned.

He was busy looking through his fire stick trying to find something to watch. He finally settled on *Barbershop 3*. By the time he turned around, Onyae was as naked as the day she was born.

"Damn, just like that, ma?" He admired her curvy figure.

She had a slight pudge, but that still didn't take away from her sex appeal.

"Just like that. So, wassup?" She threw her hands up and then let them fall to her side.

Gutta loved how outspoken Onyae was. It was one thing to be a hoe and proud, but Onyae was a freak and proud of it. Out of all the females he fucked or fucked with, Onyae was truly one of a kind. He didn't even know much about her, but her personality turned him on, and she kept his attention.

"You gon' get undressed or you gon' keep eyein' a bitch like you wanna eat me?" Onyae asked, snapping him out of his gaze.

"Shit, I'ma def do that," Gutta said and took off his jeans and T-shirt.

Onyae could already see the bulge in his black boxer briefs. She wasted no time walking over to him and they engaged one another with a kiss. Gutta grabbed a handful of Onyae's nude ass and then shoved his tongue down her throat. His fingers slipped in between her ass and her pussy was getting wetter by the moment. It was as if Gutta could sense how hot and bothered Onyae was because the next thing she knew he had stopped kissing her, grabbed her waist with both hands, and lifted her in the air. Onyae placed her legs over his shoulders and he devoured her freshly shaved pussy.

"Ooooh! Yesssssss!" she moaned with the hint of a scream.

Gutta cupped her ass and lifted her up; she was now sitting directly on his face; he licked, slurped, and ate her pussy like a freshly picked Georgia peach. Onyae had her hands on the side of his head, holding on for dear life. She had been with a few niggas in her life, but none of them seemed to be quite as freaky as Gutta, and she was loving every bit of what that nigga was giving her.

"Ooooh! Fuck!" she screamed as she came.

Gutta continued to suck her clit as he walked over to the bed and dropped her down enough so that they were face to face. His mouth and beard were covered with her cum, and when he licked it off, it turned her on so much that she had to kiss him to taste her own juices.

"Damn ma. A nigga love that freaky shit," he mentioned in between kisses.

"I know you do, and you gon' love this pussy even more. Now stop fuckin' around and give me the dick."

Gutta smirked. He loved that Onyae was a shit talker, but he was about to put her to the test. In one swift motion, he held her up with his left hand and grabbed his dick with his right hand, sliding it inside her.

"Oooh!" she gasped, being completely caught off guard.

Gutta cupped both her ass cheeks and dug his dick deep inside her with the first stroke. Onyae's pussy was already soak and wet so it made the stroke just that much more sensational, and she felt every inch of Gutta's chocolate, cream filled, eight-and-a-half-inch dick in her stomach.

Slap! Slap! Slap!

Gutta's balls smacked against her ass cheeks as their bodies slapped against one another.

"Oh! Ooh! Right fuckin' there!" Onyae screamed.

"Just like that, huh?"

"Yea, just, like, that," she moaned.

The way Gutta was stroking her had her in a fit of pleasure and pain. He continuously pounded away at her tight pussy causing her juices to drip down his balls and inner thigh area. Gutta put one knee on the bed and then laid Onyae down and laid on top of her while his dick was still inside her pussy. Her pussy was warm, wet, and gooey which made Gutta have to clench his teeth or suck in air to keep from busting early. It wasn't like Gutta to not have dick control, but he'd met his match when he came across Onyae.

"You tryna battle a nigga?" he asked, and then stuck his tongue in her mouth.

Onyae bit her bottom lip, tightened her walls, and moved her hands from holding onto his shoulders to reaching around him and pulling him so close that their skin seemed to stick together. Gutta took that as the initiative to continue dicking her down so he did just that.

Smack! Smack! Smack!

Gutta went Rico Strong on Onyae's pussy: missionary position with her legs all the way back to her shoulders as he slammed down in a violent way.

"Gutta!"

The way Onyae screamed his name was like she was punched in the stomach and it knocked the wind out of her.

Although Gutta was eight and a half inches in length, the thickness was out of this world.

"Yea, I know," he boasted all while stroking.

Onyae tried to take as much as she could before she began to try and push Gutta back.

"Okay! Okay!" she pleaded.

Gutta silenced her with a sloppy kiss and continued to power drive her causing her to squirt like water sprouting from a fountain when he finally decided to pull out. He stood up and stroked his dick while he watched Onyae's legs shake like she was having a seizure.

"Turn that ass around," he demanded.

Onyae had her right hand rubbing her pussy to try to take away some of the soreness. Her legs were weak as she slowly rolled over on her stomach and got in the doggy style position.

Smack!

Gutta smacked her ass and watched it jiggle. He positioned himself behind her, lifted her left ass cheek just a bit and slid back inside her warmth. Onyae's arch was amazing, and he could feel her walls tighten up around his dick.

"Mmmmm," she moaned.

She could feel her pussy pulsating with each stroke he gave her.

***

Meanwhile, NiNi was catching up on some *Love and Hip-Hop: Atlanta*. She shook her head at how the rapper Rasheeda was portraying herself.

"Ain't that much money in the fuckin' world," she said as she got up and went into the kitchen.

NiNi poured herself a glass of Pepsi and grabbed another bag of BBQ chips. When she walked back into the living room, she almost dropped both her chips and soda when she heard the door open. As she nervously stood there and held onto each one as tight as possible, she finally saw the big teddy bear framed male come in the living room area. NiNi still stood there startled although she realized who it was. She remembered Gutta telling her that he would be by, but she didn't believe him and on top of that, she couldn't remember being alone with any guy before.

Rayshon, on the other hand, was just standing there looking at NiNi. He could tell he had scared her by the way she was standing, but he was hoping she would have gotten it together by now.

"My bad," he said, finally breaking the silence.

"It's okay," she responded while finally taking a seat on the couch.

Rayshon walked to the kitchen, washed his hands, and got a bottle of water out the fridge.

"Where Gutta ass at?"

"Upstairs with my cousin," NiNi responded and went back to watching TV.

Rayshon walked over and flopped down beside her while helping himself to a handful of her BBQ chips. NiNi looked over at Rayshon, and he looked over at her; she smirked but tried to hide it as she took a sip of her soda.

"So, you the someone my cousin was talkin' bout?"

"Could be." She gave him attitude just in case he was on some bullshit.

Rayshon licked his lips as he admired NiNi and her curvaceous frame. Although she was sitting down, he could see that she was holding something serious by the way her hips spread in the seated position.

"Cous said they was A1 so it gotta be you," he said in the smoothest tone ever.

NiNi was nervous, but she couldn't help but to blush at what he said. Rayshon was truly a charmer so far; she thought about her cousin telling her to take her guard down a little and it allowed her to relax a bit.

"Look at you watchin' this bullshit," Rayshon said, glancing at the TV.

He could tell NiNi was shy, but he was a down to earth type of dude and he wanted to vibe with her.

"This is not bullshit. Don't hate!" NiNi shot back.

"What I'm hatin' on?"

"My show, now shut up and watch it."

Rayshon laughed and sunk into the couch trying to get as comfortable as possible. He continuously reached over for more chips as he tried his hardest to get into the ratchet television show that NiNi was watching. He couldn't get into it, so his intentions on wanting to chill with NiNi took over.

"When my cousin called and said he wanted me to come by for a lil shorty. I had no idea it would be you," he said.

NiNi cut her eye at him.

"And what the hell is that supposed to mean?"

"Oh shit, I was wonderin' when you was gon' give a nigga a lil attitude. All that shy shit was in the way, ma."

NiNi rolled her eyes. She didn't like to be judged and at that moment she felt like Rayshon was judging her. Her shyness was no act. The only people she could be herself around were her cousin and aunt. The wall she had up would come down when she was in their presence because she knew they meant her no harm.

"In the way? Oh, so you like ratchet bitches? Bitches that don't give a fuck about their actions and just act any sort of way around a nigga, huh?"

Rayshon chuckled as he fished in the pocket of his black and grey sweatpants for his cellphone. NiNi watched as he fumbled, and from what she assumed, responded to a text message. She rolled her eyes as she waited for his response because she didn't like the way he had come off on her.

"Oh, so you ain't gon' say nothing? That's that bullshit cas' it takes a lot for me to even get loud with somebody, and you done pissed me all the way off," she snapped.

Rayshon glanced at her, and then put his attention back on his phone. He could feel the tension fill the room and it came out of nowhere. He couldn't understand why NiNi got so angry just by a little statement he made.

"I can do without this shit," NiNi said. She got up from the couch and slammed her drink and chips down on the counter when she walked into the kitchen.

"Yo, you serious right now?" he asked. He got up and walked over to her.

When he saw her nostrils flared and felt the heat from her body, he knew she was more than serious. Rayshon had been with more than a few females in his life, but NiNi was different and he could tell that something was eating at her to make her snap the way she did.

"Please get away from me," she said.

NiNi took her hand and pushed him back gently. She was so upset with herself for snapping the way she did. She hated letting her emotions and personal issues get the best of her, but that was one of the reasons she stayed to herself and only dealt with her cousin.

"Nah, come here." Rayshon pulled her close to him and wrapped his arms around her.

NiNi froze up. She had never had a guy hold her to and make her feel safe. Her not knowing Rayshon from a can of paint didn't change the fact that she felt a connection with him.

"Why you so angry, ma?" he asked.

"I—I'm not," she stuttered.

"You are. Why you so angry, ma? A nigga had to hurt you for you to let one little thing make you fly off the roof like that."

NiNi held her head down low. She was embarrassed because Rayshon had pinpointed her insecurity so easily when she tried so hard to keep up a tight wall. She didn't want him to figure her out. She didn't even want to get close to him. But the moment she saw him, it was like love at first sight. No other man had ever caught her attention the way Rayshon did, and now that she was standing there with him, she didn't know what to do or how to act. NiNi was angry when she should've been happy, but all she knew was pain, hurt, and anger so when she felt judged by Rayshon all bets were off.

"Don't act like you know me," she responded in a smart tone.

"Shit, I know when a girl been hurt. I did have a mother, ya know," he told her.

"Did?" NiNi asked.

"Yeah, did. My mother died when I was locked up seven years ago," he explained to her.

NiNi felt bad for Rayshon. She couldn't imagine losing her mother. Her mother's condition scared her every day, and she tried not to think about living without her which was the main reason NiNi dealt with the abuse at home.

"I'm sorry to hear that. I don't know what I'd do without my mother," she said.

"It's cool, and I feel you. Shit, I told you I was locked up when I lost mine."

Rayshon was still holding NiNi as they talked. He didn't mind it and neither did NiNi.

"You wanna sit down?" NiNi asked.

Rayshon chuckled.

"Why? You gettin' tired of me holdin' you?" he asked.

NiNi damn near melted when she saw him smile. .

He has dimples too? He is so handsome, she thought.

NiNi didn't want Rayshon to let her go, but she also didn't want to seem too interested and get let down. She was used to guys acting interested and then it turned out to all be a front.

"No, but I would like to sit down and continue watching my show."

"Shit, it's ya fault you missed most of it. Actin' crazy and shit." He laughed, let her go, and went to sit back down on the couch.

"Oh, my god. Shut up!" NiNi said as she followed him and took a seat on the couch.

"Only one way to make me shut up," he said flirtatiously.

NiNi looked at him confused.

"And what's that?"

"Puttin' that pussy on my face." Rayshon licked his lips.

"What!" NiNi gasped.

That was one thing she had never experienced before. Onyae always bragged about having her pussy and ass ate, but NiNi couldn't relate. She knew that if she was more outspoken and vibrant then she probably would have had the chance to experience just as much as her cousin.

"Why you yellin'?" He laughed.

"I'm not. You just caught me off guard when you said that, that's all," she spoke softly.

"Caught you off guard by sayin' put that pussy on my face? You a virgin?" he bluntly asked.

NiNi rolled her eyes, folded her arms across her chest, and poked out her lips.

"No," she responded with attitude.

"Cool, so you should know about a nigga lickin' that pussy. Unless you was too scared to ever let a nigga do it." Rayshon cut his eye at her.

NiNi looked over at him.

"You ain't got no shame with what comes outta ya mouth do you?" she asked.

"Nah, not at all. I say and do what the hell I want. Ain't nobody gon' stop me from speakin' my mind."

Rayshon spoke with so much confidence that it turned NiNi on. She peeped that he wasn't trying to be disrespectful, and the way he came off was just his personality. He reminded her of a male version of Onyae. Saying what he wanted, how he wanted, and when he wanted, and didn't mind whooping somebody's ass if they had a problem with it.

"I guess you right. How old are you by the way? I just thought about you saying that you was locked up seven years ago."

Rayshon got up and walked into the kitchen. He pulled a blunt wrap and a bag of weed out his pocket and put the contents on the counter.

"Thirty-four. You smoke? Nah, you don't smoke." He laughed.

"Why you laughing? How you know I don't smoke? And you don't look thirty-four." She got up and walked in the kitchen to be nosey.

Whenever NiNi went out with Onyae, she was around guys that smoked because those were the only guys Onyae seemed to hang around. However, NiNi never tried it before, and didn't plan on it anytime soon.

"You ain't never even had ya pussy licked. So, I know for damn sure you ain't out here smokin' no weed."

"You really act like you know me, nigga. You don't know shit," she shot back.

"I know enough. I know that a nigga hurt you, and that's why you got that wall up. I know that you ain't experienced when it comes to fuckin', and I know that you nervous when it comes to bein' around a nigga. I can tell you down to earth, and it takes the right person or the right type of crowd to get you to relax and be yaself."

Rayshon had read NiNi from top to bottom. She couldn't understand how he was able to do that when that was the first time they had actually been in each other's presence. At the store they had only saw one another for a brief second.

NiNi rubbed her hand through her hair and sighed long and hard. She eyed Rayshon as he broke open the blunt and emptied out its tobacco contents. He gave her a different vibe. She wasn't an expert at reading guys but being around the niggas she met while hanging out with Onyae allowed her to tell the difference from the no-good niggas and the good ones.

"What you lookin' at?" he asked.

"Oh, so I can't look at you now?" She smirked.

"Chill out wit' all that," he told her.

"Nah, apparently I can't look at you. That's cool. I won't." She playfully turned away.

"I ain't mean it like that. I'm just sayin', you seem like you was in deep thought while you was lookin' at me. So, I'm wonderin' wassup?"

NiNi turned back to face him and almost melted at the sight of him licking the blunt to seal it. The thoughts she had went from PG-13 to naughty in just a matter of seconds. Everything about Rayshon was thuggish, but sweet at the same damn time. NiNi didn't know where the feelings she had for him came from, but all she knew was that he took her breath away.

"Nothin'."

Rayshon shook his head, pulled a lighter out his pocket and sparked up his blunt. NiNi watched him take a few pulls before coughing as he blew the smoke out.

"We gon' have to get you up outta that shy shit. I can't have my girl like that. We gon' spend a lot more time together and I guarantee all that shit gon' change," he spoke with confidence.

"Girl?" she asked in confusion.

"I don't think I stuttered. They say speak shit into existence. Well, I'm speakin' on it."

"Boy, you need to stop." NiNi giggled.

She was blushing so hard; she just couldn't control it. Rayshon was saying all the right things and she wasn't used to any of it.

"Boy?" Rayshon frowned his face up at her. "Ain't no boy over here, ma. I'm all man. I work, got my own place, my own car, pay my own bills, and this ten-and-a-half-inch dick lets me know that ain't shit boyish over here."

"Oh, my bad. I ain't mean to make you feel a way," NiNi apologized.

Rayshon took a few more pulls of his blunt before blowing the smoke out and coughing again.

"Walk outside wit' me," he said as he walked past NiNi.

She turned around and followed him outside and they sat on the steps of Gutta's house. The night wind felt good to NiNi as it hit her arms and sent chills through her body.

"What's ya story, ma?" Rayshon asked.

"What you mean what's my story?" She looked at him in confusion.

"I'm sayin'. I ain't never seen you around before and I been in Bridgeton plenty of times. Most of my family live out there and I never saw you. I saw ya cousin a few times here and there, but you, never. Why is that?" he stated.

NiNi shrugged her shoulders.

"Maybe cas' I don't come out like that. I'm more of a homebody. I always been that way. Mainly cas' my mother is sick, but even if she wasn't, I still wouldn't be out. Hell, I barely like people as it is."

"I feel you on that, and sorry to hear about ya moms," he told her.

"It's cool. She's gettin' better," she said trying to convince herself.

Rayshon nodded.

"That's wassup. So, where ya man at? How old are you? You got a baby face, so I know you a lil' youngin'."

NiNi burst out laughing and cocked her head to the side and looked at him.

"How the hell you gonna say I'm ya girl and then ask me do I got a dude and then my age on top of that?"

"Shit, maybe cas' I can? I just wanna know if I gotta beat somebody ass or not," he responded and took another pull of the blunt. "Now you gon' answer my questions or nah?"

NiNi chuckled a little this time. It was more of a dry laugh than anything. She couldn't understand why Rayshon wanted to do so much for her and they had just met one another. That wasn't something she was used to from guys, she didn't know how to feel about it, and she didn't know whether she should be accepting of it or not.

"You gon' answer a nigga?"

"What you want me to say?" she asked with a hint of frustration in her voice.

"Pipe down, ma. All that ain't even needed when it comes to me," he assured her.

NiNi folded her arms across her chest and crossed her legs in front of her.

"I don't have a man. You happy now? And I'm nineteen," NiNi smacked her lips.

Rayshon glanced over at her and took a puff of his blunt. He spoke as the smoke was released from his mouth.

"I don't wanna have to keep remindin' you about ya mouth, ma. I'ma cool, calm, and collective kinda dude. I don't take no form of disrespect from nobody and I've been givin' you respect, so I think I deserve it back, right?" he asked.

"I don't care. I been through too much to just give a nigga my respect. That's how it always starts off. Yawl be nice to reel me in, and then show me yawl true colors. I'm good on that shit to be honest. My own damn daddy showed me that I can never trust a nigga no matter how nice he seems to be."

NiNi was talking a mile a minute, and she couldn't stop herself from saying the things she said. For some reason, she felt like she could be as raw and uncut as she wanted while she was around Rayshon. It was as if he brought out a side of her that she had kept hidden for so long because she was afraid. There had been plenty of times she could let her hair down with Onyae, but Rayshon was something special. He made her feel like the naysayers didn't matter and that she could tell him her drawers were dirty if she wanted to.

"I can't even sit here and act like I don't know where you comin' from, ma. They say a father is the first man that will ever break his daughter's heart. Sucks to say I saw my sister go through that same shit when my dad walked out on us time and time again, but good thing is, she had three brothers to pick up the pieces for her. I'm assuming you ain't have that same opportunity?"

NiNi's lips trembled a little.

"I wish I did have a brother. Then maybe life wouldn't have kicked my ass like it did."

Rayshon rubbed the fire end of his blunt on the step to put it out. He then shoved the remainder in the back of his ear before folding his hands in one another.

"I'm a hood ass nigga, ma, I ain't even gon' hold you. But it def seem like you need somebody to talk to. I'm here to listen if anything."

It wasn't often that Rayshon cared about a girl and her feelings. Before he met his ex, he had grown accustomed to fucking females and moving on to the next one. During their relationship, she took him through hell and back which resulted in him being that player again.

Rayshon could peep that NiNi was a good girl. She was young, and it seemed as though she had a good head on her shoulders. All she needed was a little more guidance and stability that he was more than willing to give her if she let him.

"Nah, I'm good on that. But thanks anyway," NiNi told him.

She stood up and brushed the grit off her bottom and turned to go back in the house.

"You leavin' me?" Rayshon asked looking back at her.

"Ain't really my intentions, but what more is there to talk about? I mean, everything you said was cool, but my life is complicated. I'm not interested in telling you my secrets. I'm not interested in allowing you to get close to me. I'm way too damaged to allow any of that to happen, but like I said, thanks anyway."

NiNi left Rayshon sitting there to gather his thoughts. She went back into the house, kicked her shoes off, and sat right back down on the couch to finish watching what was left of *Love and Hip-Hop: Atlanta*. Not too long after, Rayshon came in the house, kicked his shoes off, and sat down beside her. They were both silent, but their thoughts were loud. As bad as NiNi tried to brush it off and fight it, there was indeed a strong connection between the two. She didn't know how to go about letting love in…if it was love and not just lust.

Chapter 4

When Monday morning arrived, Gutta and Rayshon got themselves together to drop Onyae and NiNi off at Onyae's house. Through the entire ride the girls sat in the back cackling and giggling about the events that happened the night before. When they finally arrived at Onyae's house, Gutta still gave her the same respectful treatment he gave her the night before.

"I'ma hit you up when I touch back in Philly, ard?" Gutta said to Onyae when he opened the back door to let her out.

"A'ight cool. I def enjoyed maself," she said with a smirk.

He leaned forward and gave her a kiss.

"Shit, I did too. I'ma def need more of that, ma."

She glanced down and watched as his dick grew in his sweatpants. As bad as she wanted to fuck him again right then and there, she had to take it like a G and keep the ball in her court.

"Tuh, I know this," Onyae said and then walked away, leaving Gutta standing there with a hard dick.

Rayshon burst out laughing as he watched his cousin drool over Onyae. He couldn't front because she was a beauty, but he had never witnessed Gutta looking at any female the way he looked at Onyae.

"The fuck you over there laughin' at?" Gutta asked and then hopped back in his ride.

"You, nigga. The fuck?" Rayshon snapped back before turning his attention to NiNi.

"Everything okay?" she asked.

"Yea, me and that nigga always poke fun at each other. It ain't nothin', but aye, look I had a good time wit' you last night, ma. Even tho' you snapped on a nigga real quick, and walked off on a nigga, left me straight stankin' and went in the house." He laughed before he continued. "You got real good conversation, real talk."

NiNi blushed. She agreed that he had good conversation as well, and she was proud of the way she handled herself being that it was her first time being alone with a guy. A guy of his caliber at that.

"Thanks honey. I enjoyed myself with you too, surprisingly," she said, and got out of the truck.

She proceeded to talk past Rayshon and head to the house until he grabbed her. NiNi had an instant flashback when Rayshon grabbed her. The frightened look in her eyes when she turned around made him let her go and take a step back; he didn't know that her mini flashback had caused her fright.

"Sorry ma. I just wasn't finished talkin' to you. Didn't mean no harm," he apologized.

"I can text you later," she responded and turned away quickly.

Rayshon watched NiNi all the way up until she entered the house. He couldn't put his finger on it, but there was something about her that made him want to get to know her more. He was intrigued by her shyness and wondered how a girl that was as beautiful as her could give off such a cold vibe. One minute she was comfortable and then the next minute she wasn't, which was highly confusing to him, and he wanted to know the reason behind it all.

"If you don't get ya sight seein' ass in here so we can go? Shit, you laughin' at me, but it look like shawty got you gone already!" Gutta said, breaking Rayshon out of his trance.

"Nigga, shut the fuck up!" Rayshon shot back.

He got back in the truck and made sure to slam the door with force just to annoy Gutta.

"Ard, you gettin' serious now. Don't be slammin' a nigga shit."

"Shut ya sensitive ass up."

"Nah man, don't slam my shit. I'll get out this truck and beat yo ass you keep fuckin' around wit' my baby."

"Yea whateva, nigga. I like to see you try." Rayshon gave him the side eye.

Gutta put the car in drive and pulled off.

"You lucky I ain't wanna embarrass you back there," Gutta said and they both broke out in laughter.

"Nigga, you stupid, but anyway, I see you def feelin' shawty back there." Rayshon changed the subject.

"I can say the same to you, nigga," Gutta said as he turned on his left turn signal.

"I'm not gon' front and act like I ain't interested in gettin' to know shorty cas' I am, but I can see love in ya eyes, cous."

"Mannnnn fuck outta here! After what I saw you go through wit' Sharee's crazy ass, ain't no way I'm takin' it there wit' any female. I don't give a fuck how good the pussy is. That bitch was crazy, and I would've been done killed a bitch if she did to me what Sharee did to you." Gutta was referring to Rayshon's ex-girlfriend.

Rayshon shook his head in response to what Gutta said. He couldn't blame him for feeling that way about women. Although, he was a street nigga, somehow, he had managed to allow Sharee to steal his heart. Not only did she crush his heart, but she took his loyalty for granted.

"I can't even blame you for feelin' the way you feel, but anyway, we gon' need to take a trip out to Cherry Hill. You know when we go, we gotta stay a few days tho', right?"

"Nigga, you act like I'm new to this shit. Understand I'm true to it. You ain't gotta keep remindin' me about shit I already know," Gutta stated as he made his turn.

"I'm just sayin', nigga. You my left, and I'm ya right so we both gotta stay on point."

"Exactly nigga, I'm ya left hand man. I earned that fuckin' spot, cous. So, understand that I'm always on my A g—"

Scrrrrrrrr!

"What the fuck!" Gutta yelled at the man in a black pick-up truck.

Rayshon immediately lifted his shirt up and went for his gun. Just by the scowl on the driver's face he could tell that he wanted problems, and he was sure enough about to get them. Gutta hopped out of the truck with his 9mm in his right hand ready to put a nigga on his ass, and he didn't give a fuck who witnessed it. Rayshon hopped out and was right on his heels with his Beretta in his hand.

"We got a muthafuckin' problem?" Gutta asked as he stood at the driver's side window.

"That's what the fuck I'm tryna figure out?" Rayshon added as he stood at the passenger side window.

Damon mean mugged Gutta, and then cut his eye at Rayshon. If looks could kill, Rayshon would be dead. He could feel the tension between him and the stranger and it caused him to grip his Beretta a little bit tighter.

"No problem here, gentlemen," Damon responded with a grin on his face.

He was disgusted, but the two gun toting men humbled him before he could think about causing any sort of trouble.

"Yea, that's what the fuck I thought. Watch where the fuck you goin' next time, bul," Gutta said before walking away.

Rayshon stood there for a moment, and he and Damon locked eyes. He didn't know where the tension was coming from, but he knew for a fact that whomever he was had a serious issue. It didn't dawn on Rayshon that there was a possibility that the man sitting behind the wheel of the black pickup truck was the cause of NiNi's mood changes. He didn't press the issue and looked at the entire situation as coincidental and went back and got inside Gutta's truck.

While Gutta pulled off, Damon turned the corner with force and sped past Onyae's house. He wanted to stop and cause a scene, but he wasn't going to go against his better judgement because Onyae was sure enough to swing as soon as she saw him.

"I got something for you NiNi. You can bet that," he spat.

Damon shook his head all while he drove home. It burned him up inside to think that NiNi was with some boy when she should have been focused on other things in life, like her mother and building a better relationship with him considering he had been there since day one.

***

"Mom, I really don't wanna talk," Onyae said to Yoshi. She was standing at the stove cooking brunch.

Onyae wasn't even in the door for a good five minutes before her mother started on her about giving Khalif a try. She didn't want to put too much pressure on her, but she at least wanted her daughter to hear her out.

"Onyae, you really need to stop with that cold ass attitude. I'm not tellin' you to welcome him wit' open arms. All I'm sayin' is give him a chance. I mean just see what he's about before you go to judge," Yoshi explained.

NiNi decided that it would be best for her to go to Onyae's room as they had their much-needed talk. She wished that she could turn back the hands of time and have her mother come to her about her now stepfather, but NiNi didn't have that chance. One day she looked up, and Damon was coming to dinner, staying the night, and the next thing she knew he had slowly moved in. Soon after, NiNi had no choice but to welcome him in with open arms, but her being young and naïve made her a target. Months passed and then years before she realized that Damon wasn't someone she wanted as a stepfather or husband for her mother.

"I gave him a chance. I spoke to him last night, didn't I?"

Some would have thought that Onyae was being sarcastic, but in all reality, that was just her personality and she was dead serious.

"Onyae, please stop it. I know how you're feeling, but please trust Mommy on this one. Give him a chance for me, and I promise you won't regret it," Yoshi said.

Although the night before was a great night for Onyae, that wasn't enough to make her feel comfortable about her mother dating. She sat in the dining room tapping her freshly manicured nails on their mango burnished walnut table. She couldn't wrap her brain around the thought of welcoming a new man into her life, but seeing how happy her mother was, made her at least give it some thought.

"I'm not gon' say no, but I'm also not gon' say yes. Just give me some time to think about it, Mom."

Yoshi gave her a simple nod, but she was smiling inside. She was happy that her daughter was at least giving it some consideration; that was all she asked for until she was ready to accept the second love of her life.

NiNi laid in bed ear hustling their entire conversation. She sighed a sigh of relief once she heard Onyae's response. She knew how Onyae felt, but she was proud of her for slowly breaking that wall down that she'd built over the years.

"Now that we got that outta the way, who is the new boo you have? Don't think I wasn't looking out the window at yawl. He got a nice ass ride too. I hope his attitude is just as nice cas' you know I'll shoot a nigga in his fuckin' kneecaps for hurting you in any manner," Yoshi said.

Onyae chuckled.

"Keep calm, Mom. He cool as hell from what I see so far. He got a nice ride, a nice house, and he nice between the legs. I mean, I'm just sayin'."

Yoshi leaned over and gave her daughter a high five.

"Yesssss! I know that's right. If you gon' fuck a nigga make sure he's worth fuckin'. Don't give ya body up to a nigga that can't take care of himself. You know I always taught you that cas' I had to learn the hard way. Mommy always went for the niggas that was good lookin', but they ain't have shit. I know I should've learned my lesson from ya father, but I was damaged and didn't know it until now."

Onyae felt every word her mother was saying, and she appreciated her honesty. Most would've looked at her and her mother's relationship as ratchet, but she didn't give a fuck. She was blessed with a down ass mother who kept it real with her no matter the outcome.

"I feel you, Mom, but stuff happens. I'm glad I can learn from you, if anything," she responded.

"You damn right, and you better not ever let any of these niggas take advantage of you. I don't care how big they dick is, how nice they house is, and how expensive the car they drive is. Don't ever let no nigga take advantage of you. And don't ever let a nigga put his hands on you. You see what I went through. I'ma continue to let you have ya fun cas' you young, but don't be like me when it comes to these niggas, baby; don't be like me. I am thankful to be blessed with Khalif, but that was years and years after being a battered woman."

Onyae listened to her mother spit knowledge to her and she took in every word. She couldn't deny that she hated men because of what her father did to them. On top of that she watched her mother struggle in relationship after relationship until Yoshi finally resulted in being a player. Onyae knew that there was a possibility that she could miss her knight in shining armor with the attitude she had, and taking on her mother's player ways, but that was the least of her worries because she didn't give a fuck.

Chapter 5

It was Wednesday, and NiNi had just gotten out of the shower. She made plans to go over Onyae's house because she hadn't heard from her much since Monday; that bothered her because they talked every day, all day. She knew that nothing major happened, but she didn't like not hearing from her cousin. NiNi figured that Onyae probably got caught up with her every day wild life. She just knew that Onyae had a crazy story to tell her once they caught up with one another.

Knock. Knock. Knock.

"Who is it?" she asked.

"Me." Damon's deep voice was heard from the other side.

NiNi's stomach started to rumble, and it felt like she had the bubble guts. She hated Damon with everything in her and she didn't understand why he didn't get the hint already.

"What do you want?" she asked as she rolled her eyes.

"NiNi, open this damn door before I break this bitch down!" he barked.

NiNi was startled by his outburst. No matter how many times she tried to act tough when it came to him, he always brought out the bitch in her.

"O—okay." Her voice trembled as she attempted to put on her remaining clothes, but the only thing she could get on was her bra before she hurried to open her bedroom door.

Damon barged in and slammed the door behind him. He grabbed NiNi by her face and squeezed tight.

"Oww!" She managed to get out through her mashed lips.

"Shut the fuck up! Who was that nigga I saw you talking to the day before yesterday?" Damon asked.

He couldn't confront NiNi right away because she didn't come home until Tuesday while he was at work; it was Wednesday morning and he was just getting home. Damon brought in good money working as a security guard for Atlantic City hotels. He even did some side jobs such as big events and parties. Point blank, Damon was the bread winner, and in his eyes, he was the head of household.

NiNi smacked at his hand and pulled away simultaneously.

"Mom!" she screamed.

"What the fuck you yellin' mom for? You know she at chemo so it's just me and you. So, tell me who the fuck that nigga was that you were talkin' to? You think just cas' you're grown that it's okay to be out here bein' a whore? You can't even work or go to school, but you out here entertainin' a nigga!"

Damon was pissed, and his flared nostrils and defensive posture let NiNi know exactly how he was feeling.

"Don't fuckin' worry about who I was talkin' to! I hate you! I wish you would fuckin' leave me and my mother the hell alone! We don't need you or your money!" she yelled.

NiNi was tired of Damon and his existence. They went at it like cats and dogs, but she couldn't deny that she was grateful that lately all they did was argue.

Whap!

Damon went across NiNi's face with an open hand slap. Her head whipped back, and she turned to look at him as her eyes watered. She wanted to grab her cellphone and call her mother, but she knew that would only leave her and her mother out to fend for themselves. What happened next was something she wished didn't happen as usual. He grabbed her and slammed her up against the dresser and pulled her towel up.

NiNi tried to turn around and push him away, but he snatched a handful of her hair and yanked her head back around. NiNi looked at Damon through the mirror with sorrow in her eyes hoping that the child like look she gave him would stop him, but she should've known it wouldn't because it didn't before.

"Don't play wit' me, bitch. You keep this tough act up, and I'ma kill ya dumb ass one of these days," he threatened.

NiNi could hear him unbuckling his belt, and the next thing she knew, Damon was pushing his thick, seven-and-a-half-inch dick inside of NiNi. He slammed his body back and forth with force.

"Ouch! Ow!" she cried.

"Shut the fuck up!" he growled.

Damon placed his right hand on NiNi's right shoulder and held her waist with his left hand as he looked down at her ass jump each time he rammed his dick in and out of her. NiNi could feel the thickness of Damon's dick split her just like all the times before. She wasn't wet, and nothing in her body could get her wet for what she endured from him. Her pussy was dry, but Damon didn't care one bit as he continued to thrust in and out of her. Beads of sweat formed on his forehead, and he was tight lipped as he focused on getting his nut off while NiNi's mother was at the doctors. Tears ran down her face as she closed her eyes as tight as she could while her body hit up against her dresser knocking things down. Her stomach was in knots and all she prayed for was her mother to find some way home and walk straight in on Damon in the act, but she knew that was just wishful thinking.

"Urgh, urghh, ugh," Damon moaned.

He held onto NiNi tight as he made sure he emptied every last drop of himself in her, and once he was finished, he pulled out and smeared the remaining semen on her ass. Damon stuffed his dick back in his dirty blue jeans and buckled his button and belt.

"Clean yaself up, and I swear you better not say shit when I go pick ya mom up and bring her home. Ya dumb ass gettin' bold but go ahead and continue to be bold. Ya mother gon' be in the fuckin' grave, and ya ass gon' be homeless, bitch," he spat, and then stormed out of her bedroom.

NiNi ran to the door, slammed it shut and hurried to lock it before she dropped to the floor with tears pouring down her face as Damon's cum oozed out of her. No matter how many times Damon used her body she felt dirtier each time and she hated the fact that there was nothing she could do about it. Her mother was her life so losing her wasn't an option.

While the tears ran down her face, and the thoughts ran through her mind, she managed to crawl over to her bed and grab her cellphone. She went to her favorites contacts, clicked on Onyae's name, and put the phone to her ear.

Ring. Ring. Ring.

Ring. Ring. Ring.

"Please answer Onyae please," she cried.

Ring. Ring. Ring.

"Hello! Sorry girl, but I'm about to beat this bitch's ass. I can't even talk right now!" Onyae scoffed into the phone.

The tears that rained down NiNi's face were gone in seconds because she wiped them away, and the pain she felt between her legs wasn't the focus anymore. Her cousin was in trouble and that was all she was worried about.

"Where you at?" NiNi asked as she got up off the floor.

She didn't even bother to clean herself. She hurried to put on a pair of dark yoga pants, and a white tank top. She put on a pair of old Nike sneakers she had in her closet and quickly tied her hair up as she held the phone in between her shoulder and cheek.

"I'm at Coastal's, girl, come on cas' I'm beatin' a bitch ass today."

Click.

NiNi unlocked her door and ran out slamming it behind her. She ran through the dining room, the kitchen and then out the door without stopping. Coastal's was a mini hike walking, but NiNi managed to get halfway there before she stopped to catch her breath. Her chest was heaving up and down, and her legs were weak from all the nonstop running, but she caught her breath and then continued down the street. Minutes later, she stepped foot into the parking lot of the store and saw Gutta's truck. She then saw Gutta standing in between Onyae and a group of girls; that seemed to give NiNi a boost of energy because she kicked dust running over there.

"We got a problem?" she asked, eyeing each of the five girls that stood on the other side of Gutta.

"Hell yea they got a fuckin' problem, sis. These bitches got me fucked up and it's all over dick. See, that's what broke bitches do! Move Gutta!" Onyae yelled.

"Nah, shawty, come on chill wit' all that. It ain't even worth it," he told her.

Whap!

The girl named Krystal slapped Gutta hard on the side of his face. "Oh, so, I'm not worth it now? Really nigga! I'm not worth it!"

He shook his head trying to keep his composure because he wanted to knock her ass the fuck out, but he refrained from doing so.

"Shawty chill, and don't put ya hands on me. This why I stopped fuckin' wit' you cas' you stay on some dumb shit that I don't got time for," he said as he looked back at her.

"Get the fuck outta here. So, now you don't fuck wit' me, but you was just plannin' on fuckin' me a couple of nights ago? Oh, I guess since you got some new pussy you don't need me anymore, huh? Hoe, he just gon' fuck you and dip cas' that's all you is, a dumb ass hoe that's good to fuck and look at. He don't want you," Krystal said while talking with her hands.

That was one thing Onyae nor NiNi played. Don't get knuck if you wasn't ready to buck, and Krystal was damn sure knucking while her friends stood by for what Onyae and NiNi assumed was protection.

Bop!

"Wassup then bitch!" NiNi swung on Krystal but Gutta managed to block her hit.

Bop! Bop!

Onyae ducked under Gutta's arm and snuck in a quick two-piece on the side of Krystal's head. He grabbed her before shit could go any further, and that gave NiNi the opportunity to finish things off, but out of nowhere she was scooped up and put to the side.

"Get the fuck off me! I'll fuck that stank ass hoe up! She got me and my cousin fucked up out here!" She kicked and screamed.

"Chill ma. They ain't worth it. Believe that," Rayshon spoke in a calm voice.

NiNi didn't know where he came from nor did she care. She wanted to beat ass and nothing was going to stop her from getting to those girls.

"Let me go, Rayshon, I'm not playin'," she warned.

"I don't care about none of that. Fuck them hoes," he told her.

"Woooowwwwww! So, I'ma hoe now, Rayshon, really?" another girl said from the sideline.

She was one of the girls that stood with Krystal, and she looked a hot damn mess.

"Sharee, shut up talkin' to me, yo. You always somewhere startin' some trouble. You too old for that yo."

Sharee was a thirty-nine-year-old, dark brown-skinned woman, with a wild, jet black, curly weave, bright green contacts, tattooed eyebrows, and a dot in the middle of her forehead. She stood at five-foot-five and popped hella noise to whoever and whenever; however, her actions never matched the bark she had.

"Nigga please. Don't tell me to shut up as if I'm some whack ass bitch off the street. You sittin' over here entertainin' this fat bitch, no wonder you ain't been answering my calls or texts." She insulted NiNi just because she thought she could.

NiNi tried to jerk away from Rayshon, but he had a tight hold on her.

"Bitch, I'll fuck you up out here, on God! Talkin' about I'm fat bitch look at you! Ol' linebacker-built bitch!"

"Whatever hoe, you ain't like that at all!" Sharee screamed back.

"Okay bitch, but I like to fight so wassup?" Onyae yelled back as she tried to get away from Gutta, but just like Rayshon, he had a tight hold on her.

Sharee waved her off and rolled her eyes.

"Girl bye, ain't nobody thinkin' about you. Get ya friend, Gutta, get ya friend," she told him.

"Don't tell me what the fuck to do. I should let her ass go so she can bust ya ass. Yawl talk so much shit, but ain't bout no kind of action. Get the fuck on, Sharee, and take Krystal ratchet ass wit' you."

Krystal stood there teary eyed and embarrassed. Her mouth was hanging wide open as she watched Gutta walk past her with his arms wrapped around Onyae just to make sure she didn't throw any sudden punches. She couldn't believe he just disowned her right in front of everyone. They had been fucking around with one another for the last five months, but Gutta had cut her off suddenly. She swore up and down she couldn't understand why he did so. But even a blind man could see that Krystal and her crew were nothing but ratchets and they were full of drama. No man wanted to deal with that, and Gutta had made the mistake of not cutting her off sooner.

"Get off me, Gutta, cas' you wild as hell." Onyae tried to wiggle out of his grasp.

"What the fuck I did?" He let her go and looked at her confused as all hell.

By now, the crowd that had formed cleared out and the girls were too busy trying to console Krystal as she cried.

"You let a bitch come at me sideways! And don't give me that shit about I'm not even ya girl cas' I don't give a fuck about that shit. If I'm fuckin' you, don't have none of those rat faced bitches approaching me about shit! They don't have the right to talk to me about anything! Handle ya muthafuckin' business as a man cas' you just about got that bitch cut the fuck up!"

"Man, I ain't want that shit to go down. I told you that I was at the store buyin' some wraps and then I was gon' come holla at you. I ain't want you to come down here cas' once I saw them pull up, I knew it would be some shit. You think I wanted you to get into it wit' them ratchet ass hoes?" he asked.

"Fuck outta here, nigga. That bitch said you was tryna fuck her a couple of nights ago, so you knew that some shit was gon' pop once we saw each other. That's how insecure bitches is. They get mad at the new female, and that's that shit I don't like. Be real about ya shit. If you got a bitch let me know, but don't have me walkin' into some shit."

Gutta shook his head in frustration. He rubbed his eyes in a stressed manner because Onyae was a cool ass girl, and he honestly didn't want to fuck up the road to a good friendship over some past pussy that he didn't want.

"I ain't even tryna argue right now to be honest. I apologize for how shit went down, but I don't fuck wit' her at all."

Onyae rolled her eyes and waved him off.

"Pssh, nigga please. Fuck you and ya apology. This why I don't take none of you niggas serious now cas' yawl all about that fuck shit. You don't fuck wit' her for the moment, but that bitch ain't just poppin' off at the mouth for nothin'!" Onyae threw her hands up and pushed past Gutta. She was so over him and the situation.

She had to walk in the store to get her a drink cas' the situation had her heated in more ways than one.

When NiNi saw how aggravated her cousin was, she looked at Rayshon who was shaking his head at the situation.

"What the fuck you shaking ya head at? You ain't no different from ya dog ass cousin. That shit is fucked up." NiNi proceeded to follow Onyae, but Rayshon stopped her.

"What the fuck you jumpin' on me for? I ain't got shit to do wit' what they got goin' on," he said in defense.

"Bull-fuckin-shit. That's ya muthafuckin' cousin, and you know what the fuck he be doin'. The least you could've did the night we chilled was keep it real about the type of nigga ya cousin was, but that's typical nigga shit. Always ridin' for ya peoples before the female you fuckin'. A damn shame." NiNi was moving her hands in all kinds of directions as she gave Rayshon the third degree.

She saw Onyae come back out the store and she began to walk over to her, but Rayshon grabbed her which sent NiNi into a raging fit.

Whap!

"Get the fuck off me!" she screamed as she slapped him hard across his face.

Rayshon was shocked and confused by her outburst. Onyae ran over and grabbed NiNi. Gutta was standing there trying to figure out what the hell had just happened. Before any of them knew it, Sharee was charging over to NiNi and Onyae like a bat out of hell.

"Oh, bitch you touched the wrong one!" she yelled.

Rayshon stood in front of NiNi, but NiNi shook out of Onyae's grasp, dipped under Rayshon's arm and clocked Sharee right in her nose. *Boop!* Instantly making her stumble back and rethink her decision of running up on NiNi and Onyae.

"This bitch just hit me! Rayshon, you let that bitch hit me!" Sharee screamed.

She was bent over holding her nose while her friends stood back in awe because they saw blood dripping on the ground.

"Oh shit," Gutta said from the sideline.

He had no clue what was going on, but he grabbed Onyae and NiNi, pulling them both to his truck.

"Yo, let's get the fuck up outta here, cous," Gutta called out.

Rayshon didn't protest because he knew why Gutta was telling him they needed to dip out. Sharee was good for calling the cops. Rayshon knew that the moment she got herself together she was going to be on the phone, and soon, the entire parking lot would be lit up with the boys. That's just how she was. The type of female that got herself into trouble but was the first one to call the cops.

Gutta opened the back-passenger door and damn near tried to throw them both in.

"Get yawl asses in there," he told them.

Rayshon hopped in the passenger seat while Gutta slammed the back door and hopped in the driver's side. Gutta started up his truck, put it in reverse and beeped like a crazy person as he backed up, praying that he didn't hit anyone.

"What the hell is goin' on?" Onyae asked, while placing her hands on the side of each seat and peeking her head in the front.

"A nigga ain't about to get locked up over no dumb shit. Uh, uh, not today," Gutta replied, and then turned down Onyae's street.

"Sharee got this thing wit' callin' the cops, and we had to dip up outta there that's all," Rayshon added.

"See, all this shit yawl done got us into," Onyae looked back at NiNi. "You good, boo?"

"Yea, I'm good. I'm just ready to go home."

Onyae sat back, reached over and began to brush her fingers through NiNi's hair fixing it for her.

"Take NiNi home first." She spoke directly to Gutta who had just pulled up in front of her house.

"Yo, why you couldn't say that shit before I turned on ya street?" he snapped.

"Nigga, shut the fuck up and take my fuckin' cousin home. You already done fucked up so taking her home first won't hurt. Shit, I need to make sure she get home safe cas' it's clear we can't trust yawl niggas," Onyae said rudely.

"What's ya damn address?" he asked.

"Nigga, don't get huffy with me cas' you fucked up!" NiNi shot back.

"Girl shut yo ass up, and give me ya damn address," Gutta snapped.

NiNi rolled her eyes and waved him off.

"Cous, give him ya address before I have to knock his ass the fuck out," Onyae chimed in.

"Pssh," NiNi smacked her lips. "34..." She gave him her address.

Gutta shook his head but went on and took NiNi home because arguing was something he didn't like to do. A few minutes later, he was pulling in front of NiNi's house. Rayshon got out of the truck and opened the back door for NiNi to get out.

"I'm not handicapped. I could've gotten out on my own," she said and smacked her lips.

"Come on wit' the attitude, ma."

"Like I said, I could've opened the door by myself, and now that I'm home safe and sound yawl can leave," NiNi said while looking at Onyae.

Onyae caught her drift and spoke up.

"I'm ready to go, yawl. So, let's go."

"Come on, bruh," Gutta called out.

Rayshon looked at NiNi who rolled her eyes at him and walked away. All he could do was shake his head, get back in the car, and slam the door in frustration. The situation that happened earlier went left, and now here he was beefing with NiNi when the shit wasn't even his fault.

As Gutta pulled away from the curb slowly, his eyes focused on the black pickup truck in the driveway of NiNi's house. He nudged Rayshon and nodded towards the direction of the driveway.

"Ain't that the same truck from the other day?" he asked.

Rayshon rubbed his beard and nodded.

"Hell yea, that's that same truck. Yo, Onyae who truck is that?"

Onyae looked from the back window and saw that their focus was on Damon's pickup truck. Before she answered any questions, she wanted to know why they were so concerned about who's truck it was.

"The fuck yawl wanna know for?" she snapped.

Onyae didn't want to make any more problems for her cousin. Her stepfather was one of the biggest problems in her life, and she didn't need to add any more fuel to the fire. So, when it came to NiNi and them questioning anything about her she became extra cautious.

"Calm that shit down, ma. The nigga who drive that ugly, ashy ass truck act like he got a muthafuckin' problem. And you can't tell me it ain't the same truck cas' it got a dent on the side of the passenger door, and them same dingy ass hubcaps on it." Rayshon had a good memory.

"What kind of problem you talkin' about?" Onyae was curious to know.

She knew who drove the truck, but she wondered what issues that Damon had with Gutta and Rayshon. She couldn't recall a time when NiNi mentioned Damon having problems with anyone, so all of this was confusing to her.

"When I dropped you and NiNi off the morning after we chilled together that nigga ran down on us like he had a problem. I wouldn't even sweat it, but the hate in that nigga's eyes made me feel some sorta way. Where I come from, you gotta watch niggas like that cas' they will try to catch you slippin' when you least expect it. I been done got that nigga before he got me," Gutta explained.

"Word up. I don't play that shit, and if anything, I'm tryna figure out where he know us from and what's the problem," Rayshon added.

"That nigga got a problem wit' everybody. It ain't just yawl," Onyae said.

Gutta jerked his head to the side and looked back at her.

"You know the nigga?"

"Long story, and I don't got time to explain shit to ya ass. So, take me home."

Onyae rolled her eyes at him, sat back and folded her arms across her chest as she pouted. She wasn't about to let Gutta off the hook just like that after the way he allowed the situation to go down at the store.

"Yo, if you know somethin' tell us," Rayshon told her.

She ignored him. "Take me home, Gutta."

Gutta shook his head and sped down the street. He didn't like the way Onyae was acting at all. He understood that she was upset, but in his eyes the fact that she was the one riding in his truck after the altercation should've spoke volumes. He couldn't understand how Onyae could pop on him when he didn't lie about anything. Yeah, he wanted to smash Krystal a few night ago, but that's all she was, a piece of ass.

Gutta couldn't see himself wifing Krystal because she was too much drama with not-a-damn-thing going for herself. He finally pulled in front of Onyae's house, and she damn near jumped out of his truck before he made a complete stop.

"Yo, Onyae!" Gutta called out.

"Fuck you, nigga! Don't call my fuckin' phone anymore!"

Slam!

She slammed his door and stormed up the walkway to her house. Gutta opened the driver's side door, but Rayshon grabbed him.

"Dog, let her cool off. Right now, ain't the time. Cas' she liable to start swingin' on ya ass and we don't need that. We don't need that shit at all."

"Pssh," Gutta sucked his teeth while slamming his door shut. "This why I just fuck bitches and leave them. All this extra shit is crazy, bruh. I'm not bouta have these bitches stressin' me out."

"I feel you. You know I do, but I also know you feelin' shorty. Just chill and give her some time. She gon' come around cas' she feelin' you too."

Rayshon tried his best to keep calm and be the rational one. He knew that everyone being upset wouldn't solve a damn thing, so he made sure to be the peace maker in all that was going on. He also made a mental note to stop by NiNi's house the next day to apologize to her for all that went on. It wasn't his character to put any female in harm's way or make her feel like she couldn't be around him without having to defend herself due to drama.

"I don't know, bruh. We was just talkin' about this shit. How I refuse to end up like you when Sharee was takin' you through it. I ain't tryna clown you, but man, shawty had you gone. I don't wanna be like that man, fareal," Gutta explained.

For a minute, Rayshon thought he heard Gutta choke up a little. He couldn't deny that Sharee took him through hell and back. She had him in and out of jail for domestic disputes and lies which was the very reason Rayshon hustled instead of having a real nine to five. His record was fucked up because he chose to love the wrong person. Though he no longer regretted it, he couldn't blame Gutta for not wanting to go down that road. However, he didn't get the vibe that Onyae nor NiNi was like Sharee or the rest of the hood rat females they dealt with in the past.

"Give her some time, bruh. Just give her some time," Rayshon responded.

Gutta didn't respond, and instead of him or Rayshon changing the subject, they both decided to stay silent and just head to their destination. The car was silent, but their thoughts were loud. Gutta couldn't care less what Rayshon was talking about; he was going to keep his same mentality and that was fuck bitches, get money. He was feeling Onyae but refused to let her have him all in his feelings. The most he was going to do was apologize for the situation, and after that the ball would be in her court. But little did he know, Onyae had the same mentality as him and she wasn't one for letting up so easily.

Chapter 6

Later that evening, Onyae was still aggravated from the fight that happened earlier. Gutta had been texting her since the incident, but she had nothing to say to him. They weren't together, but she felt like the least he could've done was not have any bitches coming at her over him, and he couldn't even do that.

"I'm not beat for this shit," she mumbled under her breath as she got off the bed.

She changed out of the tank top and booty shorts pajamas she wore and put on a white V-neck a pair of grey leggings, and her black Jordan high top sneakers. Onyae wrapped her hair up in a bun and grabbed her bat from the back of her door. She was about to go to NiNi's house so they could head back down to the store for round two of whoopin' a bitch's ass.

Her mom was out with Khalif, and she had left her car so Onyae took it upon herself to grab her mother's keys and head out. It wasn't the first time she drove her mother's car, and it wasn't like Yoshi didn't give her permission. But what her mother didn't like was Onyae going out and getting into trouble so she wouldn't have approved of what she was about to do at that moment.

She hopped in her mother's silver 2016 Beamer, started it, put it in reverse, and peeled out of the driveway. While whipping the steering wheel around, she put the car in drive and put the pedal to the metal down the street. Onyae was burning rubber, and NiNi didn't live far so she got there in no time. She became more disgusted when she saw both Damon and NiNi getting out of his pickup truck, and NiNi fixing her clothes.

"You bitch ass nigga!" Onyae yelled as she hurried to put the car in park and hop out.

She ran full speed at Damon with her bat in hand, but NiNi stepped in front of him while Damon laughed.

He smirked. "Calm down, little girl."

"I'll beat yo ass, nigga. I'm not afraid of you. You better leave my cousin the fuck alone!" Onyae yelled.

NiNi was so far gone that she didn't notice Onyae pull up so fast. She didn't realize anything until she got out the truck and saw Onyae running towards Damon with a bat.

"Onyae, please stop! You're going to wake up my mother," NiNi begged.

Damon stood there smiling. He knew that there was nothing either girl could do. The ball was in his court, and it had been in his court for a while. It brought pure joy to his ego seeing how angry Onyae was.

"I don't give a fuck, NiNi. This nigga needs to be stopped! What the fuck gives him the right to do the shit he's doin'?" she asked.

Anger filled her voice, but deep down she was emotionally hurt for her cousin. Onyae could tell that NiNi had been beat because her face had doubled in size. She wasn't sure when the assault happened, but she knew that the bruises weren't there when she saw her earlier.

Watching Onyae try to protect her hurt NiNi's soul. NiNi knew that what Onyae was doing was out of pure love, and she wished walking away was as easy as Onyae made it seem.

"Onyae, you better get the fuck on, lil' girl. NiNi knows what's best for her and her mother. That's why she sticks around. You best get the fuck on, girl, if you know what the fuck is good for you," Damon threatened.

"Nigga, I will fuckin' kill you! I swear I'll kill you and wouldn't give two fucks about doing time. You deserve to fuckin' die! Ole' dirty faggot, dick in the booty ass, pedophile ass nigga!"

Onyae was straight violating Damon, and NiNi didn't even have to turn to look Damon's way to see it. She could see him clenching his teeth from the corner of her eye, and all she could do was shake her head.

"NiNi, tell ya dumb ass cousin to get the fuck outta here like I said. And if you don't, you can forget about ya mother's doctor's appointment tomorrow," Damon warned.

NiNi lowered her head in shame. If it wasn't for her mother, she would have fought back a long time ago, but she knew there was only so much fighting she could do when her mother's health was at stake. Neosha had a doctor's appointment the next day, and Damon had to give her the money to pay for it because she didn't have good insurance.

"Please, go home, Onyae, please," NiNi begged.

Tears welled up in her eyes, and when she looked up at Onyae tears were in her eyes too.

"Please, NiNi, I'll give you all the money I have. You and Auntie don't have to live like this. You know I got you. Xoxo."

NiNi wiped the tears from her face, and shook her head no. She loved her cousin to death, but after what she went through with Damon, NiNi couldn't find herself accepting anything else from anyone.

"I'm goin' in the house. NiNi, you got one minute or ya cousin gon' make shit worse for you."

Damon turned to walk towards the house, and NiNi followed, but before NiNi went inside the house she turned back and looked at Onyae.

"Oxox," she said softly.

Onyae watched NiNi disappear inside of the house. She wanted to take the bat and bust out Damon's windshield, but she knew that would only cause more pain to NiNi. That was something she didn't want. So, just like all the other times before, Onyae had to bite her tongue and pray that things got better one day for NiNi.

Chapter 7

At 10:30am on Thursday morning, NiNi sat in the room at the doctor's appointment with her mother waiting for the doctor to come in; she was quiet as she held her mother's hand for support. NiNi made it her business to go with her mother to her appointments when she could. It bothered her a great deal when she couldn't make it, and despite the events that took place last night she refused to miss this one.

"Why you so quiet, sweetie?" Neosha asked.

"No reason. Just thinking, I guess. How are you feeling?" NiNi wanted to know.

"You done asked me that about one hundred times. I said I am fine, girl. Now, something is bothering you. A mother knows when something is bothering her child. And don't give me that 'Mom you're sick' bullshit, cas' I know something is wrong with you. What's going on? You're wearing shades and your face is swollen and bruised. Tell Mommy what's going on?" Neosha was firm with her question.

It had been a while since NiNi had gotten such a strong and forceful reaction from her mother when it came to her. She knew her mother loved and cared about her dearly, but her sickness had gotten the best of her and changed her completely. Neosha wasn't used to taking anything but blood pressure medicine, but since the cancer she was on at least three to four pills a day. It took a toll on her physically and mentally; she was barely coherent at times, and she was losing weight here and there.

"Nothing Mom. Don't worry, it's nothing."

"NiNi, don't lie to me. What's going on? I may not be able to peep everything, but when I do you know I'm going to say something. And I see those bruises on your face. Is some guy putting his hands on you? Do I need to come back out of retirement to whoop a little ass?" she asked.

If only you knew, NiNi thought. She faked a smile and gave her mother a forced look as if to say, 'mom you are tripping'.

"Mom, no. Believe me. If anybody put their hands on me, you would be the first to know. As a matter of fact, you know Onyae and Auntie would tear the city down, and let's not get started on Uncle Kick Down. So no, you don't need to come out of retirement." She laughed.

"Humph, just let Mommy know and I'm on it. I don't have a problem with kicking a little bit of ass if need be and laaawd, let's not get started on him. Speaking of him, I need to call him to see how he's doing. You know him and Tesha are forever fighting. I've been so weak lately, that I haven't had the chance to really catch up with your aunt and uncle. I'll make sure to do that today tho'," Neosha replied.

NiNi chuckled as she listened to her mother talk about her uncle. She missed him dearly. It was tough for her because she didn't get to see him often due to him always being in and out of prison. He was free now, but NiNi wondered how long that would be, considering he was always getting locked up for whooping someone's ass, violating parole or just walking down the street being black.

She always wondered how things would have played out differently if her uncle was in her life. Her father had left when she was just eight years old, and it seemed like the moment he walked out of her and her mother's lives things went downhill. Her mother couldn't get a decent job to keep the mortgage and bills paid. Yoshi would always offer to help without expecting anything back, but the way NiNi's father picked up and left, taking everything he bought, broke Neosha down. It didn't take long for Neosha to meet Damon because she was vulnerable, and he was her prince charming. From the day Damon stepped foot in their house, shit was fucked up for NiNi, and she had no control over it.

"What you over there thinkin' about?" Neosha asked.

"Just this girl me and Onyae know. She's goin' through a lot, Mom. I wish I could help her, but I don't know how." NiNi's voice became babylike.

"Well, what's going on with her?" Neosha grew concerned.

NiNi sighed and shook her head.

"Her stepfather is touching her and her baby sister. She threatened to tell her mother, but she told me and Onyae that he don't care cas' he knows for a fact that she won't believe a word they say. It hurts me, Mom, cas' she comes to us all beat up, crying, and just don't know what to do."

Neosha went from looking concerned to disturbed. She didn't like what she was hearing, and as a mother, it truly bothered her.

"She needs to tell her mother. What type of sick fuck does something like that to a child? NiNi, you need to tell your friend to go to her mother or the police, baby, this is a serious matter."

"I know, Mom, but she don't want to. What would you do if you were her mother? Maybe I can tell her what you said and then she can feel comfortable enough to tell her mother," NiNi said, just hoping her mother would catch on.

"Baby, I would be in prison cas' I will kill a motherfucker for touching you. I don't play that at all, and that's why I'm glad I found a man like Damon cas' he would never do such a thing. That man loves you like you're his own. These mothers nowadays just bring anyone around their child just so they can say they have someone. Not knowing their son or daughter is going through hell. The shit don't make no sense, and I'll be damned if I be one of those mothers. Humph, after your father, I made sure to pick the right one, and look he's been in our lives for ten years now. I thank God for him every day and that's the honest truth. Now, whenever you talk to your friend again, you tell her I said to tell her mother, regardless of the outcome."

NiNi was almost convinced that she could tell her mother the truth when she started talking, but the moment she mentioned Damon's name she felt sick to her stomach. Listening to her mother praise a man she hated so much made her angry, but she did her best to hide how she really felt. NiNi was happy that her mother was happy, and she didn't want to do anything to ruin it. Seeing her mother cry for so many days and nights after her father left them broke her into pieces. She prayed to God for many nights promising that she would do anything for her mother to be happy and to stay happy. It was after she met Damon that she had stopped praying and lost her faith and belief in God.

"Hello, Mrs. Alexander. How are you?" Dr. Sanchez greeted when he walked in.

"I'm good and yourself?" Neosha said with a smile.

"I'm just fine, ma'am. Now, seems like we have some results here for you today. How have you been feeling?" he asked.

"Hmmm, so, so. Some days are better than most, but I'm still here so I'm thankful."

Dr. Sanchez nodded as he looked inside a folder he held in his hand. NiNi couldn't tell from his facial expression how good or bad the results were because he nodded his head in approval the entire time he was reading.

"So, last time you were here we discussed your tumor on your cervix which turned into cervical cancer. Although, we stated that if this was caught at an early stage it wouldn't have been so hard to maintain, it seems as though something is still triggering it to get worse at some points which makes it difficult for us to get you at a stable point," Dr. Sanchez explained.

"Can you explain a little more to me as to what all is going on? I missed a few appointments and I definitely want to be up to date with what's going on with my mother cas' I know she be keeping things way from me to keep my mind at ease," NiNi said while giving Neosha the side eye.

Dr. Sanchez chuckled a bit.

"Of course, of course. Well, what I've explained to your mother over the last few appointments is that cervical cancer occurs when abnormal cells on the cervix grow out of control. The cervix is the lower part of the uterus that opens into the vagina. However, cervical cancer can often be successfully treated when it's found early. It is usually found at a very early stage through a Pap test which is how we found your mother's," he explained.

"But wait, you said it can be treated successfully if it's found early. So, basically you're saying that you found my mother's early? But from my understanding, my mother found out that she had this sometime last year," NiNi mentioned as she gave Dr. Sanchez a confused look.

Dr. Sanchez gave a puzzled look.

"Can we please get to my results from my last visit, please," Neosha chimed in.

None of this makes sense. How could she get treatments for something she knew nothing about? NiNi thought to herself.

Dr. Sanchez scratched his head before looking at his charts. NiNi, on the other hand, could tell that her mother had been keeping too much information from her and she didn't like it. She wasn't going to jump down her throat just yet, but she made a mental note to confront her about this doctor's visit.

"Mrs. Alexander, things are up and down with your condition. The tumor grows, and then it shrinks, and then it grows, and then it shrinks. Now, as I said before, if we can get the tumor to shrink naturally then we won't have to do surgery because the cancer will be gone," Dr. Sanchez explained.

NiNi looked over at her mother who had a faint smile on her face. Although, she looked weak she never stopped smiling. It was as if nothing ever got her down, and regardless of her feeling a way about her mother possibly lying to her about her health, that was something NiNi loved about her mother.

"You know I don't want any surgery. I've been doing just fine. I would like to stop taking chemo, and just do things naturally from this point on. I will continue with my doctor's visits, and take my medicine as needed, but the chemo must be stopped. I feel like if anything, that's killing me before my time is actually supposed to be up." Neosha responded in the most delicate voice.

"Are you sure, Mrs. Alexander?" Dr. Sanchez asked with raised eyebrows.

"Yes, I'm sure. I praise a mighty God, and I know I will be okay," she responded.

"Alright, I can't argue with you because you are the patient. So, chemo will be removed, and you will continue with your standard medicines. I adore your strength, Mrs. Alexander. Take care. I'll see you next month," Dr. Sanchez said with a smile before giving Neosha a firm handshake.

"Thank you. I'll see you then, Dr. Sanchez." She smiled.

Dr. Sanchez walked out of the room and left NiNi and Neosha alone to gather their things. NiNi stood up to help her mother stand, and when she did, Neosha looked at her.

"You still didn't tell me what happened to your face, missy."

"I was fighting, Mom. I didn't say anything cas' I know how you are about violence," NiNi explained.

Neosha sighed and shook her head. She gave her daughter a once over before walking towards the door. She opened the door and looked back at NiNi.

"No, I don't condone fighting, but I also know that you only fight when you're with Onyae. Yawl two better stay out of trouble before me and my sister have to kick yawl's ass, and don't think yawl too grown to get an ass whooping. Remember, yawl our daughters so yawl can fight cas' of us."

NiNi laughed. She was so happy to see her mother make light of the situation. She didn't want her to be stressed over anything that could jeopardize her health more. As she closed the door behind her and followed her mother to the front desk she felt her phone vibrate.

Zzzz.

NiNi reached inside of her hoodie and pulled her cellphone out. She saw Rayshon's name flash across her screen in a text message notification. She rolled her eyes, but still decided to read it.

Rayshon: *Wassup ma? I know you still prolli mad at me, but I wanted to apologize for that bullshit Sharee pulled.*

NiNi tucked her lips in her mouth as she read the text message. She appreciated his apology, but she had nothing to say to Rayshon after that situation. She felt like he knew what type of guy his cousin was and could have at least told her so she could warn her cousin.

NiNi: *Thanks.*

Her text was dry, simple and straight to the point. NiNi didn't want to give off any mixed signals making Rayshon think they were back on good terms. She refused to deal with a guy that could possibly have her out in the streets looking stupid and dumb in love.

"You ready, baby? Damon is outside," Neosha said.

"Can I just take a cab home?" NiNi asked.

Neosha sucked her teeth and rubbed her forehead. For the life of her, she couldn't understand the beef between Damon and NiNi. All she wanted was for her family to be happy, but their feud made it very difficult at times.

"NiNi, no. I can't deal with this bickering between yawl. Now, it's been ten years and you still don't like him? Baby, I know you think he's going to walk out like your father did, but I can assure you he is not like that. It's been ten years too long, and honestly, I'm tired of it. I don't know how long I have left on this earth, but what I do know is that I want you to stop giving him the cold shoulder. I'm not saying call him dad, but I am saying show him some respect for once. Although you don't accept it, he does give you anything you want, gives me anything I want, pays all the bills and puts food on the table." Neosha gave NiNi the third degree.

NiNi stood there looking at her mother with a distressing look on her face. She didn't have to say anything because her facial expression said it all. Just when she thought she could muster up the courage to finally tell her mother what was going on, Neosha snatched it away in no time causing NiNi to feel alone once again.

"I don't mean to come off so firm, but baby, it's time for a change. All that anger you have in you from your father leaving is just driving you crazy. I can feel that negative energy, and baby, Mommy don't like it. I love you with everything in me, but I need you to love me the same and give Damon a chance. Will you do that for me, please?" Neosha gave NiNi the sincerest look.

Neosha was unaware that NiNi had already sacrificed more than enough because of the love she had for her mother. She never accepted Damon, but she dealt with him feeling like she had no choice of her own. All she could do at the moment was give in to her mother's wishes because she didn't want to disappoint her.

"Yes Mom. I'll do that for you," NiNi responded while holding back tears.

Neosha smiled and hugged her daughter tight, and NiNi slowly wrapped her arms around her. When Neosha pulled away, she kissed her on the cheek and nodded towards the first exit of the doctor's office.

"Let's go. Damon is waiting."

With no response, NiNi opened the first door for her mother, and they walked through the waiting room of the doctor's office to the second exit. NiNi opened the door and allowed Neosha to walk out first. She was dreading going out there to face Damon knowing she couldn't stand the ground he walked on. She slowly shut the door behind her and walked like a snail behind her mother. When they both got closer and closer to the door that would lead them outside, they were confused because Damon was parked, waiting for them in a 2017 Pacifica Limited instead of his black pick-up truck.

"Damon, boy, what is going on? Where the hell did you get this from? Where is your truck?" Neosha asked back to back questions.

Damon got out of the sparkling blue car smiling from ear to ear. He walked around the car, placed both hands on each side of Neosha's face and stuck his tongue in her mouth. NiNi felt sick to her stomach as she watched her mother and Damon make out. Everything about him made her nauseous.

"There's plenty more where that came from, beautiful," Damon said when he finally pulled away from Neosha.

"Well, I would hope so. The way you got me feeling now, but enough of that. Where in the hell did you get this?" she asked.

Neosha was excited and even if she didn't say it, her entire mood proved it.

"Shit, I bought us a new ride. My truck is at the house where it should be, but I told you plenty of times before I want to give you and my daughter nothing but the best." Damon looked at NiNi with flirtatious eyes.

Neosha didn't catch it, but NiNi didn't care if she did. At this point, she felt like nothing would be done.

"Aw, NiNi, did you hear that?" Neosha looked over at NiNi who forced a fake smile.

"Yea Mom, I heard it. Thanks Damon," she said dryly.

"No problem. Now let's get home so I can take something out for dinner tonight." Damon opened the passenger side door for Neosha.

She gave him a quick peck before getting in, and Damon closed the door behind her. Before he opened the back door for NiNi, he grabbed her shoulder and squeezed tight.

"Fix ya face. Don't fuckin' play wit' me," he warned.

NiNi straightened up her face, and Damon nodded as he let her go. He opened up the door and she quickly got in while he closed it with force.

"Mom, can I go over Onyae's when we get home?" she asked.

NiNi didn't know why she was asking permission for something she'd always done. Whenever she got around Damon her mind was so jumbled that she couldn't think straight. She was always afraid to say or do the wrong thing when he was around. She wished she hadn't even brought it up because whenever her mother got around Damon, she became a different person.

Neosha sighed.

"NiNi, didn't you just hear Damon say he was cooking dinner tonight, and you wanna leave? Girl, you are a piece of damn work."

"Please Mom? I ain't seen her in a few days," NiNi lied, knowing she had just seen her last night, but she didn't dare bring it up. "Besides, it's almost twelve; no one eatin' this early, so why can't I got over there for a few hours and then come back home?"

"NiNi no. I just made a huge decision to stop taking chemo from this point on and Damon just bought us a new family van. Things are going good today, and I want to enjoy my family. You can see Onyae any time, but you barely want to spend time with ya own damn family. That's a shame, NiNi, but I tell you this much, the shit stops today," Neosha said in a firm tone.

Damon had just gotten in on the tail end of the conversation. He looked over at Neosha who seemed aggravated, and then looked back at NiNi who was sitting back with her arms folded against her chest pouting.

"Everything okay?" he asked.

"Yes, everything is fine. Now, let's go home so I can take a nap. My damn head hurting now," Neosha said, and then adjusted her seat so she could be comfortable.

Damon shrugged his shoulders, put the van in drive, and then pulled out of the parking lot. The eight-minute car ride home was dead silence, and the tension was thick. NiNi grabbed her phone and decided to text Onyae. She hadn't heard from her since last night, and she knew she was still upset about everything that had gone on.

NiNi: *Hey, I wanted to see how you were doin'*

Damon pulled in the driveway of their home, parked, shut the van off and got out. She watched as he ran over to the other side of the van and opened the passenger side door for Neosha. NiNi rolled her eyes as she watched her mother be all smiles as she got out.

"Thanks babe." She heard her mother say.

Before Damon could even think about opening NiNi's door, she was already halfway out of the van. She slammed the door shut, walked past Damon and her mother and walked up the mini walkway to their home. She went to reach in her hoodie pocket for her house key, and heard her phone go off.

Ding. Ding.

NiNi looked down at her phone and saw that Onyae had texted her back.

Onyae: *I was waitin' for yo ass to text me. You know how I'm feelin' about that shit that went down last night, but I'm not even gon' talk about it cas' I know you don't want to. But just so you know, I'm good. Still pissed about that Gutta situation but these niggas for everybody cous.*

NiNi felt relieved that Onyae let last night go. It was bad enough she had to deal with the physical and mental memories of it. She didn't need to have it repeated to her on a new day. NiNi stuck her key in the door and unlocked it. She took a quick glance at her mother who was all hugged up with Damon as if they hadn't been around each other in days. She took this moment as the opportunity to go in her room, lock the door, and figure out a way to get out of the house. She knew she was not about to spend the rest of the day with them; it was something she just didn't want to do.

She kicked off her shoes, pulled her hoodie over her head, threw her shades on the dresser and plopped down on her bed. After wiggling her toes to stretch them a little, she finally texted Onyae back.

NiNi: *Nah, I don't wanna talk about it, and thank you for understanding. As far as Gutta, don't even sweat that shit cous. He gon' hit you up beggin' and pleadin'.*

Knock. Knock.
Knock.

"What!" NiNi called out in an irritated tone.

"Don't answer me like that, girl. There is someone at the door for you," Neosha responded from the other side of the door.

Onyae: *Fuck that! And fuck him! I refuse to feel disrespected by any of these niggas. I never even let my damn daddy disrespect me, and that bitch ass nigga walked out like the bitch he was!*

NiNi couldn't respond to Onyae's text right away. She was confused when her mother said someone was at the door for her. The only people that came by for her were Yoshi or Onyae. It was rare for her uncle Kick Down to visit her; the more she thought about it a smile spread across her face because she hadn't seen him in a while. NiNi hopped off the bed with her phone still in her hand. She unlocked her door, opened it and ran straight past her mother in a hurry to see who she thought was her uncle.

When NiNi finally got to the door she was greeted by Rayshon standing outside with his hand in his pocket and the other hand scrolling through his phone. NiNi was shocked and lost for words. For a second, she forgot how he knew where she lived, then she remembered that he had dropped her off at home the other day.

"Wha—what are you doin' here?"

Rayshon gave a pearly white smile, but it quickly turned into a frown when he saw her face.

"What the fuck happened to ya face?" Rayshon was quickly defensive.

NiNi had forgotten all about putting her shades back on, and she was embarrassed once Rayshon mentioned her bruises, but she was thankful that it wasn't her uncle because all hell would've broken loose.

"Rayshon, you shouldn't be here," she told him.

"Well I'm here now. What the fuck happened to ya face?" he asked again.

NiNi bit her bottom lip and looked back at her mother who was coming to the door.

"Rayshon, you shouldn't be here. You should go," she insisted.

"NiNi, introduce me to ya friend." Neosha folded her arms across her chest with a smirk on her face.

"Mom, no, he's just leaving," she responded.

"Actually, I came to apologize to you for the other day, ma. I def ain't mean for shit to go down like that, and when I texted you and you responded wit' just, *thanks*. I knew I had to come by personally and give you a sincere apology," Rayshon explained.

"I like him already, NiNi," Neosha said with a look of approval on her face along with a raised eyebrow.

NiNi rolled her eyes and shook her head.

"Rayshon, can you please leave?"

"Not until you accept my apology and tell me what happened to ya face," he stated seriously.

"That's none of ya damn business, now can you please leave!" NiNi's voice got louder.

"Girl, if you don't calm down, and go outside and talk to that boy. He seems nice, and that's something you need in your life. Now go on outside. Damon is getting the grill started on the deck back there, so you have some time to yourself without any one of us all in your face," Neosha told her as she gently pushed her outside the house.

Before Neosha could even close the door behind her, Damon appeared out of nowhere. He caught the door in mid-swing with his hand and forced it back open while pushing Neosha to the side in a gentle but firm manner.

"Excuse me, NiNi. I don't mean to be rude, but as I said before, I want to spend time wit' my family today. I'm afraid that ya lil friend has to leave."

"Pssh, since when the fuck did you have the right to tell me what to do?" NiNi snapped back.

She was so tired of Damon trying to play the father role in her life when all he had done was fuck up her life from the moment he came in it. Although, she didn't know Rayshon was going to stop by, and she didn't want him there, she still felt like Damon had no right to say who could or couldn't come by her house.

"NiNi!" Neosha yelled.

"What!" NiNi looked over at her mother.

Neosha could feel the anger and tension as she peeked her head past Damon. NiNi's eyebrows were curved inward, and her eyes seemed to have gone dark.

"Calm down, ma. I don't wanna cause no problems. I'ma leave, but just be lookin' out for my text," Rayshon was talking to NiNi, but staring at Damon the whole time.

He remembered the truck, and once he saw Damon's face again everything came back to him, and he quickly thought about the day he and Gutta dropped NiNi and Onyae off after they had spent the night together. He didn't realize he was having a flashback until Damon spoke again.

"Ya friend got amnesia?" Damon asked while looking at NiNi. "I said he needs to leave, or I'll make him leave."

Rayshon snapped out of his trance and chuckled when he heard what Damon said. He looked over at NiNi, then peeked at her mother, before finally giving Damon his attention.

"This ain't what you want bruh bruh," Rayshon said as he shook his head and then turned to NiNi. "Look for my text, ma."

He said as he bent down and gave her a kiss on the cheek. NiNi was loss for words as she watched Rayshon walk off her porch and down the walkway of their house.

"Who the hell does he think he's talkin' to?" Damon asked with flared nostrils.

NiNi rolled her eyes and pushed past Damon. He was a complete joke to her because he could abuse her, but didn't think about stepping to Rayshon until he walked away.

"Where the hell are you goin', NiNi? Don't walk away from me," Damon said as he turned to follow her.

"Damon, calm down." Neosha grabbed his arm.

"No, Neosha, that's why she disrespects this household. There's no stability, and we do too much for her to allow her to just have some random fuckin' guy come here and disrespect us as if we ain't shit. NiNi!"

Damon walked through the kitchen, dining room, and into the hallway to go in NiNi's room, but was disappointed when he ran straight into a locked door.

Bang!

"NiNi, open this damn door!" Damon yelled as he banged on her door.

"Damon, what the hell is wrong wit' you? Leave her alone! She ain't done nothin' wrong, and I won't stand here and pretend she did." Neosha was standing right beside him, looking up at him with a distorted face.

Bang! Bang!

Bang!

"Damon stop! I'm not dealing wit' this shit today!"

NiNi jumped when she heard the bang. Her heart was beating fast, and her palms got sweaty. Although, she knew that Damon wouldn't do anything crazy and violate her while her mother was home, she still didn't take any chances because his temper was just that bad.

However, she still was going to stand her grounds. If Damon thought he was going to say fuck that her mother was there and harm her anyway, then she was going to do all that she could to fight back. Even though her mother made her feel like shit earlier, she still felt that if her mother saw the way he really was, she would get rid of him with no problem.

NiNi: *Ughhh! I swear I can't stand him! Damon gets on my nerves Onyae and I swear I can't wait until somebody off his ass!*

Onyae: *I'm gettin' dressed now. I'm bouta come over there and fuck that nigga up. Tired of this shit! And if Auntie want some she can get some too. Fuck all the dumb shit and fuck them too!*

NiNi didn't even look surprised when she read Onyae's text. She knew exactly how her cousin was, and Onyae was very overprotective over her. Not to mention, Onyae always had a bad feeling about Damon from the beginning. The dislike quickly turned into hate when she found out what Damon was doing

NiNi: *Nah, don't.*

"NiNi, I'm not gonna tell you again! Open this door!" he yelled.

NiNi rolled her eyes and waved her hand as if he could see her. She wasn't going to front and act like she wasn't scared because she was, but she refused to entertain Damon. He had already proved how bitch he was when Rayshon showed up.

"You ain't gotta open shit! I don't give a fuck who pays what! My name is on that muthafuckin' lease and don't you forget that! I done gave her the fuckin' third degree about you, and now you sittin' here running down on her like she's a damn man. That shit ain't right, Damon. That shit ain't right at all, and regardless of how much you do around here, as your woman, I'ma tell you when you're right and when you're wrong," Neosha stated while pushing him away from NiNi's bedroom door and into the dining room.

NiNi smiled when she heard her mother defending her. It felt good considering she never witnessed her doing it. She sat down on her bed and read Onyae's text as she tuned out her mother and Damon's arguing. She didn't really hear Damon say much because her mother would barely let him speak.

Onyae: *Fuck outta here NiNi. I'm tired of this shit. I'm tired of all this bullshit. Fuck these niggas. Fuck all of them! Our dads left us to fend for ourselves. We gotta*

have each other's backs cas' we don't have no father figures to protect us. We all we got! So, like I said I'm comin' over there wit' my bat and I'm fuckin' shit all the way up!

NiNi read Onyae's text, and she didn't know whether to cry or woman up and go out there and finally beat Damon's ass. Their hatred for men came from their fathers walking out on them at such a youthful age. While NiNi was getting touched by Damon, Onyae watched her mother get her ass beat by her so-called boyfriends. They watched their mothers get taken advantage of by men and vowed to never be like them. That caused their attitude to be 'fuck niggas' no matter who they were to them, except for their uncle, Kick Down. He was the only man they had any sort of respect for, and he had earned that for continuing to be real with them no matter what.

NiNi: *I feel you, and I don't blame you at all cous. But I just don't want my mom and auntie to be beefin'. I can't lose you too and I know that's gonna be the outcome cas' auntie prolli wouldn't want me there anymore.*

Chapter 8

Knock. Knock.
 Knock.

Yoshi had just gotten finished washing the dishes when she heard a knock at the door. She smiled thinking it was Khalif surprising her. He was just that type to pop up at her house with some roses or jewelry and she accepted every bit of it. She walked to the door as she dried her hands off on her pink and black sweatpants.

Yoshi peeped out the little curtain that hung over the window of the door and raised her eyebrows when she saw a fine ass man standing on the other side. She shook her head as she opened the door because she assumed that he was for Onyae.

"Can I help you?" she asked with her arms folded across her chest.

"Actually, you can. I'm lookin' for Onyae," he said.

"And you are? Shit, I know you don't think you just gon' walk yo big, fine ass up here and not introduce yaself.

I don't give a fuck if you fuckin' my daughter or not, you show Mama some respect or get cussed the fuck out and sent on ya way."

When Yoshi spoke, she had so much spunk and confidence with her demeanor. It made whoever she was talking to humble themselves quick. Her stance and attitude read that she was clearly not the one to be fucked with.

"I see where she get her mouth from," Rayshon mumbled. "Anyway, I'm Rayshon, Gutta's cousin. I came here to talk to Onyae for a second if that's okay."

"Excuse me? I heard what the fuck you said. You better watch it before you see this door get slammed in ya face. Now, either you want to talk to her or you don't?" Yoshi asked with a raised eyebrow.

Rayshon sighed long and hard. "I apologize, ma'am. Yes, I would like to talk to her if that's okay," Rayshon said.

"Onyaaaaeeeee! Somebody at the door for youuuu!" Yoshi turned her head and called her name.

Onyae was just putting on her sneakers when she heard her mother calling her. She hurried and texted NiNi back before she ran out of her bedroom.

Onyae: *Girl bye. Yoshi will never disown you, and I don't give a fuck what happens. She ride for you just like I do. She knows you don't like Damon, but she doesn't know why. I would never tell her unless I have to but hold on somebody at the door.*

"Who is it, Mom?" Onyae asked when she walked into the kitchen.

"Some guy named Rayshon," Yoshi responded, and then walked away from the door.

Onyae frowned. She walked to the door and had attitude written all over her face. She wondered why Rayshon had popped up all of a sudden, and she was hoping that it wasn't to get her to talk to Gutta because she was going to curse his ass out and send him on his way.

"The fuck you want?" she asked.

"Man, I ain't come over here for all that shit. I done already got cussed out by ya mom, and I refuse to go through the same shit wit' you when I came over here in peace and shit," he said.

"Rayshon please. Ain't nobody thinkin' about you or what the fuck you sayin'. You and ya dirty ass cousin got a lot of damn nerve."

"Pssh! Man, stop disrespectin' me for one. I ain't one of these lil' young buls, ard? Chill wit' all that extra shit. I came by here to speak to you about a situation and that's it. All that rah, rah you spittin' you can save that shit for Gutta," he told her.

"Whatever nigga. Anyway, get to the point. Why you here?" she asked after she smacked her lips.

"What's goin' on wit' NiNi?" he asked.

Onyae raised her eyebrow.

"Why?"

Her guard instantly came up when he questioned her about NiNi.

"Relax ma. I ain't tryna hurt her or get her hurt. I texted her earlier apologizin' for the shit that went down the other day, and she responded wit' a *thanks*. I know how yawl jawns be so I knew she was still bothered. Me being me, I popped up, and her moms answered the door. After that, shit got real," he explained.

"What you mean shit got real? What happened? I just got finished textin' NiNi. She ain't tell me shit about you stoppin' by so what the fuck is really goin' on?" Onyae gave him the side eye.

"Look, like I said her moms answered the door and then the nigga that acted like he wanted a problem wit' me and Gutta popped up. We passed a few words and he acted like he wanted to get tough when I walked away, but I ain't even trip cas' I had already pulled his bitch card."

"You said somethin' to him?" she eagerly wanted to know.

Rayshon's eyebrows went inwards. He felt like Onyae was questioning his gangsta, and he really wasn't the one to do too much talking. He allowed his actions to speak up for him which was why he didn't like drama because shit would get real on his end.

"The fuck I gotta lie for? I looked that nigga in his mismatched ass eyes and told him he ain't want no problems. He tried to get tough when I walked away talkin' about who the fuck am I talkin' to. Clearly, I was talkin' to his stupid ass, and to be honest, I could've knocked his fuckin' head off right then and there, but NiNi and her mother was standin' there. I couldn't risk shit happenin' to them. She already had a black eye and bruises on her face."

Onyae's mouth was wide open. She couldn't believe that Rayshon had gone at Damon the way he did, and she was impressed that he wasn't afraid to go toe to toe with Damon's bitch ass.

"Fuck that! You should've blew his bitch ass head off!" Onyae spat.

She was pissed. Damon was truly a bitch in her eyes. There was nothing manly about him.

"Onyae! Watch ya mouth!" Yoshi yelled.

"My bad, Mom," she responded and then turned her attention back to Rayshon.

"Yawl don't get along wit' bul or somethin'?" Rayshon was curious.

"Who yawl talkin' about?" Yoshi walked up and intervened in their conversation.

"Damon, Mom, translation for nobody important," Onyae replied.

"Ooh, his bitch ass. What done happened now? Seems like him and NiNi argue every day. I swear all my niece has to do is say the word, and I will move her ass right on in here," Yoshi stated seriously.

Rayshon rubbed his hand through his beard in a concerned manner. By no means was it his place to step in if anything was going on in NiNi's household. But considering that he had vibed with her that night at Gutta's, and he could see that she was a good girl with a messed up past, he felt obligated to protect her.

"So, what yawl sayin'? The nigga need to be handled?" he asked.

Yoshi jerked her head back with a surprised manner on her face.

"I wouldn't say all that. They just don't get along, baby, no need to bring anything else into it. I mean, they argue but that's it. Nothing more and nothing less, but I'll leave yawl two to finish talking," Yoshi said before walking away and heading back in her bedroom.

Onyae wished she could tell Rayshon what was really going on, but she knew NiNi would be pissed at her and would never forgive her, so she kept her response as simple as she could.

"Yea, my mom is right. Ain't too much to it but some arguin'." Onyae winced when she said that.

It was like it hurt her to lie about what Damon was really taking NiNi through.

"You tellin' me she just dislike the nigga for no reason? I was there today. I saw how NiNi snapped at bul, and I could tell she ain't fuckin' wit' him or anything that he bringin'. The shit seemed mad tense, and considerin' I fucks wit' NiNi, I wanna make sure she's good at all cost."

"Pssh, nigga you barely know us. So, how you fucks wit' her like that?" Onyae asked.

"I'ma street nigga at heart, and I can tell when I come across somebody that's genuine and ain't about no bullshit. NiNi ain't about no bullshit, and if I have to put a nigga down for her I will. So, wassup wit' the wassup?"

Onyae sucked air through her teeth and shook her head. There was only so much she could tell Rayshon, and the truth just wasn't in that equation.

"I just feel like you should leave it alone. If shit was deeper than what you thinkin', me and my mother got her back."

"Basically, you tellin' me ain't nothin' goin' on?" he asked just to be sure.

Onyae nodded.

"That's exactly what I'm tellin' you. Just leave well enough alone. NiNi is good, don't worry," she assured him.

"So, what about the bruises?" he mentioned again after realizing Onyae never reflected on that matter.

"Me and NiNi always gettin' into fights wit' bitches that's all. It ain't even that deep my nigga."

Rayshon stood there looking at Onyae. He wasn't convinced that NiNi's bruises came from her and Onyae getting into a few fights; especially after seeing how she was ready to tear Sharee and Krystal into pieces, the shit just wasn't adding up. In his heart, he knew that more was going on, but had no proof of his assumptions. He would have never assumed that NiNi was in harm's way if she didn't show the same actions as his mother did years back when she was getting abused. Although, he had no proof, Rayshon knew shit wasn't sweet under NiNi's roof.

Chapter 9

Beep. Beep.

    Beep. Beep.

"Damn nigga, get yo ass out here!" Gutta said impatiently.

He sat outside of Rayshon's house waiting for him to come out so they could bust a move. It was 11pm and they had business to handle, but like always, Rayshon was never on time.

"You drawlin' out here beepin' all crazy!" Rayshon yelled as he came out of the house.

"Nah, you drawlin'. We be havin' specific times to go handle shit and ya ass always be late. You a ol' female ass bul. Always makin' sure you got ya fuckin' make up on before you leave." Gutta laughed.

"Shut the fuck up, nigga." Rayshon laughed as he got in Gutta's truck.

"Fareal nigga, but wassup wit' you? I ain't heard from ya ass since that shit went down wit' Krystal's dumb ass," Gutta asked as he drove off.

"Maannn, let me tell you bout what happened. I meant to hit you up the same day, but my mind was on NiNi that whole day and night, and then I had to make a quick run to Cherry Hill on Thursday, so I was tied up," he explained.

"Why you ain't hit me up to take that ride wit' you?" Gutta asked.

He headed down Southeast before making a left turn onto Pattison Ave. About ten minutes later he was turning onto South Front Street until merging onto i-95 North toward Central Philadelphia.

"I only picked up one package, so it wasn't no need for me to hit you up when I was already makin' a drop round that way anyway," he explained.

Ring. Ring. Ring.

The conversation was interrupted due to the ringing of Rayshon's phone. Rayshon looked down at his phone and got agitated when he saw Sharee's name flash across his screen. There was no way he was going to answer the phone for her; not only because there was business that needed to be handled, but also because he didn't understand why she was calling him. They didn't even fuck with each other on that level anymore.

He swiped left on his phone, sending her right to voicemail. Soon after that, his phone was ringing again. Rayshon swiped left once more, sending her to voicemail again.

"Who dat you bangin' on? Must be Sharee's ass. Her and Krystal two crazy ass jawns." Gutta laughed.

"I swear I'm tired of her ass. I done blocked her numerous times and she still find a way to contact me. I store her number so I can know what call not to answer," Rayshon said honestly.

They conversed for the next half hour until Gutta pulled up on Diamond Street.

"There go them niggas right there. I told Ron Ron that I'ma light this block up if I caught 'em on it. Guess these muthafuckas thought I was jokin'," Gutta said as he pulled up one car back from the guys they were targeting.

"I don't know when these young buls gon' learn. Sellin' another nigga shit on a block that's ours? Fuck outta here," Rayshon said as he made sure his 9mm was cocked and loaded.

"They gon' learn tonight. I can guarantee you that," Gutta said as he parked and shut his truck lights off.

Rayshon counted each guy and came up with a total of seven males. He wasn't looking to kill them all, but he was looking to make a statement being that he was tired of the disrespect.

"Pull ya cell out and act like you talkin' on the phone while you walkin' up. The moment you get on the other side of them niggas, it's on. We can't run up on 'em too wild cas' that's how niggas gettin' rocked." Rayshon ran everything down to him.

"The fuck you breakin' shit down to me for, like I don't know what to do?"

Rayshon looked over at Gutta.

"Nigga, cas you too fuckin' hot headed. I gotta tone ya ass down sometimes. I need shit to go sweet at all times, and when a nigga a hothead he allows his temper to get the best of him. We don't need that shit."

"Ard. Let's just handle shit. We doin' too much talkin' as it is."

Rayshon agreed and they both put their hoodies over their heads; simultaneously, they quietly got out of the truck making sure to close the doors just enough so they wouldn't be wide open, but not closed all the way. They didn't want anything to slow them down. When they made their move, they wanted to just hop back in the ride and peel off without any extra hassle.

Rayshon allowed Gutta to walk ahead of him. He watched him reach in his hoodie pocket and pull out his cellphone. He watched Gutta bop up and down as he approached the group of guys at a quick but steady pace.

"Shawty you trippin'. I ain't even got time for the shit that you talkin'. Either you gon' let me fuck or you ain't. It really don't matter cas' I'm stickin' my dick in somethin' tonight. Whether it's from you or the next jawn." Gutta pretended to be on a phone call as he approached the crowd.

"Ahhhh, bul on the phone beggin' for the pussy." A light-skinned guy, in dire need of a haircut, laughed.

"Jawn bad as fuck, hell yea I'm beggin'," Gutta replied as he attempted to turn the corner but doubled back.

Click.

Clack.

In one swift motion, Gutta had replaced his cellphone with his .44 Magnum and had it aimed at the head of the light-skinned male that was talking shit. Two of the guys tried to reach for their guns, but Rayshon popped up like a thief in the night.

"I dare you," he warned.

"Yawl niggas drawlin'. Fuck yawl want wit' us?" A dude who looked to be about sixteen years old spoke up.

Whap!

"Speak when the fuck you spokin' to, muthafucka!" Rayshon smacked the boy across his face with his gun.

"That's the problem wit' you young buls. Yawl lettin' these fake ass gangstas boost yawl head up. When a nigga say stay off his fuckin' block, that's what he mean!" Gutta spat.

"Fuck that. We eatin' too, regardless what yawl fuck boys say. This our block now!" The sixteen-year-old said.

Boc! Boc! Boc!

Rayshon let off three rounds into the young boy's face, splattering brain matter on the guy that was standing the closest to him. He was all for a guy having heart, especially the young ones, but there was a difference between having heart and being hardheaded, and Rayshon had to make an example out of him real quick.

"Anybody else? Or is shit clear?" Gutta asked.

Everyone was silent. They were so silent you could hear a pin drop. The young boys were hard up until some real OGs came their way to set shit off.

"Get the fuck off this block before I have my homie empty his clip into one of you lil' muthafuckas," Rayshon demanded.

The remaining six boys scattered like roaches in different directions. Rayshon and Gutta casually turned around and walked back to their ride, getting in and peeling off without drawing too much attention. They did what they had to do when it needed to be done. Disrespect was a no, no, and when they gave orders, they expected for them to be followed. The young boys didn't take their threat seriously which resulted in one of them losing their life and adding another body under Rayshon's belt.

Chapter 10

"You sure you missed ya period?" NiNi asked while sitting on the bathroom countertop swinging her legs back and forth.

"Bitch, I'm positive. It's March third. The last person I fucked was Gutta and we ain't use no condom. It's been three weeks and five days, maybe more, maybe less, but my damn period still ain't came the fuck on. This some bullshit," Onyae spat.

Onyae sat on the toilet as she peed on the third pregnancy stick while NiNi bit her bottom lip and gave a not so concerned look. It was evident that Onyae was pregnant from the first two pregnancy tests.

"Damn, it's really been that long since we talked to them?" NiNi said in disbelief.

"Yea, it has. It don't even seem like it tho', but I told that nigga he wasn't about to play me. Especially, for some trash ass bitch like her ass," Onyae said as she thought about how busted Krystal looked.

"Niggas don't give a fuck, cous, I swear they don't. But what you gon' do?" NiNi asked.

Onyae looked at the results for the third pregnancy test and cursed as she looked up at the ceiling as if to say, 'really Lord?'

"Abort this shit, the fuck? I don't got time to be havin' a nigga's baby. Fuck that shit, and Gutta a no-good ass nigga too, paleeze. I'll be doomed from the start if I keep this shit."

"You gon' tell Yoshi?" NiNi asked knowingly.

Onyae shrugged her shoulders.

"Yea, I mean, why not? I tell her everything else anyway."

"True, but are you gonna tell Gutta? Regardless of how fucked up he is, I still think he deserves to know."

Onyae rolled her eyes at both NiNi and the third positive pregnancy test. She was pissed at herself for slipping up. For as many times as she fucked, and for as many niggas she had fucked, something like getting pregnant had never happened. Although, Onyae wasn't the type of female to just go around fucking guys raw; she also had a few guys from her past who she got down with on that level.

"Nah, I'm not tellin' him shit. I told Rayshon I was done wit' that fuck nigga when he came by last month."

"Onyae he deserves...wait a minute. You talked to Rayshon? Why didn't I know about this?" NiNi asked with her eyebrow raised in suspicion.

It didn't slip Onyae's mind to tell NiNi that Rayshon came by. She didn't want NiNi to completely blow

Rayshon off once she found out that he was asking about Damon and what he was about. She wanted NiNi to be happy, and even though she wasn't on good terms with Gutta, Rayshon played no part in what went down.

"Girl, he just wanted to know why you was actin' cold on him the day he apologized." Onyae didn't lie, but she didn't tell the full truth.

"A'ight so if it was somethin' simple, why didn't I know about it? We tell each other everything so why stop now?" NiNi was becoming agitated.

Trust meant a lot to her. There were very few people that she trusted, and besides her mother, Onyae was top dog. Feeling like she could have possibly kept something away from her, bothered her something serious.

"Cous, you really bout to trip over somethin' old as fuck? I ain't keep shit from you, I just forgot to tell you because it wasn't no big deal."

Onyae didn't want to squabble with NiNi over something that was small in her eyes. With everything she was going through, arguing with her best friend was the last thing she wanted to do so she did her best to ease NiNi's mind.

"It's not old. The shit happened last month. I'm not trippin', but damn, can a bitch know wassup? He came to you askin' why I did somethin' instead of comin' to me?" she asked.

"He said he came to ya crib and shit got real. So, he knew that me and you mad close and he wanted answers. You happy now? I told you. Now can we please drop this fuckin' subject cas' I really need you right now."

Knock. Knock.
Knock.

"Yawl come out that damn bathroom and see who came by to see yawl." Yoshi banged on the door a few times.

NiNi couldn't respond back like she wanted to, so she dropped the subject. She hopped down off the counter and helped Onyae put the pregnancy tests away as quickly as possible. Once the girls were finished, Onyae scooted past NiNi and opened the bathroom door.

"Oh my God! Uncle Kick Down! Where the hell yo hoe ass been?" Onyae asked as she damn near jumped into his arms.

NiNi was right behind her jumping into his arms. He almost fell back with all the joy and happiness they tackled him with while Yoshi stood back smiling with her arms folded across her chest.

"Why I gotta be a hoe?" He laughed.

He released both girls from his grasp while allowing their feet to touch the ground again. Onyae playfully punched him in the left arm.

"Awwww, don't act like we don't know how you get down, Unc." She laughed.

"Shiddddd, well yawl know how I do." Kick Down flexed for his nieces.

Lorenzo 'Kick Down' Alexander was easy on the eyes. At the age of forty-four he didn't look a day over thirty-five. Standing at a mere six-foot-one with a Hershey's dark chocolate skin complexion, Kick Down rocked a low-cut, high top curly fade. The grey patch of hair in the front of his head drove the ladies crazy as well as his Sunni beard which was always trimmed nicely. Kick Down could dress his ass off from head to toe. He stayed in nothing but the latest brand clothing. His own style was smooth, and everybody and they mama knew that he was a player. But that didn't stop them from wanting to try the anaconda that hung between his legs, and his mean tongue game.

"Unc, you is too much. What made you stop by? And how you know I was here?" NiNi asked.

"I talk to my big-headed ass sister all the time. She keeps me up to date wit' yawl crazy asses, and I know you be here more than you be home so this where I came. I missed my nieces and the moment I had the free time, I stopped by," he explained.

"Dang, Auntie can't keep nothin' a secret, huh?" NiNi joked as she looked over at Yoshi.

"Girl shut up. You practically my second daughter fuck bein' my niece. You always here and that ain't no secret."

"I'm just kiddin', Auntie, but I do gotta get home soon. Onyae needs to talk to you anyway. Unc, can you take me home?" she asked him.

"Yea, I wanna see my sis anyway. She doin' good?" he asked.

"Yea, she's doin' better. Auntie, did yawl talk? I don't like tellin' her business, but I know I can trust yawl when it comes to her well-being," NiNi said.

"I've been talkin' to her here and there, but when Damon is around, I can barely have a full conversation wit' her," Yoshi revealed.

"Fuck that nigga. I only respect him because of Neosha, but if it was up to me, I wouldn't give two fucks about him.

He treatin' my sister, right? Shit, is he treatin' you right?" Kick Down asked.

NiNi looked at Onyae who looked back at her, and then gave a fake smile. When it came to them, Yoshi and Kick Down was all up and through their life. If anything was an issue, they would be the first ones to handle it, but NiNi was so prone to keeping things to herself. It didn't matter if she had people that would actually protect her in her corner.

"Everything is good, Unc, don't worry. If somethin' was goin' on, you would be the first to know."

"I hope so. You know how I get down. I don't got a problem wit' runnin' in a nigga or bitch shit wit' that blocka!"

Yoshi, Onyae, and NiNi all burst into laughter. Kick Down was the best of both worlds. He was a jokester, but he also knew when to get serious.

"Unc, you still funny wit' ya doofy self." Onyae laughed.

"I wouldn't be me if I wasn't makin' light of every situation. Life would be hella borin' if a nigga couldn't joke and make people smile and laugh. No matter how gangsta I am, there's many sides to me that allow me to get through life every day," he told them.

That was just like Kick Down, always kicking knowledge in the spare of the moment. No one had a problem with it though; whenever he spoke, everyone listened.

"Ain't that the truth. See, I be tellin' these girls that life ain't so bad. It's what you make it. Yawl know what Kick Down crazy ass been through. He stayed locked up and for him to always be happy means a lot and makes a strong statement," Yoshi added.

Onyae nodded, but NiNi didn't; she didn't feel like there was too much to be happy about considering she had been through so much.

"I hear you, but Mom, I really need to talk to you about somethin'," Onyae told her.

"Alright girl; and Kick Down you make sure you drive safe wit' my baby in the car. You know how you just don't give a fuck," Yoshi warned.

"Man, shut up. I got my niece. She forever gon' be good when she wit' her unc. You ready?" he asked NiNi as he looked down at her.

"Yea, I'm ready," NiNi responded and then turned to Onyae. "Text me later. Oxox."

"I got you, boo. Xoxo."

"Yawl and that damn hugs and kisses bullshit. I swear yawl been doin' that shit since yawl was little," Kick Down said to them.

"They sure have. The bond they have is unbreakable and sometimes it scares me," Yoshi spoke truthfully.

"It's good that they like this. It's sorta like how me, you, and Neosha was when we was younger. We still close, but the bond could be a lot stronger," he stated.

"You right, but when you get over there maybe you can tell her how you feel so we can get shit back on track."

"We'll see, but if anything, I'ma let you know what it is. Love you, sis. Love you, niece." Kick Down gave them both hugs.

"I love you too, bro."

"I love you more, Unc."

Chapter 11

NiNi only lived down the street and around the corner so Kick Down pulled up to her house in no time.

"Who van is that in the driveway?" he asked.

NiNi poked her lips out and waved her hand with attitude.

"Damon claims he bought it for the family."

"That nigga be doin' the most," Kick Down said as he shook his head left to right.

"I guess so," NiNi responded dryly.

Being the street dude that he was, Kick Down could sense that something was bothering NiNi. However, he assumed she was having typical girl problems just like every other teenager.

"So, how everything been wit' you, niece? You ain't been dealin' wit' none of these knucklehead ass lil niggas, have you?" he asked as he pulled up behind Damon's pickup truck.

"Nah, Unc. I ain't been dealin' wit' none of these lil knuckleheads out here. Don't even worry about that," she said.

"Cool, cool. Well, when you do, they better treat you right. Always know your worth and know that you deserve nothin' but the best. Don't be like these other bitches out here giving up the pussy, sucking a nigga dick and getting a fuckin' happy meal from McDonald's and sent on their fuckin' way. You too good for that," Kick Down told her.

NiNi laughed.

"Thanks, Unc. I appreciate it. I don't even eat McDonald's. I prefer Wendy's to be honest."

Kick Down laughed and then shut off his car.

"I thought you was driving ya work van around?" NiNi asked.

"This my girl car. I gotta get my tire fixed on my work van so I been cruisin' in her shit. Hell, she don't mind. As much dick as I'm slangin' to her, she better let me drive this raggedy shit."

NiNi laughed so hard she was in tears. Kick Down got out the car, and NiNi followed as she continued to laugh. It felt just like old times with her uncle. Usually when she came back to her house, she would feel sick, but for some reason her stomach was at ease.

Knock.

"I got my key. You ain't gotta do that." NiNi stuck her key in the lock, but when she went to turn it, it didn't work. "What the hell?"

"You must got the wrong key. Try the other one," Kick Down suggested.

NiNi looked down at her keys to make sure she had the right one which she did.

"Unc, I only got two sets of keys. This one is for my house and the other one is for Onyae's house. Ain't no way I got the wrong key. Mommmm!" NiNi yelled as she banged on the door.

Bang! Bang!

Bang!

"You want me to kick this shit in?" Kick Down asked.

"Nah, Unc. You shouldn't have to do that. Mommmmm!"

Bang! Bang!

Bang!

NiNi and Kick Down could hear loud walking. It was almost like someone was stomping as they were walking to answer the door.

"Damon, I'll answer it!" Neosha yelled out.

She sounded like she was one room away from the door, but NiNi and her uncle could still hear her. NiNi was hurt as she listened to the locks being unlocked. She looked over at Kick Down who didn't look happy at all. Before her mother could even open the door, the tension grew thick.

"Girl, why you bangin' on the door like you the damn police? You scared me half to death." Neosha laughed a little while she grabbed her chest.

"Mom, why is the locks changed?" NiNi asked.

She really didn't need an answer because Damon was standing right behind her mother and she knew he had something to do with it. The dislike they had for each other got worse by the day.

"I'm sorry, sweetie. I forgot to call you and tell you that Damon was getting the locks changed. Don't worry, you will have a key," she assured her.

NiNi didn't get a chance to get another word out before Kick Down stepped in. He had his hands in his pockets, but his head was held high and his demeanor was tense, making it known that he was aggravated by what was taking place in front of him.

"Fuck the key. Why was the locks changed in the first fuckin' place? Come on now, Neosha, you know damn well NiNi should've known prior to this happening. I came by to see how you were doin' because I know I've been neglecting yawl, but I be damned if I ain't run into some bullshit."

Damon stepped around Neosha and stuck his arm out towards Kick Down; it was his way of telling him to chill.

"Aye, relax yaself. I'm the one who changed the locks, and to be honest I had every damn right to. Since you're chastising me, you need to talk to ya niece about some respect. This house may be in Neosha's name, but I pay all the damn bills here and put food on the fuckin' table. The least she can do is respect me and my rules."

"What the hell are you talkin' about? I don't do anything but go to Onyae's house when I'm not takin' care of Mom," NiNi stated.

"NiNi, you ain't gotta say shit cas' I know damn well I ain't been gone that long to where you became a disrespectful person. That's never been ya character, and furthermore, muthafucka don't you ever tell me to chill. This my fuckin' sister and my fuckin' niece. If some shit is goin' on, I need to know what it is so I can see how we can solve it," Kick Down said and took it upon himself to take a step closer in Damon's direction.

"Alright now yawl calm down. I don't have the time or strength for this," Neosha said as she stood between the two men. She then looked at NiNi. "Baby, Damon meant no harm, but the coming and going is a bit much. That's all."

"Mom, I'm nineteen. All I do is help take care of you. I'm not out here messin' with no boys or doin' anything that you wouldn't approve of. I'm with Onyae and Auntie, Mom, that's it," NiNi pleaded.

Neosha rubbed her hand through her hair in a stressed manner. She was caught between trying to be a good mother and a good wife. All she wanted was her family to stick together because she wasn't sure how much longer she would have considering she made the decision to stop taking chemo. She wasn't sure what kind of effect it would have on her body, and the last thing she wanted was to be rolling over in her grave because her daughter, who was her world, and the man she loved couldn't get along.

Neosha checked the watch around her wrist to check the time.

"Look, it's 5:55pm. Let's have dinner and discuss it then. Kick Down, you're welcomed to stay. Despite all this mess, I missed you like hell so you know we need to catch up with each other."

"I missed you too, and you know I don't mind stayin' for dinner. A nigga like to eat, but I'm tellin' you now, I ain't for no fuck shit," he warned.

"Neosha, seriously? I'm sick of this shit," Damon snapped before storming away.

"I'ma knock that nigga the fuck out one of these days. I promise you that, sis," Kick Down said.

He pushed past Neosha and walked in the house. His attempt was to follow Damon to see just what the fuck his problem was, but Neosha grabbed him.

"Kick Down, please don't," she begged.

"Sis, that nigga ain't right. I'm tellin' you he ain't right. Ain't no way he should be comin' at NiNi like that or you for that matter."

"It's not like that. He just doesn't want NiNi to feel like just cas' she's grown that she doesn't have to respect this household," Neosha explained.

Kick Down shook his head.

"Sis, NiNi ain't out runnin' these streets, and I know that because I keep in contact wit' Yoshi often. If you would pick up ya phone when I called, you would know that," Kick Down shot back.

"I just want them to get along. Damn, Kick Down, is that too much to ask for? I want my fuckin' family to get along! That's it!" Neosha's tone grew loud.

The creases in her forehead were deep. The stressful energy that came off Neosha started to make NiNi stress. She hated to see her mother bothered about anything, especially if it concerned her. NiNi's intentions were never to cause any unnecessary stress to her.

"No, Mom it's not!" NiNi's voice was louder than she intended it to be. "I love you wit' everything in me, and I never want you to feel like the little things you ask is too much. I don't mind making things work because of you. That's all I've been doin', but lately, I've been feelin' like it's me against him when it comes to you. It seems like you've been choosin' him over me and it's all because I don't rock wit' him like that."

"But why, NiNi? Why don't you rock wit' him like that? Is it cas' you are still angry cas' ya father left? And why would you think I would choose Damon over you? That will never happen. NiNi, I'll die before I choose a nigga over you. I love Damon, and I appreciate everything he do for me, you, and this household, but he damn sure don't come before you, and I'm sayin' that loud enough for that nigga to hear me."

Neosha was spot on because Damon was right in the bedroom eavesdropping at the door. He was pissed to hear the way Neosha was talking about him and directed every word towards him.

Smack!

He pounded his fist in his palm and swung at the air. He paced back and forth in the bedroom in a furious state. All he wanted to do was go out there and strangle Neosha, and handle NiNi the way he normally handled her, but there was nothing he could do while Neosha was in her right mind and Kick Down was around. At that moment, all Damon could do was sit down on the bed, and finish ear hustling.

NiNi, on the other hand, was a little surprised at how her mother was coming. She knew that she had it in her, but it wasn't often that the 'no nigga or bitch better fuck with me' side of Neosha came out.

"I appreciate that, Mom, and no it ain't got nothin' to do wit' Dad walkin' out. I'm over that, okay? It ain't that I hate Damon. I just rather not get too close."

NiNi responded as best as she could without giving away too much. She knew that her mother was only as hype as she was because she hadn't taken her meds yet, and NiNi knew that it was only a matter of time until the words her mother had just spoken would mean nothing.

Zzzzz.

Onyae: *Be waitin' outside in like twenty minutes. I decided to tell Gutta's bitch ass about the baby. I told him we needed to talk in person so him and Rayshon on they way.*

NiNi was relieved to read Onyae's text. The tension in her house was getting worse as the conversation went on, and she wanted no parts of it. Nine times out of ten, Damon was bound to take it out on her, and she was going to avoid an encounter with him as much as possible.

"Mom, I'm gonna be leaving soon. Onyae is comin' to get me, okay?" she said while looking at her mother.

"Psssh," Neosha scoffed as she threw her hand up. "NiNi, this is what I'm talkin' about. You come and go like it ain't nothin'."

"Mom, cas' I don't..."

"Wait a minute, wait a minute, wait a minute. Now, I stopped speakin' to let yawl have yawl mother and daughter moment, but I feel like it's only right that I step in again. Neosha, you know I love you. You my lil sis, but sis, I'ma tell you when you right and when you wrong, and right now you wrong. You can't cripple NiNi for her whole life. She's been there for you nonstop, and I don't give a fuck if Damon pays ya medical bills or not. I can bet my life that he ain't did as much as NiNi did for you, and that's facts." Kick Down cut NiNi off and gave Neosha nothing but the harsh truth.

Tears welled up in Neosha's eyes. She fumbled with her nose as she folded her right arm across her chest while her left arm rested on her hand.

"Have a good time tonight, baby," she said through a cracked voice.

"Mom, don't cry." NiNi held her arms out to embrace her in a hug.

"I'm fine. I know that Kick Down is right and crippling you was never my intentions. I just want you here wit' me cas' I don't know what life has in store for me, sweetie. It ain't got nothin' to do wit' Mommy tryin' to stop ya life, and if you ever felt that way, I'm sorry," she apologized.

"It's okay, Mom. Please don't cry. It's okay," NiNi cried.

She hated her home life, but she hated seeing her mother hurt more which was one of the reasons she dealt with the abuse from Damon. She didn't want to see her mother sad or hurt; if anything, she'd rather it be her.

"I'm okay, baby, but I want you to gon' head and have a good time. Kick Down will keep me company, don't worry." She assured her while wiping the tears from both her and NiNi's face.

"I got her, NiNi, don't worry. You gon' out and be a teenager like you should be doin'," Kick Down told her.

He tugged on NiNi's shoulder to gently pull her away from Neosha. He could see their strong bond, that had been evident since NiNi's father had walked out on them, but somehow, some way he could see it weakening. Kick Down knew it was Damon breaking the girls away from one another. While Neosha was fighting for her family, Damon had other intentions. But Kick Down just couldn't put his hands on it. He always had an eerie feeling about Damon, and he knew he didn't like him for a reason. Out of respect for his sister and niece he tried his best to tolerate him.

"NiNi, let me walk you outside," he said and then looked to Neosha. "Sis, fix us a plate. I'll be back in here shortly."

"Okay," Neosha agreed.

NiNi walked past her uncle, and he followed her outside closing the door behind him.

"Is that nigga makin' you feel uncomfortable in anyway?" he asked.

NiNi was so caught off guard by her uncle's question that she stuttered a bit when answering. She had never been confronted about anything when it came to Damon, not even from her mother.

"Nah, nah, Unc. Why you ask that?"

"I'm just makin' sure. The nigga too damn disrespectful for me, and it seem like ya mom only catch the tail end of shit. I don't like the vibe I get in that house or from that nigga. I'm tellin' you, NiNi, if that nigga ever try to put his hands on you or try some slick shit wit' my sister, let me know. I'ma put that fuck nigga in the ground."

NiNi fumbled with her phone. The conversation put her in an uncomfortable setting. Her mind was telling her to tell on Damon, to reveal everything he'd done to her for the last ten years, but her heart told her to continue to look out for her mother. No matter how sick and tired she got of being sick and tired, nothing would make her give up on her mother. Her love and loyalty lied with Neosha; and regardless of NiNi's pain and suffering, her mother was still breathing because Damon made sure she got some of the best help.

***

An hour later

Gutta was pissed. He looked at Onyae in disgust because of what she had just said to him. In no way, shape, form or fashion was he ready to be a father, but for her to say she was aborting his child as if it didn't matter made him feel a way.

"Onyae, get the fuck outta here wit' that stupid shit. I ain't even tryna hear it, shawty, fareal," Gutta waved her off.

"Nigga, you get the fuck outta here wit' that stupid shit. Fuck you and this baby!" Onyae spat.

She was so fed up with Gutta and, in her eyes, he was putting on a front. Onyae felt like every guy was full of bullshit and the only thing they could do for her was give her dick when she wanted it and buy her shit if she wanted it.

"Ard, ard, come on now, ma. You trippin'," Rayshon stepped in.

"Nah, ya nigga trippin' if he think I'm keepin' this baby by his no-good ass. Better call that stank, dirty, mixed mutt in the face ass bitch Krystal, so you can put a baby in her!" Onyae snapped.

"Shawty, I'm not even bouta do this shit wit' you. You talkin' reckless as fuck right about now. You gon' text me talkin' about you pregnant, but then when I come pick ya dumb ass up, you talkin' about abortin' it? What kinda shit is that?" Gutta asked.

"Who the fuck you callin' dumb, pussy? You got some good dick and all, but don't you ever disrespect me like I'm one of them dust bucket ass hoes you deal wit'!"

Gutta's leg was tapping impatiently as he stood in the kitchen, leaned over the counter rolling his blunt. Onyae had his nerves shot like a motherfucker, but he was trying his best not to come out of character and treat her like a bitch. Gutta respected women, but bitches were another story. He didn't mind smacking a bitch upside her head if need be.

"Shawty, I'm tellin' you now. Get ya cous before shit get real hectic in here," Gutta said to NiNi.

"Yawl both need to calm down. It's a baby involved now so it really ain't about neither one of yawl, and that's real shit," NiNi said while looking back and forth at the both of them.

"Like I said before, fuck that nigga and fuck this baby," Onyae repeated.

"Onyae, stop fuckin' disrespectin' me!" Gutta threw the blunt and weed on the counter and stood up.

With the way he started in Onyae's direction, it seemed like he was on the verge of snapping. There was nothing but rage in his eyes; Gutta's hands were damn near around Onyae's throat before Rayshon stepped in.

"Nah bruh. This shit ain't goin' down like this," he told him while pushing him back into the kitchen.

"Oh, nigga, you tried to put ya fuckin' hands on me? Let that bitch ass nigga go, and I'ma cut him the fuck up, think I'm playin'!"

Onyae had pulled out her blade, and NiNi grabbed her.

"Onyae, you need to chill the fuck out! This shit is outta fuckin' control!"

"Move, NiNi! I'm bouta fuck this nigga up!"

Onyae quickly looked around, bent down and grabbed a controller from one of Gutta's game consoles. She pulled her arm back with force before throwing it at him.

Crash!

Rayshon and Gutta ducked right in the nick of time; the controller hit the wall behind them and fell onto the dining room table.

"Watch out, bruh. She really fuckin' tryin' me." Gutta tried to push Rayshon out the way.

"Nah, I'm not about to let you hit that girl. Fuck what she sayin'. Yawl need to come together right now."

"Let that pussy ass nigga the fuck go! I'll beat his ass in this muthafuckin' house!" she yelled.

NiNi stood there looking disappointed in her cousin. She knew Onyae could be cold and heartless at times, but this was beyond that, and she didn't like it.

"Cous, you wrong as hell. That baby didn't ask to be here, and you and Gutta didn't think about strappin' up when yawl fucked, so ain't no need to take that shit out on the baby."

"Word ma. I got love for both of yawl, but yawl both wrong and this shit is gettin' outta hand. If yawl don't wanna deal wit' each other than cool, but disrespectin' each other and tryin' to fight each other is doin' what?" Rayshon looked at Gutta and then Onyae for a response but got none. "Right now, yawl need to talk about what decision yawl gon' make."

"I was tryna talk man, but I ain't havin' nobody disrespect me and that's real shit," Gutta stated.

"I feel you, but right now throw all that shit out the window. Is you good? Because I'm not gon' leave yawl alone if you ain't," Rayshon told him.

"I'm good, bruh. Long as shawty cut that fuck shit out, I'ma remain good."

Rayshon looked over at Onyae.

"I ain't even gon' ask you is you good cas' I see you the type that'll keep shit goin'. All I'ma say is get on ya grown woman shit right now. Discuss the baby and what decision yawl gon' make. Me and NiNi gon' go upstairs so yawl can have some alone time."

Onyae rolled her eyes, but she didn't say anything back. That let both NiNi and Rayshon know that she was willing to talk things out regardless of her actions prior.

NiNi followed Rayshon upstairs to the bedroom he occupied whenever he spent the night at Gutta's place. He opened the door and allowed NiNi to walk in first. She sat on the bed and wasted no time speaking about the situation that had just taken place.

"I know my cousin like the back of my hand, and I know you know Gutta like the back of yours. How you think shit gon' play out?"

Rayshon took of his sneakers and laid down on the bed behind NiNi. He yawned loudly before responding.

"He gon' hear her out. Might not seem like it on both ends, but I think they gon' chill and get through this shit like they should."

"I hope so cas' this shit is crazy. I don't think things would've been this bad if it wasn't for that stuff that popped off at the store wit' Krystal and ya ex Sharee."

"I feel you, and Gutta was wrong for that shit, but he ain't a bad dude. I wouldn't fuck wit' him if he was. Family or not if you a fucked-up person, I can't rock wit' you," Rayshon spoke honestly.

"Well, that's good to know," NiNi said with her back turned to him.

Rayshon sat up on the bed and then stood up. He walked down by NiNi and sat next to her on the edge of the bed. She gave him a weird look as she looked over at him wondering why he was so close.

"I know shit hectic between them, but I def don't want that to stop what we could possibly build, ma," Rayshon said.

"I mean. It doesn't have to, but Onyae is my cousin, more like my sis. My loyalty lies wit' her." NiNi didn't bite her tongue when responding to Rayshon.

"I respect that, but don't let ya loyalty to her control ya life, ma, real shit. But off that, I wanna take you out tomorrow. So, be ready around 5:00pm or better yet 6:00pm just in case, cas' I know how yawl females be when it comes to gettin' ready."

"So, you takin' me on my first date?" she asked.

"I'm honored, ma," he said.

NiNi nodded with a small smile. She was glad that she was finally letting her guard down and coming out of the timid shell she was in and agreed on the date with Rayshon. She wanted to know more about the man she had such a hidden love for.

"That's a plan then."

***

Meanwhile, Gutta had finally finished rolling up his blunt, and he had it sparked. He had to take a couple of pulls to get his mind right so that he could have an open mind and remain calm while talking to Onyae.

"Look shawty, I ain't gon' front and act like I'm ready for a child cas' I'm not. But at the end of the day, I fucked you raw and wouldn't mind doin' it again. I knew the outcome of it, and I wasn't thinkin' about it nor did I care. If you gon' keep the baby then let's do what we gotta do to be the best parents we can be, but if you don't want to keep it, at least let it be a mutual agreement."

Onyae bit her bottom lip as she watched Gutta smoke and talk. She appreciated him stepping up, but she couldn't see herself being anyone's mother. Not only was she living young, wild, and free, Onyae couldn't stomach the fact that she would be having a baby by a guy she just fucked for fun. She also didn't want to risk her child being fatherless, because in her eyes, that's all a man did was walk out on their family. She didn't want her child to experience the feeling that her and NiNi had many years ago.

"Gutta, I wanna get an abortion," she blurted out.

Chapter 12

Saturday evening, NiNi sat in the dining room all dolled up waiting for Rayshon to come and get her. Since everything had kicked off with Damon the night before, she and Kick Down decided it was best to spend a couple of nights at Onyae's house. Deep down, she knew she was in for a rude awakening once she officially went back home to stay.

"Okay, bitch, look at you lookin' like a snack." Onyae smirked while giving NiNi a once over.

The weather was still cold so NiNi rocked an off the shoulder burgundy *GUESS* sweater. A pair of black, acid washed, destroyed, *GUESS* skinny jeans along with a pair of MUK LUKS Nikki fuzzy boots to complete her outfit. NiNi wore light make-up which consisted of black eyeliner, Blistex and lip gloss to add the shimmer. She wore a simple pair of hoop earrings which complimented her hair that Onyae had bumped to perfection.

"You is stupid." NiNi laughed.

"Cous fareal. You is lookin' too beautiful tonight. That nigga gon' be droolin'. He gon' try to get that pussy tonight, chick!" Onyae snapped her fingers in the air.

"Girl! Shut up! He ain't gettin' none of this pussy."

Onyae waved her off.

"Girl bye. You better let that nigga get some. I know you like him, and I know he likes you. You need to give your body to the man of your choice, and I think Rayshon is indeed the one."

NiNi couldn't have agreed more. Rayshon was hardcore, but he was doing and saying all the right things. He didn't just speak upon it; his actions backed everything up.

"I feel you, but I'ma just let things flow. You know my past and my present. I just can't do that with anyone. Never really had the chance to." A hint of sorrow filled her voice.

Whenever NiNi or Onyae spoke about, mentioned, or reflected on anything that hinted around the things that were happening to her, it made her emotional no matter how much she tried to not let it affect her.

Onyae threw her hands up as if she was praising and shook her hand back and forth no.

"Bitch, I refuse to let you cry over that fuck nigga and the fuck shit he's been doin' to you," Onyae said as she placed her hands on each side of NiNi's face. "Cous, I love you. You know I'm not the mushy type, but you've been there through my struggles just as much as I've been there through yours. Our fathers leaving our mothers to raise us, broke us. I mean yea, we're girls and we needed our mothers, but we also needed our fathers, and now, our mentality is fuck niggas."

NiNi couldn't help but to tear up. She loved how Onyae understood her without judgment. It made her incomplete life feel complete at times.

"Yea, the shit sucks, but it's life, I guess. But I promise that I'll do my best to have a good time, and not think of the fuck shit." NiNi laughed a little.

Onyae had no intentions to cry as she talked, but the words she spoke hit her heart as well.

"Don't try, do it. And while you're at it, NiNi, don't let Damon's bitch ass break you anymore. Don't let that faggot ass bitch take your power anymore. He's done it for so long, and he mentally broke you down; now Rayshon, your dream guy, is here to sweep you off ya feet and you don't know how to let him."

They both wiped the tears from each other's eyes.

"How do you know he's my dream guy?" she asked.

"Girl, you know how many niggas I done been wit'? A bitch know when a nigga is one hunnid. Rayshon, that nigga is one hunnid, boo, and don't mess this up. Regardless, of what me and Gutta go through, don't miss out on love."

Yoshi walked in on the tail end of the conversation. She could tell that whatever they were talking about was a serious and emotional conversation.

"What yawl crazy asses in here talkin' about? Cryin' and holdin' hands and shit." Yoshi laughed.

Onyae turned to her mother and playfully pushed her.

"Don't be tryna play us, Mom." She laughed.

"Ain't nobody tryna play yawl. It's just weird to see yawl hardcore asses emotional that's all, but, NiNi, you look beautiful. I can't wait to see this mystery man." Yoshi overexaggerated her words while putting her hands in the air and doing spirit fingers.

"Mom, you met him already," Onyae told her.

"When?" she asked.

"Remember a month or so ago when that big dude came here to talk to me? That's who NiNi goin' out wit' tonight." Onyae tried to refresh her mother's memory.

"Whattttt! Lemme find out my niece done pulled her a keeper. That young man was too concerned about you, so I know he likes you."

"How you know this?" NiNi asked.

"You ain't just hear, Onyae? He came by a lil while ago, and he was not happy wit' the way certain shit was goin' down over there." Yoshi talked while pulling out leftovers from the night before.

"Onyae, you said he wanted to know why I was actin' cold on him the day he tried to apologize. What Auntie talkin' about?" NiNi asked curiously.

Onyae went into the kitchen where her mother was grabbing a few pots and pans from underneath the cabinet next to the stove. NiNi followed her.

"Mommy walked in on the tail end of the conversation like she always do. It wasn't nothin' deep, cous, I promise you if it was you would know," Onyae assured her.

"I hope so. I don't want him tryna pry in my personal business without me tellin' him myself." NiNi made sure to give Onyae a stern look.

The last thing she wanted was for Rayshon to find out about her home life. In her eyes, she was used goods, and she was sure that no man wanted her. She normally wouldn't even let any man get close to her in the way she was allowing Rayshon to; in her mind, the moment he found out about who she truly was, he wouldn't want anything to do with her.

"I got you, boo. Don't worry," Onyae assured her.

She wanted to smack her mother over the top of her head for having loose lips. Onyae didn't want NiNi to know that Rayshon was concerned about her. If she did, Onyae knew NiNi would sure enough shut Rayshon down, and block him out from getting to know her.

Knock. Knock. Knock.

"I got it!" Onyae hurried to the door.

NiNi grabbed her purse and ran to the bathroom to make sure her eyeliner wasn't smudged due to her crying. When she realized she could use another coat she quickly reached in her purse and fished out her NYC black liner and reapplied it under her eyes. Once she was satisfied with how she was looking, she put the liner back in her purse, closed it and left out of the bathroom.

"I ain't gon' sugarcoat shit. You fine as hell. My niece pulled a good one, and I don't get no bad vibe from you cas' if I did then yo big fine ass wouldn't even be takin' her out on this date," Yoshi said with her arms folded across her arms.

Rayshon rubbed his beard and laughed.

"I see where Onyae gets her outspoken personality from."

"Like mother, like daughter and we ain't ashamed one bit," Yoshi stated with confidence.

"He better know it," Onyae chimed it and gave her mother a high five.

"Yawl funny as hell." He laughed again.

"I hope yawl not in here harassin' my date," NiNi said, walking into the kitchen.

"Girl bye, we just keepin' him company. Why ya ass dipped off before I could even open the door?" Onyae glanced back at her.

"Shut up. I had to fix my eye liner." She playfully pushed her.

"Don't worry, NiNi. We just tellin' him how sexy he lookin'," Yoshi added.

Rayshon was blushing from ear to ear. All he could do was laugh which kept revealing his pearly whites.

"Nah, they good, ma," he assured her.

"Good, and I have to agree wit' my aunt, you are lookin' mighty handsome tonight," NiNi complimented him.

Rayshon stepped out in a pair of DSquared, distressed, blue graffiti jeans, a long sleeved, white, Burberry button down shirt, and a pair of white, leather Burberry shoes to complete his outfit. Rayshon didn't have on any flashy jewelry to NiNi's surprise. The only thing he had on was an earring in his right ear.

"Thanks, beautiful. You ready to go?" he asked.

"Yes, I'm ready," she said.

"Cool," Rayshon extended his hand, and NiNi placed her hand in his.

He walked her out of the house, and Yoshi and Onyae couldn't help but to smile as they followed them. They stood on the porch, watching them like proud parents.

"Damn, this you?" NiNi admired his truck.

Rayshon chuckled.

"What, you thought I was broke or just ridin' off Gutta? I got my own shit, ma. Believe that."

Rayshon walked over to his all black Ford F250 and opened the passenger side door for NiNi.

She got in without hesitation and raised her eyebrows in an impressed manner. Rayshon's truck was spotless, and it smelled just like his cologne. When Rayshon got in the car, he noticed her facial expression.

"What's wrong?" he asked.

"Nothin'. I was just lookin' at how clean ya truck is."

He laughed. "You drawlin', ma. A nigga ain't dirty. I keep my shit nice and tidy at all times. You'll prolli catch me slippin' as far as not washin' the dishes at my crib, or leavin' my hoodie around, some clothes on the bed, but that's it," he told her, and then started up the truck.

Beep. Beep.

Rayshon beeped at Yoshi and Onyae before pulling off.

"So, where you takin' me?" NiNi asked.

Rayshon glanced over at her.

"Why you can't just sit back and ride, ma?"

"Cas' I wanna know where you takin' me. Is that too much to ask?"

Rayshon bit his bottom lip as he made a left turn on Route 49.

"You feisty, but I like it." He flirted but continued to drive without answering her question.

"Rayshon, you gon' turn this big muthafucka right around if you don't tell me where you takin' me!"

"Chill, ma, damn, a nigga can't even surprise you." He shook his head back and forth. "I thought takin' you out to eat, lettin' you explore South Street, and pick up a few things if you want, would be nice for a first date."

"I'm not too fond of surprises. Never had them so why start now? Anyway, dinner is nice, but why be so quick to spend money on me when we still gettin' to know one another?" she asked.

"Baby, stop thinkin' so negative. If you don't do anything else, promise me that you'll just sit back, relax and enjoy yaself." Rayshon reached over and rubbed underneath her chin.

NiNi gave a fake smile. She leaned back in the seat, closed her eyes, and took a deep breath.

Relax NiNi, just relax, she coached herself.

The car ride was silent, but Rayshon didn't mind. He wanted NiNi to be as comfortable as possible. Once they hit Philadelphia, he made sure to slow down in certain areas so NiNi could sightsee. He could tell she didn't get out much, and if she did it wasn't outside of Bridgeton.

They arrived on South Street in about an hour. NiNi had only been to South Street a couple of times before, but it wasn't packed like what she was witnessing at that moment.

"I'ma find a close parking spot, but we still gon' have to do a lil bit of walkin'. You don't mind that do you?" he asked.

"Not at all. Hell, my fat ass could use the exercise," she told him.

Rayshon had to literally press on the breaks in mid-traffic to look over at NiNi.

"You drawlin', ma. Ain't shit fat on you except for that ass, titties, and I know that pussy fat too."

NiNi's mouth was wide open. His response had completely caught her off guard and she couldn't help but to blush. She didn't have what society thought was the perfect model body; although she didn't have the worse body, NiNi wasn't used to getting compliments as such. It wasn't like she had never gotten them before, but it was never a genuine compliment. It was always from guys who wanted to fuck her.

"I don't even know how to respond to that, silly."

"You ain't gotta respond. I can see how you really feel all in ya face," Rayshon said with a sly smile.

"Ooh whatever!" She laughed.

She sat back while Rayshon parked his truck. He shut the truck off, took off his seatbelt and got out, closing the door behind him. NiNi took off her seatbelt, and grabbed the handle attempting to get out, but Rayshon snatched the door open.

"What you touchin' the handle for?" he asked.

"I was gettin' out the car," she told him.

"Nah, don't play wit' me, ma. That's not for you to do. When I get out the car you sit tight until I come round and open the door, ard?"

NiNi was appalled but flattered at the same time.

"Well okayy then," she said before getting out of the car.

Rayshon closed the door behind her, grabbed her hand and they started down the sidewalk.

"It stay packed out here," NiNi stated as she looked around.

"Ooh, so you been out here before?" he asked.

"Yea, a couple times whenever I felt like goin' out with Onyae and my aunt."

"Ard, so you know where you wanna eat then? Cas' right now a nigga starvin' like marvin," he said.

NiNi looked up at him and laughed.

"I don't remember the exact food spots out here, but it's wherever you wanna go."

"Ard, they got Fat Tuesday, Copa's, Johnny Rockets, His and Hers, and plenty other spots. Those just a few I thought of right quick." He ran down a few food spots that came to mind.

"Okay, well we can go to Johnny Rockets. I could go for a burger and fries right now," she told him.

"Ard ma, say no more," Rayshon said, and led the way.

He pointed out different stores to her as they walked to their location. On the way, different guys and girls spoke to Rayshon and some of the females shot NiNi daggers. She started to have an issue with it, but Rayshon held onto her tight and made it well known that they were out together.

Moments later, they arrived at Johnny Rockets. Rayshon held the door open for NiNi and she walked in.

"Hello, table for two?" the hostess asked.

"Yea for two," Rayshon responded.

"Great, follow me." She directed them.

NiNi and Rayshon followed the brown toned hostess to their seats. She placed down two menus on the table.

"Alright, here are your menus, and your waitress will be over here soon. Enjoy!"

"Thank you," both Rayshon and NiNi said in unison.

They opened their menus and began to browse their choices of foods and drinks.

"Oooh they got all kinds of milkshakes!" NiNi exclaimed.

Rayshon looked up from his menu and chuckled.

"You hype about a milkshake, ma?"

"Oooh, don't try to play me. I just love milkshakes, big head."

"Damn, you gotta come for a nigga head?" He laughed. "But, I'm just playin, ma. You can order however many milkshakes you want."

"Awww fareal?" NiNi asked as she leaned her head to the side while rubbing her thighs. "Ya head not big no more."

"You funny as fuck." He laughed.

"I am, huh?" she said and glanced back down at her menu. "What you gettin'?"

"Shit, they only got burgers and fries."

"Boy! They got salads and sandwiches as well," NiNi told him.

"I know but come on now, ma. They don't really have a big variety of anything. I'ma take you to The Cheesecake Factory next time or a spot in Cherry Hill. Philly really ain't shit to be honest, but for the first date I wanted you to be as comfortable as possible," he explained.

NiNi nodded her head in agreement. She appreciated the fact that he made sure she was good at all times. It wasn't often that she ran across people of his nature besides her auntie, uncle, and cousin.

"Hello, I'm Kim, your waitress for the evening. Can I start you two off with a beverage of your choice?" she asked.

"Go head, beautiful. You can order first," Rayshon said looking in her direction.

NiNi blushed again before taking a peek at her menu.

"Um, I'll have the Oreo cookies and cream milkshake, and for my meal I'll have the Route 66 burger, and please make sure it's well done because I refuse to eat a bloody burger. I don't care how healthy it is."

After NiNi finished giving her order the waitress and Rayshon laughed at her bluntness.

"What about you, sir?" Kim asked.

"Lemme get a water with lemon, and a half and half mixed iced tea. For my meal, I'ma have the Original burger and the bacon cheddar burger without the bacon. I don't want no swine on my plate. Make sure it's well done, and don't put my tomatoes and lettuce on my burger. Bring it to me on the side." Rayshon ordered.

"Boy you greedy!"

"I'ma big dude that love to eat. Chill on me." He laughed.

The waitress laughed.

"I can tell that yawl are a couple. Neither one of you play when it comes to yawl food," Kim said. She made sure to write everything down in the order they gave it to her.

"Yea, she get it from me," Rayshon said with a sly smile.

"Ooh shut up," NiNi told him.

Kim smiled at their cuteness before taking their menus.

"I'll be right back with your drinks," she told them, and walked away.

NiNi had her hands between her legs. It was something she used to do to stay warm, but it became a habit, so she started to do it naturally.

"Talk to me, ma," Rayshon said, and then placed his cellphone on the table.

"What you wanna talk about?" she asked bashfully.

"Anything, you…"

"Okay, I have drinks! A delicious Oreo milkshake for you, and a water with lemon and a half and half mixed iced tea for you." Kim interrupted Rayshon when she came back to the table.

"Thank you," they both said in unison.

"No problem. Your food will be out shortly," she said and walked away.

NiNi opened her straw and took a long sip of her milkshake; her eyes were closed, her body caught chills, and she moaned.

"Mmmmmm."

Rayshon took a small sip of his water and then sipped a nice amount of his iced tea as he watched NiNi have an orgasm. When she opened her eyes, he was looking directly at her.

"Must be good." He had a smirk on his face.

"It def is," she replied, and then took another sip.

Once she was done, she put her glass down, and stared at Rayshon for a second. He was so handsome, but yet he was still so mysterious to her.

"What's wrong, ma?" Rayshon asked, noticing that NiNi was deep in thought.

NiNi placed one hand over the other and looked at Rayshon.

"I don't want to offend you or anything so I'm not gon' ask," she told him.

Rayshon laughed.

"You might as well ask cas' you done already said it."

"Shut up." She laughed as well. "I really don't want to be rude or anything. I don't want our date to be cut short cas' of a question I asked."

Rayshon took a sip of his drink.

"I don't get offended easy, baby, and I damn sure won't cut me spendin' time wit' you in half all cas' you speakin' ya mind," he assured her.

NiNi was impressed with each word that came out of Rayshon's mouth. It was like he didn't have to try at all; everything was so natural about him which made her fall for him more and more even when she tried to fight it.

"How did ya mother die?" she asked.

She remembered him telling her that his mother passed when he was locked up, but they never got into how.

"My father killed her. Growin' up he always abused her in any way he could. Physically, mentally and emotionally. She got the strength to leave him a few times but lost it and took him back time and time again. I blamed myself for years when she was murdered. I felt like if I never would have got bagged then she wouldn't have taken that nigga back, lookin' for moral support and shit." Rayshon looked disappointed as he reflected on his past.

NiNi reached across the table and grabbed his hand. She wanted console him, and for some strange reason she felt like she needed to be there for him.

"Crazy thing about it was she act like she ain't have two other sons that she could've got support from."

"I'm sorry to hear that. I wish you didn't have to go through that," NiNi said as she rubbed his hand softly.

"Nah, I had to go through that. The streets, watchin' my moms get her ass beat, and gettin' bagged prepared me for any and everything. Thankfully they allowed me to go to her funeral. Seein' my moms in that casket made me numb to life. That was until I met Sharee," he stated.

NiNi quickly rolled her eyes at the mention of Sharee's name, and Rayshon caught it. He knew how it was when talking about a female he dealt with in the past to a female he was currently dealing with. But honesty was all he knew, and if NiNi was feeling him then she was going to have to accept the truth regardless of how she felt.

"Chill ma, it ain't even that type of party. I'm just bein' real wit' you. You asked a question so I'm gon' answer it the best way I know how. And that's by givin' you the real from start to finish."

"I ain't said nothin'," she told him.

"You ain't have to. Ya actions spoke for you, ma, now you want me to continue or nah?" he asked while leaning his head to the side as he stared at her waiting for an answer.

"Continue, Rayshon," NiNi spoke in a soft voice.

She didn't know whether she should've been offended or turned on by the way he checked her; either way she appreciated his honesty, and she was going to listen to him talk until her face turned blue.

"Ard, well like I said, I was numb to life until Sharee came in the picture. I thought she was the one cas' that's what she showed me, but that bitch took me through hell and back. I don't even disrespect females, but I'll disrespect a bitch in a minute. Sharee is a bitch so don't get offended when I refer to her as a bitch cus' I call it how I see it," he explained.

"I'm not gon' judge you. Whatever went down between yawl made you feel that way so it is what it is. I know she's a bitch, but I'm glad you agree too, but continue," NiNi said.

Rayshon licked his lips and shook his head before continuing.

"Sharee was decent at first, but then her true colors came to light. Shorty was vindictive than a muthafucka, and I had already been through a lot, so a nigga was in love. I kept givin' her chance after chance because she was there for me at one point or at least that's what it seemed like. That's prolli why she think she entitled to keep callin' me the way she do, but that Rayshon is long gone. That bitch ain't never gettin' that close to me again."

NiNi didn't like the fact that Sharee and Rayshon had been together, but he wasn't her man, nor did they know one another at that time. She could spot a snake ass bitch a mile away, and she knew when she saw Sharee that she would probably have to beat her ass every time they saw one another. Especially now that she and Rayshon were dealing; she was sure it would be a problem.

"How long was yawl together for?" she asked.

"Like two years on and off. She cheated on me a few times, and I did the same with her, but that wasn't until I knew that I was gon' leave her because of the shit I had found out. I was slowly weenin' myself away from shorty because that bitch was a nut," he explained.

"What you found out?" NiNi asked in curiosity.

She wanted to dig as deep as she could so that she could build a strong bond and trust with Rayshon. Knowing that Sharee was vindictive let her know that she would go over and beyond to get what she wanted or better yet, who she wanted.

"You nosey," he joked.

NiNi raised an eyebrow.

"Damn right. When it comes to you, I am." Her clapback game was serious.

"Ooh, really? I like that, ma."

"Mhm, I bet you do, now continue."

"She set me up once, cheated and brought me back a fuckin' STD, stole money from me and tried to burn my damn house down. Not to mention the many times she flattened my tires and busted out my windows."

NiNi looked shocked. Rayshon didn't look like the type of man that would allow a female to do the things Sharee did to him. He seemed like the type that would cut a bitch off the first time he saw her make a funny move.

"That shit is crazy. I see why certain niggas don't trust females, but anyway, off that situation. When did you get locked up , and what was it for?" she asked.

"I got bagged when I was twenty-six, and my mom died like four months after my twenty-seventh birthday. I ain't get out til I was twenty-nine. I got bagged for some light shit, but I still had to do that time cas' there ain't no way I was snitchin' on my cous," he told her.

"I can tell yawl close. Gutta seem like cool peoples, he just got a lot of baggage, somethin' that we don't accept when it comes to a guy. You lucky to even get this close to me to be honest," NiNi confessed.

"I feel you, but Gutta A1, ma, fareal. We used to get into mad shit together when he was livin' in ATL, that's where he's originally from. Hence the way he speak. I say shorty, he say shawty so his accent is still wit' him. He a loyal ass dude, but when he saw what Sharee did to me he was like fuck relationships. And before you even ask, no, him and Krystal is not together. Never was and never will be," he said honestly.

"I guess that's understandable." NiNi shrugged her shoulders.

They both got quiet for some reason, and soon after they did, Kim was walking over with their food.

"Sorry for the wait," she apologized as she sat their food in front of them. "It's pretty busy in here, but the good thing is your food is hot and fresh. You two enjoy your meals."

"Thanks," Rayshon said to her.

NiNi didn't even touch her food yet. She was too busy thinking about everything that Rayshon had just told her, and his mother's death stood out to her the most.

"So, what happened to ya dad?" NiNi asked.

Rayshon had given her the entire run down about his mother's death, her funeral, his time in jail and his relationship with Sharee, but he didn't speak on his father any further.

Rayshon was in mid-bite of his burger when NiNi asked him the question. It seemed as though he had lost his appetite when he put his burger down, took a sip of his drink and cleared his throat before responding.

"I got out of prison and murked him."

NiNi wasn't too fond of the streets, but she knew street terms when she heard them, and she was aware that the term murked was another way of saying killed. Rayshon had killed his father, and she didn't have to wonder or ask why. It was because of the love he had for his mother, and the pain he had watched her endure growing up.

NiNi was hoping that the love Rayshon would have for her someday would somehow have the same outcome, and he could get rid of her problem forever.

Chapter 13

NiNi was on cloud 99, and it was all because of Rayshon. She was so happy because of how perfect her first date was that she told him to drop her off home instead of back at Onyae's. NiNi was on such a high that she felt like nothing or no one could ruin it. Things were going good for her and she couldn't have been happier. NiNi couldn't remember a time where she was genuinely happy, and it wasn't forced. Here she was looking through her clothes in her closet for tomorrow night's occasion. No matter how much she tried to stop it, Rayshon was persistent when it came to her. It had only been a month since they had been knowing each other, but it felt like years to NiNi.

Rayshon: *I hope ya moms ain't too mad that I brought you home late. I'm lookin' forward to tomorrow night ma. I had a good time wit' you tonight so I can only imagine how tomorrow gon' be.*

NiNi smiled as she reread Rayshon's text twice before responding to it.

NiNi: *Nah, she's sleepin', and she wouldn't have been mad if she was up. I had a great time as well. You so sweet, and I can't wait until I see you tomorrow. I guess this time I'll finally be able to go to ya place.*

Rayshon: *You already know ma, but a nigga bout to get some sleep. So, you get some sleep beautiful. Goodnight.*

NiNi was smiling from ear to ear when he called her beautiful. It felt so real and seemed so natural for him to do so.

NiNi: *Goodnight handsome.*

Once NiNi sent off the last text message to Rayshon she put her phone on the dresser and changed into her night gown and a pair of cotton shorts. When she was finished, she stepped into her bedroom slippers, and left out of her bedroom and headed in the kitchen to get a glass of juice. By the time she stepped near the sink, she ran straight into Damon, who had just walked in the house. He reeked of liquor.

"Get downstairs," he demanded.

NiNi began to back away. Her intentions were to run to her mother's bedroom and wake her up as quick as she could. Damon must had read her mind because he cracked his knuckles and clenched his teeth.

"NiNi, get downstairs now. I'm not gon' tell ya stupid ass again. I'll kill you and ya fuckin' mom tonight, bitch, don't play wit' me. Get ya ass downstairs in that muthafuckin' basement now," Damon's mouth barely moved as he spoke.

She was so afraid that she was in a frozen state. NiNi put her hands up in defense while she spoke.

"Damon, please," she begged.

"Pssh, you really think shit is a game?" he scoffed.

He walked towards NiNi and grabbed her by the neck while pushing her towards the basement door. Tears started pouring from NiNi's eyes like a waterfall. She went from a happy teenager to a frightened little girl in a matter of minutes knowing that her pleas went unnoticed.

Damon damn near pushed her down the stairs all while his hand was still tightly wrapped around her neck. Once he had her in his domain, there was nothing she could do. The basement was Damon's mancave when he wasn't working, upstairs spending time with her mother or making NiNi's life a living hell.

The basement was fully furnished. If one wanted to, they could live down there, sort of like what Damon did in his spare time. He pushed NiNi on his Cailon queen sofa sleeper, which was a bed and couch all in one, kicked off his shoes, and unbuckled his jeans. NiNi laid there praying for some sort of miracle that she was sure would never come while Damon climbed on top of her.

He lifted up her nightgown and went to push his dick inside her when he got a disappointment.

Whap!

Damon punched NiNi in her face as if she was a man.

"You tryna be funny, bitch!" He snapped when he saw that she had shorts on.

She couldn't get a word out as she swallowed the salty blood that came from her mouth being busted open. Damon snatched her shorts off and forced himself inside her.

"Oow!" she cried.

"Mmmm," he moaned.

Slap. Slap. Slap.

Damon humped and jumped on top of NiNi at a fast pace. She held her breath to keep herself from smelling Damon's scent; hoping that would help her get through the encounter. He looked down at her and licked her face while digging deep inside her.

"You like this shit, huh?" he grunted.

NiNi didn't say a word. Her eyes were tightly shut as Damon slammed in and out of her with force. She wanted to die right then and there. No matter how many times Damon raped her over the years, she could never prepare herself for it.

"Answer my question, bitch. You like this shit, huh?" he asked again.

NiNi still didn't answer. She couldn't allow herself to stoop so low. However, that only made things worse. Damon put his arm around the back of NiNi's head, lifted her left leg over his arm and began to pound at her vagina. A fresh batch of tears flowed down NiNi's eyes as she punched and scratched Damon wanting him to get off her.

"Please stop," she cried.

"Tell me you like it," he told her.

"I like it," she whimpered.

Slap. Slap. Slap.

"Tell me you want me to keep doin' this."

NiNi felt so dirty, but there was nothing she could do.

"I want you to keep doin' this."

"Mmmm, I know you do, baby." He moaned.

NiNi wanted to throw up. She wanted to die. Damon's sweat from his forehead had dripped on her face. Her pussy hadn't got wet once for him, regardless of how many times he'd violated her. NiNi could feel the wetness and she knew it was from his semen, and probably blood from him ripping her.

"You want ya mother to live?" he asked.

NiNi wasn't confused by the question. Damon always made it clear that she was the key to her mother's life. She was sickened by the fact that he relied on that threat.

"Yes." She cried harder.

Slap. Slap. Slap.
Smack. Smack. Smack.

"Mmmm," he moaned. "You sure?"

NiNi nodded, and it was as if Damon was turned on by her weakness. Soon after, she felt a warm feeling inside of her, and she knew he had released inside her once again.

"Uhhhh, urgh," he grunted, and then pulled out.

The moment Damon sat up on the side of the sofa, NiNi pushed his semen out of her. She felt so dirty and unwanted, and to think she had an amazing time just a few hours ago with the man she had unknowingly fallen in love with.

"Get the fuck out," Damon said with his back to her.

Tears ran down her face as she laid back on the couch with her night gown above her stomach. She slowly sat up while wishing she had a knife to stab Damon in his back until her arm got tired. NiNi slid her bottom off the couch, grabbed her shorts off the floor, and slowly walked towards the stairs. Her vagina was sore and with each step she took she winced in pain. When NiNi finally made it upstairs, she went down the hall and peeked in her mother's room. More tears rolled down her eyes as she watched her mother sleeping peacefully. She glanced over at her nightstand that was full of medicine.

"I love you, Mommy. I'll continue to do anything for you," she whispered.

NiNi turned around and held the bottom of her stomach in pain as she walked. Before she could make it to her room, in one swift motion, Damon had his hand around her neck as he pushed her in her bedroom.

"Please don't," she begged.

"NiNi, don't fuckin' play wit' me. The fuck you in ya mom room for?" he asked.

"I—I—I just wanted to check on her," she cried.

Damon squeezed her neck just a bit tighter to let NiNi know he wasn't playing any games.

"Bullshit!" he spat and spit flew in her face. "I swear to God if you keep playin' wit' me, I'ma kill ya mom and then I'ma kill you. All that dumb shit you doin' tryna make shit obvious is only gon' hurt you in the long run. Keep fuckin' around, bitch."

Damon let go of NiNi's neck and stormed out of her bedroom making a left to go to the room he and her mother shared.

NiNi grabbed her bath towel off the back of her door, reached back and grabbed her cellphone off the dresser, leaving out of her bedroom and going into the bathroom. She made sure she locked the door behind her. NiNi was in so much pain. It was beginning to be unbearable, and the only thing she could do was run herself a hot bath.

She turned on the hot water and put the stopper down. NiNi couldn't sit to wait for the water due to the pain she was in, so she stripped out of her night gown and slowly eased her body in the tub. NiNi could see streams of blood floating in the tub. The only thing she could do was continue to sob. She couldn't run to her mother, she couldn't run to her aunt, she couldn't run to the police, and she couldn't run to the hospital. NiNi had to nurse herself back to health when it came to everything she endured.

While trying to calm her nerves, and get her body under control, NiNi had to text Rayshon. She knew he told her he was going to sleep, but there was no way she was going out with him in the condition she was in.

NiNi: *I can't go tomorrow night. I'm sorry.*

Tears poured down her face. Happiness didn't live with her, only pain and suffering. Regardless of how much she tried to put everything she was going through behind her, things just continued to get worse.

Rayshon: *Huh? What happened that fast ma? We was just talkin'.*

NiNi read his text but she didn't respond. Instead, she threw her phone on the rug beside the tub, covered her face with her hands and cried until she couldn't cry anymore. A woman's love for their child was unconditional, but a daughter's love for her mother went beyond measures.

Chapter 14

Neosha was feeling like her old self again, and even got up that morning to make breakfast which wasn't something she did often due to her being sick the majority of the time. She sat at the dining room table drinking her coffee and scrolling through Facebook on her cellphone.

"I tell you one thing. They don't need the got damn news cas' leave it to Facebook they know everything," Neosha said, shaking her head.

"Yea, that's social media for you, bae," Damon responded.

"You right. It's a gift and a curse," Neosha said while taking a sip of coffee.

She looked up when she heard NiNi's door open. Neosha was ready to greet her daughter with a big smile and good afternoon until she saw NiNi barely able to walk on her way to the bathroom.

"NiNi, baby what's wrong?" Neosha asked with concern in her voice.

NiNi looked over at her mother in an attempt to say something but stopped when Damon looked at her with daggers. NiNi swallowed hard and forced a fake smile at her mother.

"I'm gettin' sick, Mom. I think it may be the flu," she lied.

"NiNi, what happened to your face!"

NiNi had stayed up most of the night putting ice pack after ice pack on her mouth to take the swelling down. She was hoping that it wasn't as bad anymore, but from her mother's response she was wrong.

"Mom, I tripped and fell the other night. I didn't say anything because it wasn't a big deal."

Neosha eyed her daughter for what seemed like an eternity.

"Come here let me feel ya head," she said.

Damon blew loudly when he saw NiNi struggle to walk over to Neosha at the table. He made sure to keep direct contact with NiNi, watching her every move, making sure she knew not to say one word.

"You don't feel warm. What's ya symptoms?" she asked.

Neosha gently grabbed NiNi's face with one hand to examine her bruises. She wanted to assume that the guy NiNi was talking to was the cause of it, but instead, she accepted what her daughter told her.

"Mom, I'm fine. I'm gonna take some medicine," NiNi told her.

"I don't like how you can barely walk. I'm hoping it's the flu because you know how this weather is. I don't need it being anything else," Neosha said while she examined NiNi.

"She's fine, Neosha. Chill wit' babying her. I'm sure if somethin' serious was wrong wit' NiNi she would say it," Damon chimed in.

"Damon, don't tell me what to do when it comes to my child. If I feel like somethin' is wrong wit' her, nine times out of ten I'm right because a mother knows," Neosha said with attitude.

"This is why she walk around wit' no fuckin' respect for me. Every time I say somethin' concerning her here you go tellin' me you know her best," Damon snapped.

Neosha took her attention off NiNi and jerked her neck around so fast it could have broken. She didn't like how Damon was coming. He may have been NiNi's stepfather, but she was her mother.

"I get you sometimes, Damon, but right now nah you not even about to get this one. My daughter looks like shit, and you got the nerve to talk some stupid respect shit? Tuh, you can get the hell on with that one."

Damon got up and stormed from the table. NiNi wished that she could hurry and tell her mother what was really going on with her, but she knew there would be consequences and repercussions if she did.

"Mom, I don't want yawl to argue," NiNi said.

"Don't worry about him, girl. Him and his bitch fits will be fine," Neosha said, waving her hand in the air in an 'I don't care' manner.

"You sure?" she asked.

"NiNi, I'm positive, and I waited for you to get up so we could go over Yoshi house. She wanna see me, and since I'm feelin' good today I said I'll go over there and chill with her for a few."

"Gimme a few minutes," she said quickly.

NiNi's eyes lit up like a kid on Christmas. She couldn't wait to get out the house, and she couldn't wait to be around her cousin. She was in pain, but she hurried back to her room, got out a pair of black and yellow, cloth, snug fitting pajama pants, a yellow tank top and her all black Nike sneakers. She wanted to take another bath, but the pain between her legs, and the eagerness to leave the house told her otherwise.

NiNi hurriedly got dressed and put on her shoes. She couldn't bother to fix her hair so she threw on her scarf, grabbed her cellphone and left out her bedroom.

"Mom, I'm ready!"

"You ain't waste no time, did you?" Neosha laughed as she got up from the table.

She was already dressed and ready in a pair of army fatigue leggings, with a tan tank top, and zip up hoodie with her black Laverne and Shirley sneakers.

"Nope. You drivin' today?" NiNi asked in a surprised tone.

"Yup. Momma is feelin' good, and I'm takin' advantage of it," she said, grabbing the keys to the van.

NiNi had an awful night but seeing her mother back to her normal self for a little while made her feel a tad bit better. They left out the house, and Neosha locked the door behind them. She hit the unlock button on her keypad, and they got in the car.

"I know she gon' have so much to say considering I ain't been over there in a while. You know ya aunt," Neosha said while putting on her seatbelt.

"You know she is, but she'll be happy to see you more than anything." NiNi made clear.

"Yea, I know. I do miss her. Things just ain't the same anymore. Especially, since I've been sick," Neosha stated, as she started up the car, and pulled out of the driveway.

NiNi grew quiet. Her mother was right so there really wasn't much to say in response. She knew that things had changed since she'd been sick, and since she and Damon had been together. Lately, NiNi had become aware that she wasn't the only one that had a dislike for Damon.

They drove in silence which neither one of them minded considering it wasn't often they had mother and daughter time. It took a few minutes to get to Yoshi's house. A smile spread across Neosha's face when she parked backwards in front of her sister's house. Just the sight of Yoshi's house brought joy to Neosha's heart. She didn't realize how much she missed being around until that moment, and she hadn't even seen Yoshi yet.

"Mom, you ain't changed a bit cas' you know you can't park like this." NiNi laughed.

"Chile, ain't nothin' changed but my health. You know ya mama don't give a fuck, and I know every damn cop up in Bridgeton. I wish I would get a damn ticket for parkin' in front of my sister's house," Neosha said while shutting off the car, and taking off her seatbelt.

NiNi chuckled, and then took off her seatbelt. Her body was in excruciating pain. It seemed as though the more she stayed still the worse it got. She was hoping that taking some pain meds, and another hot bath would do because she refused to go to the hospital no matter how bad she felt.

Meanwhile, Onyae had just got finished texting Gutta when she came out her bedroom. Her stomach growled loudly after smelling the aroma of the good food her mother was cooking. She sat at the dining room table and grabbed an apple that was sitting in the fruit dish in the center of the table.

"Mom, you need to hurry up. Ya girl starvin' over here," Onyae said.

Yoshi spun her head around.

"Onyae, you better get ya greedy ass on. Ain't nobody tell you to be grown and open ya legs," she shot back.

Onyae waved her off.

"Dang, why you gotta be all extra? Can't I just get a plate without all that back talk." She laughed.

"You better get gone! The food is almost done, greedy! And while you waitin', go get my charger out the car," Yoshi said.

Onyae got up from the table and walked in the kitchen. She threw the remainder of the apple in the trash, and then opened the door. When she made it to the porch stairs, she saw NiNi and her aunt getting out of the van.

"No, the hell it's not! I know that's not who I think it is! Awww shit! Mooommm! Auntie is here! Like she really here!" Onyae yelled.

Before NiNi could even get out the van good she heard screams. She closed the passenger door and looked over at her mother who had tears in her eyes.

Yoshi had just gotten finished cooking dinner which consisted of fried chicken, baked chicken and gravy, string beans, baked macaroni and cheese and fresh rolls with a lemon pound cake for dessert. When she heard Onyae scream that Neosha was outside, she wiped her hands on her pants and ran outside.

"Oh my gosh! I missed you so much!" Yoshi ran with open arms towards Neosha.

"Ugh, I missed you too, baby." Neosha embraced Yoshi in a tight hug.

NiNi wiped the tears that had formed in her eyes. It wasn't often that she was able to see something so pure. She could tell that her mother and aunt missed each other dearly.

"Hey boo!" Onyae greeted NiNi.

"Hey babes," she responded.

Onyae gave her a hug, and NiNi winced causing Onyae to pull away.

"Sss, ah." NiNi groaned.

NiNi didn't even have to speak. The look Onyae gave her let her know that she already knew what had happened to her. All Onyae could do was sigh loudly as she combed her hair with her hand and flared her nostrils.

"NiNi, you sure you don't wanna go to the emergency room? I don't like how stiff your body is," Neosha asked while eyeing her daughter.

NiNi didn't even realize that her mother was paying attention to her. She thought that she was still hugging Yoshi, but she caught her off guard with the question.

"Nah, Auntie she good. I told her not to be messin' around wit' this weather. It's probably just a lil cold or somethin' because we always wearin' our lil spaghetti strapped shirts with no jackets tryna be cute." Onyae fake laughed.

"Yea, this weather ain't no joke," Yoshi added.

"That's why I'm concerned. It could be pneumonia or anything, and I refuse for my baby to be sick to the point of no return. People dying every day because of this fucked up ass weather," Neosha shook her head.

"Mom, I'm fine now can we get in the house? I smell some good ol' food and I know Auntie cooked." She laughed.

"What happened to ya face, NiNi?" Yoshi asked. It was slightly swollen, and she saw a few bruises.

"Clumsy ass fell," Neosha said with a chuckle. Yoshi eyed NiNi for a moment as she thought about the excuses she made when she was getting physically abused. She quickly shrugged it off figuring that something like that could never happen to her niece.

"Come on, Neosha. It's been a while since you had ya sis cookin' and I know you miss it," Yoshi said.

They all walked back into the house and shook the cold off. Yoshi wasted no time washing her hands, getting plates out and filling them with hot food.

"Oooh, sis, this smells so good," Neosha said, and then took a seat at the dining room table.

"I know right, Auntie. She tryna act like I couldn't eat just a few minutes ago," Onyae added.

"Humph, did you tell her why not?" Yoshi glanced back at her daughter.

"Tell me what? What's goin' on wit' you girl," Neosha asked.

Yoshi brought plate after plate to the table, and drink after drink before sitting down.

"I'm pregnant, Auntie, but I ain't keepin' it. I'm not ready to be nobody's mom, and the dude I'm pregnant by ain't somebody I wanna have a baby by," she explained.

Neosha nodded her head as she stuck a forkful of mac and cheese in her mouth. There wasn't a judgmental bone in her body when it came to anything her niece said because she was once young.

"Well, it seems like you got it all figured out. You know we're against abortions, but what I don't want you to do is bring a child into this family knowing you're not ready. That's the problem wit' a lot of these young moms. They have these kids to keep these men, and the shit backfire. That's when you have kids dyin' and in foster care or some shit. It just ain't right, and neither is abortion, but sometimes the best decision is the wrong one." Neosha said a mouthful.

Her and Yoshi both were young mothers. They weren't teens but having a baby in their early twenties was just as bad considering the fathers didn't even wait until they were grown to walk out of their lives.

"That's what I told her. Shit just a lot worse nowadays. More than it was back then," Yoshi added.

"Mhmm." Neosha took another forkful of food to her mouth. "I know you and NiNi experienced the same thing which is yawl fathers bein' bitches and bailing out on yawl. I'm not kickin' their backs in cas' yawl saw the shit for yaself. Now, take that and times it by ten. These young men these days ain't bout too much of shit either. Now don't get me wrong, it's some good ones out here, you just gotta hold on to him when you get him."

Yoshi took a sip of her juice and then took a bite of her biscuit.

"I think they both found some decent ones. It sucks to say I'm gonna meet Onyae's lil boo during the trip to Cherry Hill, but things happen," she said.

"Ooh, you met NiNi's friend?" Neosha asked with eyebrows raised.

Yoshi nodded. "Yup, and he's a sweetheart. You can tell he really cares about you, NiNi. Don't miss out on love, baby, especially when it's right there in ya face."

When Yoshi met Rayshon, she could tell he was a good man with a few flaws. She didn't know all that NiNi was going through, but she did know she was suffering from low self-esteem, and she was aware that she felt alone at times because her mother was sick. Yoshi looked at Rayshon as the man and friend that could take NiNi to explore different things and have the chance to experience life.

"That's nice and all. I wish I would have met the side you saw cas' he came to the house, and it went from a nice meet and greet to a whole damn argument." Neosha shook her head. "He might be a nice dude and all, but I don't want any man around that can't respect my household."

The house got quiet. It was so quiet that one could hear a pin drop. NiNi's mouth grew dry when she saw Onyae's facial expression to what her mother had said.

"What exactly happened, sis, cas' he seemed real thorough to me. He the type of nigga that don't come outta pocket unless he's provoked, and I can say that cas' that's how my boyfriend is," Yoshi stated.

"Boyfriend? When did this happen?" Neosha asked completely ignoring Yoshi's question.

Yoshi shrugged her shoulders.

"Sis, if you came around more often you would know what's goin' on. I know you sick and all, but that shouldn't stop you from bein' around family." Yoshi threw her hands up. "If you ask me, I think Damon is the real cause of you not comin' around anymore."

Neosha frowned her face.

"What the hell makes you say somethin' like that?"

"Just by the way shit is. Ain't no way we live around the damn corner from each other and haven't seen each other in months, shit, a year. The shit don't make any sense," Yoshi told her straight up.

"You know what. If I would have known comin' over here would give you the open opportunity to ride down on me, my ass would've stayed away. I don't have time for this, Yoshi, I really don't," Neosha told her.

"Neosha, I'm not tryna ride down on you. Now, you know me better than that, sis. All I'm sayin' is that nigga ain't right, and I don't care how long yawl been together. I know a snake when I see one."

Neosha slammed her fork down on the table with force.

"What the hell is it about him that yawl hate so much?" she asked with tears in her eyes.

Onyae and NiNi sat back witnessing two bold, black women who loved each other dearly going head to head. Neither one of them jumped in because they knew the conversation was much needed.

Onyae: *Uncle KD, Auntie and NiNi is here at our house. I think you should hurry up and stop by. Shit is gettin' heated and I'm sure you got a lot to say as well.*

Onyae took it upon herself to text their uncle because the situation was getting out of hand, and she knew that he had a lot of issues with Damon as well. She was hoping that them hashing out their differences and opening up her aunt's eyes could possibly help NiNi in the long run.

Onyae knew that her mother and uncle didn't know exactly the pain and suffering NiNi endured. But she knew that they got a negative vibe from Damon and that was good enough to let them know that he wasn't the man he was pretending to be.

"Who said I hated him? I just don't like him, and it's evident that NiNi doesn't either. Sis, I know that you've been through a lot, and I know you want love. Hell, I'm just now findin' love after all these years. I've been givin' this good pussy and my good heart to the wrong ones for a long time, but that was until I met Khalif," Yoshi explained, and reached over to grab her sister's hand. "I'm not tryna hurt you by tellin' you that you need to peep game when it comes to Damon. I just want you to see that you're hurtin' yaself more than anything. Love ain't supposed to hurt, and I don't give a fuck if that nigga payin' ya medical bills. I got money, and you can come live wit' us if you don't wanna be alone."

Neosha pulled away from Yoshi to wipe the tears from her eyes. She heard everything her sister said, but she didn't agree with any of it.

"I see it was a mistake comin' here. NiNi, let's go, and for future references, stop discussing my household wit' your aunt," Neosha said as she pushed her chair back and stood up.

NiNi sat there looking at her mother in disappointment. She loved her mother to pieces, but she couldn't tolerate that she was so in denial about things.

"Mom, I'm not leavin' and neither should you. For once, stop bein' so stubborn. Auntie ain't said nothin' bad to you, and I know she ain't tryna hurt you. Just listen to her," NiNi said.

Neosha frowned her face upon her daughter and shook her head. She grabbed her car keys off the table and headed for the door; the moment she opened it, she ran right into Kick Down.

"Who called him?" she snapped as she whipped her head around.

Onyae raised her hand without a care in the world.

"I didn't call him. I texted him; I feel like yawl got a lot to talk about. So, now that he's here, me and NiNi gon' go in my room so yawl can talk."

Neosha knew how her niece was; at times she hated how she was so bold and honest.

"Chill sis. I only came to talk," Kick Down assured her.

"There ain't shit to talk about, okay?" Neosha attempted to push past him, but he stopped her.

"Neosha, shit is gettin' outta hand, and it's time to put shit on the table. Regardless if you like it or not you gon' listen. It's been a long time since we got together as a family, and to have this nigga keepin' you hostage ain't sittin' well wit' me at all. I shouldn't have to go through my niece to see how you doin'," he stated.

"This shit is ridiculous. You chose not to come around, it wasn't my fault! How long have you been gone Kick Down, huh? It wasn't me who stopped talkin' to you so don't go there actin' like Damon is the cause of us losin' touch cas' he's not!" Neosha felt attacked, and she was fed up.

It was clear to everyone in the house that Neosha was oblivious to the fact that they were trying to help her, not harm her.

"You right. I've been in and out of jail, and on top of that I was doin' some illegal shit that I didn't want to bring around my sisters or nieces. So, nah, I didn't come around, and I think you should respect me for that instead of actin' like I didn't want to come around at all," Kick Down shot back.

"Let me add that I never stopped talkin' to you either, but I got tired of reachin' out to you and you barely wantin' to talk. Or, I would hear Damon in the background tellin' you to get off the phone. What type of shit is that? You a grown ass woman, and he has entirely too much control over you and I don't like it," Yoshi added.

When Yoshi said her piece, Onyae and NiNi took that as their opportunity to remove themselves from the table and head straight to Onyae's bedroom. Before they could reach Onyae's bedroom Kick Down spoke up.

"Why the hell you limping, NiNi? What happened?"

NiNi stopped in mid-step and looked directly at Onyae who was already looking back at her.

"Um, I'm sick, Unc. I might have the flu to be exact."

Kick Down saw through the bullshit. He looked over at Neosha.

"What's wrong wit' my niece?"

"Didn't you just hear her say she might have the flu? I'm just as concerned as you, but she doesn't want to go to the hospital."

NiNi looked at Onyae with pleading eyes.

"Unc, she's fine, okay? Now let us go in the room so yawl can talk."

Onyae didn't give Kick Down a chance to respond before she turned back around and headed to her bedroom with NiNi right behind her. As soon as NiNi closed the door behind them, Onyae started on her.

"That fuck nigga touched you again?" she asked.

NiNi whipped her body around fast.

"Shhhh." She put her finger up to her lips. "You loud as fuck."

"Fuck that, NiNi! You can barely fuckin' walk, and you tellin' me to shhh? I'm goin' out there and I'm tellin' Auntie right fuckin' now," Onyae said before trying to push past her.

"Onyae no." NiNi shoved her back. "Don't do this. Please, don't."

NiNi begged and pleaded hoping that Onyae would just leave well enough alone.

"NiNi, I'm tired of this shit. This nigga is fuckin' you up, literally, and you expectin' me to continue to keep quiet? NiNi, you can barely walk!" Onyae broke down.

NiNi was lost for words. Being emotional wasn't a part of Onyae's character so to see her break down broke NiNi's heart. She didn't know what to do at that very moment, and it felt like her mind and heart was having a tug of war battle. On one hand, NiNi agreed with Onyae and she wanted to run out there and tell her mother what was really going down, but on the other hand, she felt like it would backfire. Before NiNi could get another word in to calm Onyae down, they heard a loud noise.

The sound of glass shattering interrupted NiNi and Onyae's dispute. Neither one of them thought twice before they damn near stumbled over each other trying to get out of the door. When Onyae and NiNi finally made it to the kitchen, they saw Neosha in tears.

"Mom, are you okay?" NiNi's tone was worried.

Neosha wiped her face before responding.

"No, I'm not okay, but I will be," she sniffled. "I refuse to ever need a man again. Your father took everything from me, and I'll be damned if I depend on anyone again. Yes, Damon does help pay my medical bills, and he helps pay the household bills, but he never holds it over my head. NiNi, your father took everything and left us with nothing. I've been with Damon for ten years and he has yet to give up on me. So, yawl can hate him all you want, but he has proved his love for me."

"Pssh!" Yoshi smacked her lips and threw her hands up in aggravation. "Neosha, he is keepin' you away from ya damn family! I mean, I understand NiNi's dad made you depend solemnly on him and then snatched everything away from you when he left, but what do you think I went through with Onyae's dad? That nigga cheated, beat my ass and had the nerve to leave as if he didn't have a family to take care of. Every nigga after that felt like they could beat my ass, but what did I do? I got my power back! I started workin', and savin' up so that me and my daughter would never have to depend on a man again! The nigga I'm wit' now does shit for me, but it's a bonus cas' I take care of myself. If he leaves me today or tomorrow I'ma be good and so will Onyae. If Damon leaves you today or tomorrow what's gon' happen, sis? That nigga ain't no better. He just doin' shit in a different way."

Neosha stood there looking at her sister with a mixture of sorrow, hate, and hurt in her eyes.

"Yoshi, thanks but no thanks," she said and then looked toward NiNi. "Stay here if you want, but I'm leavin'. I can't deal wit' all this extra stress."

Neosha didn't give NiNi a chance to respond before she pushed past Kick Down and stormed out of the house.

Kick Down walked over to his niece and placed his hand on her left shoulder.

"NiNi, you good? Is somethin' goin' on? Cas' I don't like that nigga at all. I don't like the attitude he got when it comes to my sister. Like, I told you before, if that nigga ever say one thing slick to you, put his hands on you, or do anything that make you feel uncomfortable, don't hesitate to let me know, and it's off wit' that nigga head." Kick Down's tone was serious.

Onyae looked over at NiNi who looked back at her. Before NiNi even told Onyae about the horrific encounter that she and Damon had last night she already could tell that something happened. Onyae was so accustomed to what NiNi was going through that she had begun to read her body language long ago. That allowed her to know beforehand that NiNi had been touched once again, and she hated that there was nothing she could do to protect her.

"Nah, it ain't nothin' like that, Unc. I just don't like how he tries to control my mother just cas' he pays her medical bills." NiNi did her best to lie with a straight face.

Although, she had succeeded in covering up her secret for so many years. She didn't know if she was capable of doing so when it came to her uncle because he was a street nigga who could pinpoint a lie a mile away.

"A'ight, I'ma take ya word for it," Kick Down told her.

Yoshi placed her hand on her forehead and shook her head back and forth in a stressed manner.

"Girls, help me clean up in here, please?" She glanced at Kick Down. "Go home, get some rest. We'll figure this shit out along the way."

***

Forty-five minutes later, Yoshi was finally settled in her Queen-sized bed with her Jacquard five-piece plum comforter set. She picked up her cellphone, took it off the charger and scrolled through her favorite contacts. Once she found the contact she desired to call, she placed the phone to her ear.

Ring. Ring. Ring.

"Hey baby," Yoshi said when Khalif picked up the phone.

"Wassup beautiful. Everything okay?" he asked, sensing something was wrong because of the stressful tone of her voice.

"Can you come over, please? I need you right now."

"You ain't gotta say please, baby. I'm on my way," he said before ending the call.

Chapter 15

That evening, Khalif sat on Yoshi's bed rubbing her feet with warm oil. She laid her head back on the pillow with her eyes closed trying her best to get her mind right after the conversation she had with her sister.

"What's on ya mind?" he asked.

"Remember, I was tellin' you I got an older sister and brother?" she asked, making sure he remembered. "My sister is the one fightin' cancer right now."

"I listen to everything you say to me. So, yea, I remember. Wassup wit' them? Somethin' happened?"

Yoshi smiled just a little. She loved how overprotective Khalif was when it came to her although they were still building a solid foundation.

"Yea with my sister. Remember, I briefly told you that we've been in and out of one another's lives since she got sick and been wit' the guy she's wit' now?"

Khalif nodded.

"Yea, but you also said yawl gon' be close regardless, so what's the problem, ma?"

"She popped up about an hour or so ago, and I was so happy to see her, but things went left real fuckin' quick." Yoshi sighed.

"Went left how? Considerin' yawl don't see each other often there shouldn't have been nothin' that fucked up yawl time together," he spoke honestly.

Yoshi rolled her eyes.

"Damn, can I get a word in?" she asked.

"My bad, bae. You know how I feel about shit like this. If I would have ended the beef wit' my brother a long time ago maybe he would still be alive. You told me that ya sis was sick so time is a precious thing right now," he explained.

Khalif used to be a cold-hearted street nigga. He was the type that just didn't give a fuck; if you crossed him, you lost him. He kept that mentality for years, and the same rules that he applied to the streets, he also applied to the ones he loved. His brother ended up fucking him over, and that was the end of their relationship.

"And I get that, but can you at least let me explain?" she asked.

Khalif nodded and continued to rub her feet.

"A'ight ma," he said.

"Thank you. Now, like I was sayin', shit just went real left. I was happy to see her. I missed my baby so bad, but all I could think about was how long it's been since we actually spent time together as a family. I know she's sick, but a lot of the time we lost together has a lot to do wit' that nigga she's wit'," Yoshi explained.

"And you told her that?" Khalif asked.

"Hell yea. The fuck?"

Khalif shook his head and chuckled.

"You should've let that one slide, Yoshi. If anything, you should've enjoyed yawl time together, and then when she came around again that's when you should've said somethin'. Not when yawl just now seein' each other for the first time in how ever long it's been."

Yoshi kicked Khalif and snatched her foot from him. She appreciated how he tried to give her advice, but right now she felt like he was seeing all the wrong in something that was right.

"What the fuck, Khalif? I mean, damn can you actually understand how much I fuckin' miss my sister? She could die any day, and that mismatched eyed bastard's only interest is keepin' her away from those who love her most!" Tears filled Yoshi's eyes.

She was overwhelmed from the situation with Neosha, and Khalif didn't make it any better by pointing out that she was wrong for being concerned for her sister.

"Baby, come here." He scooted over to her. "Don't cry, ma. I'm just tryna help. If anything, I'll go over there and talk to this guy man to man. I know it's not my place, but damn, seein' you cry do somethin' to a nigga."

Yoshi managed to chuckle a little. Khalif wiped her eyes, and then kissed her deeply.

"I'm not tryna hurt you or make the situation worse. I just know what it's like to lose a loved one, and you can never get that lost time back," he explained.

"I know, and that's why I'm fightin' so hard for her to open her eyes before it's too late," Yoshi told him.

The more time went on, the more Yoshi sensed that Damon just wasn't the man for Neosha regardless of how long they'd been together. No man or woman should want to keep someone away from their family, especially if their life is at stake.

"I got you ma, and I understand you. I'ma help you in every way that I can. While I help you wit' that situation, we can also work on Onyae finally lettin' me in and allowing me to show her how a man should treat a woman and her daughter. We've been dealing for a year, and we're serious, but how can I further things if ya daughter don't approve?" he said.

Yoshi bit her bottom lip. Khalif was right about everything he said, and her daughter was a tough egg to crack. She assumed that Onyae would gradually let him in, but the most she did was give him a hi and bye as she went about her business.

"We'll take it step by step and day by day until Onyae is ready, but in the meantime, can you just hold me?" she asked.

Khalif moved down to the bottom of the bed, pulled Yoshi's panties off, and spread her legs apart.

"I can do better than that," he said and went to town licking and sucking her clit.

"Oooo, fuck," Yoshi moaned.

He reached between her thighs and parted her pussy lips with his fingers. Khalif sucked on her clit and Yoshi's legs began to shake uncontrollably, but he didn't stop there.

He fingered her pussy and flicked his tongue back and forth at a fast pace.

"Shhhhiiiiittttttt!" she moaned.

She placed her hands on the sides of Khalif's head, and he reached underneath her and cupped her ass. Khalif had a mean tongue game, and Yoshi loved every bit of it.

Chapter 16

The weekend was bittersweet for Yoshi, and after a long, dreary Monday she dreaded the arrival of Tuesday morning, but it was here and there was nothing she could do about it.

Yoshi, Onyae and NiNi had gathered their belongings before heading outside. Yoshi locked the door while the girls got in the car. She grew nauseous the more she thought about the appointment they were headed to, but she supported her daughter one hundred percent. She knew sooner or later she would run across a situation like this with Onyae, and she prepared herself for it. Yoshi couldn't blame Onyae for wanting to get an abortion. She didn't like it because it would have been her first grandchild, but she respected her daughter's wishes.

"You ready for this?" Yoshi asked when she got in the car.

Onyae shrugged her shoulders. "Yea, I am. I know you don't want me to do this, but Mom, I'm not ready to take care of no one's kids."

Yoshi started up the car and deeply sighed.

"I know, baby, I know."

She pulled out of the driveway, and stopped once Onyae saw Gutta's truck pull up behind them.

"He made it, I see," she said while checking her cellphone for the time. It read 10am.

"I knew he would," NiNi said, reaching to the front, and rubbing Onyae's shoulder.

Zzzz.

Just then, Onyae's phone made a ding sound then vibrated. She looked down to see Gutta's name and number flash across the screen.

Gutta: *We gon' trail yawl ma.*

Onyae rolled her eyes. He hadn't said anything bad, but just the fact that he texted her made her nauseous. Her nose was tooted up when she responded to him.

Onyae: *Whatever.*

She threw her phone down as soon as she sent the text. Yoshi placed a hand on her shoulder for support before driving off. The car ride had an awkward silence which wasn't something that happened when the three ladies were together.

They arrived at Cherry Hill Women's Center at exactly 11:02am. Yoshi put the car in park and shut it off. She looked over at Onyae.

"You ready, sweetie?" she asked again.

"Yea, Mom. I'm good. Don't worry," she said and then got out of the car.

NiNi opened the back door and got out.

"Good luck, boo. Oxox," she said. NiNi and Onyae embraced one another in a tight hug.

"Thanks boo. Xoxo."

"Wassup ugly," NiNi said when Gutta walked over.

"Shut ya short ass up." He laughed.

NiNi wanted to lighten the mood because it was dark and dreary, and she knew that Gutta was the last person Onyae wanted to be around.

"Don't be in there gettin' on my nerves," Onyae said with an attitude.

"I'm just tryna be there for you, ma. I ain't tryna argue," he told her.

"That's good to know, and we both thank you, although Onyae ain't gonna say it right now. But with that bein' said, let's get in here cas' the wait be long, and she's already aggravated," Yoshi said.

NiNi got back in the car, and watched Yoshi, Onyae, and Gutta walk into the clinic. She looked over and saw Rayshon staring at her from inside the truck, but she turned her head and put her attention on her phone.

Inside the clinic, Onyae had to sign in and wait to be called. To her surprise, the wait wasn't long because the place wasn't full. She had to go through a list of things before the actual procedure such as, getting an ultrasound to determine the gestational age of the pregnancy and lab testing to determine RH blood type, hemoglobin level, and vital signs. They also had to do a history and physical to review her medical history, current physical state, and birth control options. And lastly, she went through the support and education process to address questions, concerns and expectations.

Gutta was right there with her through the entire process, and as bad as Onyae wanted to hate him, she couldn't because he was man enough to support her through it all. Onyae, Yoshi, and Gutta sat patiently waiting in the procedure room. It was all too quiet, so Yoshi took it upon herself to break the ice in a strong way.

"So, what's this thing you have wit' my daughter? Yawl just fuckin' or it's more?" she asked while looking Gutta straight in the eyes.

Gutta looked a bit surprised. He knew that Onyae was outspoken and up front, but now he saw where she got it from. This was his first-time meeting Yoshi, and it was as if he was looking at a replica of Onyae. Same face and voice.

"Me and ya daughter cool, ma'am."

Yoshi waved him off.

"That's not what I asked, sir. I said what's up wit' yawl. Yawl just fuck buddies or what?" she asked again.

"Mom, we fucked a few times in the same night. I've been done wit' his ass every since. The dick is good, but the baggage he got is unacceptable. Besides, I'm not tryna be wifed up right now. That shit is dead," Onyae chimed in.

Gutta scratched his head. He even went as far as taking his ponytail out and putting it back in just because. Onyae's mouth was reckless and it took everything in him not to start an argument.

"Look ma, I like ya daughter. She ain't like the rest of these girls, but I'd be lyin' if I said I'm tryna be in a relationship wit' anyone right now. Do I still wanna kick it wit' her? Hell yea. Regardless if we together or not, if I'm only dealin' wit' her ain't no other female bein' entertained cas shit like that cause problems. Yea, I might respond to a bitch text, but that's it. I'm not gon' be stickin' my dick in another bitch cas' again that cause problems, and to be honest, my shit too precious to just be givin' away to any and everyone."

Yoshi looked at Gutta and then over at Onyae. He was blunt, but she liked his style. She respected the fact that he didn't beat around the bush and try to pretend that he wanted a relationship when he didn't. That was something most guys lied about just to get in a girl's pants.

"Nigga please, if that was the case then you wouldn't have been hittin' that ugly bitch up askin' to fuck her just days before me," Onyae shot back.

"What the fuck, Onyae, do you hear yaself? The shit was before you. Chill the fuck out yo, fareal. That bitch don't mean nothin' to me!" Gutta was frustrated.

He knew he shouldn't have snapped the way he did, but he couldn't keep allowing Onyae to blame him for a female that he was dealing with way before her.

"A'ight yawl calm down. Right now, isn't the time for yawl to be goin' back and forth over dumb shit. I just asked a damn question and yawl about to tear each other's heads off," Yoshi said.

Before either one of them could get another word in, a sandy-brown haired woman walked into the room.

"Hello, my name is Susan. I'll be the doctor performing your procedure today. As standard protocol I'm going to ask you a question. I have to ask just in case you're having second thoughts as we get closer to the actual procedure," Susan explained.

"Okay," Onyae said.

"Are you sure you want to go through with the procedure?" Susan asked.

"I'm sure that this is what I want to do," Onyae answered without giving it a second thought.

"Alright, and they went over all the options with you, correct?" she asked.

Onyae nodded. "Yup, I'm aware of everything."

"Great, well let's go over a few more things before we get started," Susan told them.

***

While Yoshi, Onyae, and Gutta were inside of the abortion clinic, Rayshon took it upon himself to get out of the truck and inside of Yoshi's car. He couldn't stomach the fact that NiNi was ignoring him as if they hadn't had a connection. He was hoping that after a while NiNi would get out and come talk to him, but he was wrong.

"Why you won't talk to me, ma? Did I say or do somethin' you ain't like?" Rayshon wanted to know.

NiNi had been avoiding him since their date, and it confused him. From his knowledge their date went great, but her actions proved otherwise.

"No, Rayshon. You didn't do anything. You did everything right to be honest. I'm just goin' through a lot right now, and I didn't want to be around you while I was goin' through it. I still like you, and hopefully you still like me even after how I've been treatin' you."

"Hell yea. I just wanted to know what was goin' on. Everything was goin' so good between us and then shit just stopped. Shit caught me off guard to be honest, not to mention the next time I saw you ya face had bruises on it. You care to share what happened?"

"I fell, that's what happened okay? But again, I apologize for bein' so cold towards you. I was goin' through a lot and still am."

Rayshon knew NiNi wasn't telling the truth about what happened to her, but he didn't want to pry any longer. He felt as though once she was comfortable enough to tell him she would, but in the meantime, he was just going to have to accept the answer she gave him.

He caught NiNi off guard when he leaned over, gently and grabbed NiNi's chin and pulled her close to kiss her. Her body caught chills.

"Shit happens, ma. Next time just don't forget about a nigga," he told her.

NiNi melted inside. Everything about Rayshon was perfect, but imperfect. He made her heart dance for him without even knowing it. It was as if she loved him more than she loved herself, but she knew she couldn't have him due to the life she lived.

***

Onyae was finally done, and instead of Yoshi driving back, Gutta told Rayshon to drive his truck, and he drove back with Yoshi and Onyae after the procedure. Onyae was weak and in a little pain, but she took it well. Yoshi pulled into Coastal's to get Onyae a ginger ale. Onyae didn't understand why, but as a black mother that was the cure for everything.

"You want me to go in?" Gutta asked.

"No, sweetie, I got it. Stay in the car wit' Onyae," Yoshi said and then got out.

When she disappeared in the store, Gutta looked over at Onyae who had laid her head on the door.

"You good, Onyae?" he asked.

"I'm fine. I just wanna lay down to be honest," she told him.

Gutta scratched his head. This was all new to him. He had fucked plenty of women, and some told him that they were pregnant by him. Although he didn't believe them, he threw them money anyway. He'd never actually gone to one of the abortion clinics with them to support them through the procedure because he really didn't give a fuck, but Onyae was different.

"You want me to stay the night wit' you?" he asked her as he rubbed her shoulder.

Knock. Knock. Knock.

"Really Gutta! You still wit' this bitch!" Krystal banged on the window.

"What the fuck!" Gutta spat.

He hated how every time he was at the store, Krystal popped up. Her cousin lived a few houses down from the store, so they always knew when he was around.

"Get the fuck outta here wit' that bullshit, yo. Now is not the time," he warned.

Onyae rubbed her forehead in a stressed manner. She didn't have the time or strength to be fighting with one of Gutta's ex bitches.

"Gutta, get this dirty bitch away from my mother's car before it be problems fareal," she told him.

Gutta shook his head because once again Krystal was making him look like a fucked-up person when he wasn't fucking with her anymore. He got out of the car, but NiNi beat him to it and she was on Krystal's ass.

"Bitch, you got a lot of muthafuckin' nerve. I know you better get the fuck on before you get yo ass beat the fuck up out here!"

"Bitch, fuck you! Who the fuck you talkin' to!" Krystal spat.

"That's what I'm tryna figure out!" Sharee added.

NiNi frowned. She couldn't understand why Rayshon and Gutta's exes were so hardheaded. She had just put hands on Sharee, but they still wanted to act tough.

"Bitch, I guess you ain't learn from last time, huh?" NiNi asked.

Rayshon was already on his way out the truck, but he sped up when he saw NiNi's body posture change. He could tell that shit was about to go down, and he wasn't about to let it happen.

"Nah, nah, chill out wit' that. Yawl need to get the fuck on. Every time I look up yawl pop the fuck up wit' some bullshit. Like damn, don't yawl got somethin' better to do?" he asked.

"Shut the fuck up, Rayshon! This shit ain't got nothin' to do wit' you!" Krystal yelled.

Yelling at him made NiNi furious and before anyone knew it, she had leaped and punched Krystal dead in her face. She tried to grab her hair to give her more work, but Rayshon intervened.

"Ah, ah, what the fuck is goin' on!" Yoshi ran out the store.

She'd dropped the bag she had in her hands and went in hood chick mode. Without waiting for a response, Yoshi was out there squaring up.

"Wassup? What yawl bitches wanna do?" she asked.

"Wassup bitch!" Sharee threw her hands up.

Onyae didn't give a fuck what she had just been through. When she saw her mother run out the store and square up all bets were off; she got out the car with the quickness.

"Shawty, get back in the car," Gutta told her.

"Fuck outta here. What yawl bitches wanna do? I'm sick of this shit!"

"Chill, shawty, I'm not lettin' yawl fight," Gutta said while holding onto Onyae.

"Don't protect that bitch!" Krystal screamed.

"Bitch, you still talkin'!" NiNi tried to break away from Rayshon, but the hold he had on her was too tight.

Boop. Boop.

Yoshi hitting Krystal in her face twice made the sound of a wet rag being tossed and flicked in the air as if to sting someone.

Krystal quickly grabbed her face in shock. Sharee attempted to swing, but NiNi managed to grab a handful of her hair and yanked her to the ground. When she tried to kick her, Rayshon spun NiNi around to the other side.

"Come on lil bitch I'm bout all that action!" Yoshi yelled.

Rayshon yoked Yoshi up as well and pulled both her and NiNi to Gutta's truck.

Krystal regained her composure and tried to run up and swing on Yoshi while Rayshon had her. Onyae snapped and kicked and squirmed to get out of Gutta's grasp.

"Chill Onyae! I'm not lettin' you go!" he yelled.

"That dirty ass bitch gotta death wish on her! I'll fuckin' kill that bitch. Don't you ever in ya fuckin' life square up to fight my mother, bitch!" Onyae's face was turning red from anger.

"He got the clap anyway, bitch!" Krystal blurted.

All eyes were now on Gutta. What made the situation far worse was that Coastal's was semi packed so more than one person heard Krystal's outburst. Rayshon's mouth had dropped wide open. He needed answers because that was the first time he'd heard that accusation.

A dark sound came out of Gutta, and he went from holding Onyae back to blacking out and beating Krystal like a man on the street. Rayshon had to let Yoshi and NiNi go to break up the situation, but by now the cops had arrived. The next thing he knew, Gutta was arrested, and put in the back of the police car.

Chapter 17

It was almost 7pm in the evening when Khalif looked at the text message that Yoshi had sent him earlier. He then squinted his eyes to double check the address on the house; once he saw that it was a match, he got out of his car. He took his time walking up the sidewalk to the house to figure out how he was going to approach Damon.

Knock. Knock. Knock.

Khalif stood there waiting patiently for someone to answer. After a few moments, he heard someone unlocking the door; he took a step back when the door slung open.

"Who you?" Damon asked with a snarl.

Khalif remembered Yoshi calling Damon a mismatched eyed bastard so he knew that was him.

"Wassup man. I'm Khalif, Yoshi's boyfriend. I don't mean no disrespect, but I would like to speak wit' you man to man, if that's okay," Khalif asked.

"Speak to me about what?" he asked with a look of disgust on his face.

"Look bruh, I'ma get straight to the point. I think that you should really think about what it is you're doin' when it comes to keepin' Neosha and Yoshi away from one another. That shit ain't cool," Khalif told him.

Damon was taken aback by what Khalif had said. The nerve of him to come confront him like it was an okay thing to do.

"Nigga, I suggest you get the fuck off my porch. Ain't nobody keepin' Neosha away. Her family is fucked up, and she can see the shit for herself." Damon scoffed.

Khalif didn't like the tone Damon was taking with him or the fact that he had taken a step forward. He was trying to keep a leveled head, but he could see why Yoshi disliked the man that stood before him.

"I think you better take a step back. I ain't come here to disrespect you. I just think you need to realize the shit you doin' ain't right, and for you to say her family is fucked up shows a lot about ya character," Khalif said while looking Damon straight in the eyes.

Damon didn't like how Khalif was trying to read him. He felt disrespected, and he was seconds away from turning a verbal confrontation into a physical one.

"Get the fuck up outta here, nigga. You got me fucked up. You and that bitch Yoshi better get the fuck on and go about yawl business!" Damon yelled.

Neosha was on the couch when she heard Damon yell. She quickly got up and ran through the dining room and kitchen to get to the door.

"What's goin' on?" she asked.

"Ya sister done sent this nigga over here on some fuck shit!" Damon snapped.

"I ain't come over here to disrespect you or ya dude, but Yoshi don't like how he's keepin' yawl apart," Khalif said to Neosha.

Neosha was furious, pissed wasn't the word to describe how upset she was that Yoshi had gone behind her back. Yoshi was discussing her personal life with a man she knew nothing about.

"Are you fuckin' serious? Go back and tell her to mind her fuckin' business!"

Slam!

Neosha slammed the door in Khalif's face.

"I can't believe she would do some shit like this!" She yelled.

"Calm down, bae. Don't get yaself all worked up. I'm just glad that now you see why I don't want you around her, and I think you should stop NiNi from goin' over there," he said.

"I'm about to handle this shit right now!" Neosha went back into the living room and got her cellphone.

She called Yoshi and as soon as she picked up, Neosha started on her.

"Hello?"

"How fuckin' dare you send that man over here to comfort Damon about the way he's so called treatin' me!" She snapped.

"Wait, calm the fuck down. First of all, Khalif just wanted to see if he could help. He ain't mean no harm so chill," Yoshi told her.

"Don't fuckin' tell me what to do, Yoshi! I'm so fuckin' tired of you thinkin' you can tell me when to eat and shit. Stay the fuck out of my life if you can't respect me and mine!"

Click.

Yoshi pulled the phone away from her ear and looked at it. She had never witnessed her sister being so angry, especially with her. Khalif had just walked in the door, and he didn't even get a chance to say anything. He could tell by Yoshi's facial expression that she knew things didn't go as planned.

"I'm sorry, bae. I tried, but ya sister ain't tryna hear shit and neither is that nigga. I walked away before I emptied a clip in his ass, and I don't wanna go back to the old me," he explained.

Yoshi couldn't stop the tears from pouring from her eyes. She meant no harm or ill intentions, but Neosha saw otherwise and that bothered her.

"I'm done. I'm done wit' trying to help her, I swear I am. I'm gon' let God give her the reality check she needs, but I wash my hands on her."

Khalif walked over to Yoshi and wrapped his big arms around her to console her. He did what he could as her man and her friend, and although things didn't go well, he still did his part. That's all that mattered.

"Don't stop lovin' her tho'. She needs you; she just doesn't know it yet."

Yoshi hugged Khalif tight. Those were the realist words he spoke, and she needed to hear them. She knew that sooner or later, Neosha would realize just how much Yoshi and Kick Down tried to help her.

Chapter 18

A long week and two days went by and it was now March 21st, NiNi was meeting up with Rayshon again and she wasn't happy, but she wasn't sad either. The past week was trying for her and all she wanted to do was have a good time. This time, she made the decision to go back to Onyae's house after her date with Rayshon.

"What you wanna do today, ma? It's early in the afternoon, but we can still do anything you want," Rayshon asked when NiNi got inside his truck.

"Let's just get some food from Wendy's and go to the park. I don't really feel like doin' much," she told him.

Rayshon looked at her and shook his head side to side.

"What's wrong?" she asked.

"You know for a fact a nigga got money, but yet you so easy to please. I love that shit about you ma, and that makes me wanna give you the world. I swear it do," he told her, and then pulled off.

"You so sweet." She smiled.

"Only for you." He flirted.

NiNi laid back on the seat and relaxed while Rayshon drove into the Wendy's drive thru.

"Welcome to Wendy's would you like to try our new chicken sandwich today?" the woman said through the speaker.

"Nah, give me a second tho'," he told her.

"Okay, let me know when you're ready to order," she said.

"What you want, ma?" he asked.

"A spicy chicken sandwich with cheese, but I want the meal tho' and make sure it's a large," she told him.

"Damn, you come here often, don't you? Got ya order down packed and shit." He laughed.

"Shut up." NiNi playfully punched him.

"Ouch!" Rayshon acted like he was hurt.

"You so silly. Hurry up and order the food. I'm hungry," she told him.

Rayshon went ahead and gave the woman their order and she gave him his total. He drove up to the second window to pay and get his change and receipt.

"We goin' to the Bridgeton park?" he asked while pulling up to the second window.

"Yea, that's the only one I know besides the one in Millville, but ain't no need to go all the way over there. We can stay here," she said.

"Ard," Rayshon said as he was getting the food.

"Let me make sure everything is in here before we pull off," NiNi said and checked the bags.

Once she was sure that all of their food was there, she gave Rayshon the okay to pull off. It took them a good seven minutes to get to the park because it wasn't far. Rayshon parked and grabbed the food.

"Don't touch that handle, girl," he told her.

NiNi laughed and put her hands between her legs. Rayshon got out of the truck and walked to the other side. He opened the door for her, and she got out.

"You make me feel like a little girl touchin' a hot stove when it comes to that damn handle." She chuckled.

"I should put a damn shock charge on it so whenever you try to touch it you feel a jolt of electricity."

NiNi burst into laughter.

"You better not do no shit like that!"

"Keep ya hands off then," Rayshon replied and then sat down at one of the benches.

He placed the food on the table, and they both said grace before sinking their teeth into their juicy burgers and chicken sandwiches.

"I love they chicken sandwiches, but I gotta have ranch sauce wit' it. They so nasty without it," NiNi said, and then took another bite.

"Yea, that's how I had to eat it before, but I'm not really a fan of the chicken period," he said.

"Boyyyy. You don't know what you missin'," NiNi told him.

"Girlllll, yes I do." He mocked her.

"Oooh, I can't stand you!" she joked.

Rayshon smiled at her and continued to eat his food. They went from having great conversation to silence. Rayshon's thoughts were roaming while NiNi was enjoying the sounds of the birds chirping.

"Be real wit' me, ma," Rayshon said out of nowhere.

"About what?" she asked.

"Why you always at ya cousin's? Somethin' gotta be goin' on at ya house for you to always be wit' Onyae."

NiNi knew that Rayshon was going to keep pressing the issue so she figured she'd just tell him part of the truth just to ease his mind a little.

"My mom's boyfriend, Damon. He hit me a few times recently. So, ever since then my aunt let's me stay at her house. I guess it's just until things cool down," NiNi told him.

"The day I saw you wit' the black eye?" he asked.

"Yea, that was the first time," she lied.

Rayshon slowly chewed his food as NiNi revealed that Damon had put his hands on her a few times. It brought back bad memories of his mother getting abused by his father, and it made him angry to know that she had experienced such a thing.

"Are you okay? I knew I shouldn't have said anything. I was just trying to be honest and tell you why I didn't like him," NiNi explained.

She could tell by Rayshon's facial expression and body language that he wasn't happy.

"Ya mom home?" he asked.

"No, she's at her doctor's appointment," NiNi told him.

"Cool, I'ma drop you off wit' her. I gotta go handle some business, ard." He got up from the bench and grabbed the leftover food and threw it in one of the garbage bens.

"Okay," NiNi said and got up and did the same thing.

She'd lost her appetite when Rayshon lost his. He walked ahead of her to the truck, but he still made sure to open the door for her.

"Thank you," she said.

Rayshon didn't respond. He just closed the door and walked to the other side. He put the key in the ignition, put the truck in reverse and sped out of the parking lot violently. NiNi was so mad at herself for telling Rayshon anything; he hadn't said a word to her the entire way to the doctor's office.

He pulled up on the hill in front of the doctor's office, put the truck in park, and hopped out. Rayshon jogged to the other side of the truck and opened the door for NiNi. When she got out of the car, he leaned down and kissed her.

"I'ma hit you in a few days, ma. Go in there and make sure ya moms good," he said and closed the passenger side door.

NiNi didn't say anything as she watched him get back in his truck and speed off. She wiped the tear that had fallen from her eye and went into the building. She walked down the two long hallways before she made it into the waiting room where she saw her mother.

"What you doin' here? Neosha asked.

"I just wanted to be here wit' you, Mom, that's all," NiNi said, but she didn't get a response from Neosha.

Meanwhile, Rayshon had picked Gutta up from the South Side of Bridgeton and let him know why he needed him on such short notice. If it wasn't important Rayshon would've never pulled Gutta away from business. He pulled onto Harrison Street which was the street that NiNi lived on. He was in luck because he saw Damon walking up the sidewalk to the house. Rayshon didn't hesitate to press on the gas with his arm out the window.

Boc. Boc. Boc. Boc. Boc. Boc. Boc.

Damon dove on the porch as the bullets came at him. He scattered on the porch like roaches did when the lights came on. His heart was beating fast knowing that he'd almost lost his life in just a matter of seconds.

Rayshon sped off down the street and made a sharp turn. All he could think about was NiNi when he emptied the clip of his gun on Damon.

***

Ring. Ring. Ring.

On their way out of the doctor's office, Neosha's phone rang. She picked up her cellphone smiling from ear to ear which let NiNi know that Damon was on the other end. She didn't hear anything, but yelling from him, and for a moment she went in defense mode until she saw her mother sobbing.

"Oh my God! Damon, are you okay?" Neosha broke down in tears.

NiNi looked concerned. Her mother was distraught, so it only made her wonder what was going on.

"Mom, what's wrong?" she asked.

"Somebody shot at Damon while he was goin' in the house, but he's okay. Thank God," she told her.

NiNi frowned. She was upset at how crazy her mother got when she got the call from Damon, and she was also upset that Damon turned out to be okay. It never dawned on NiNi that the moment Rayshon dropped her off, Damon unexpectedly got shot at.

Chapter 19

The next day, Onyae received a text for Gutta telling her to come outside. They hadn't talked since Krystal caused the scene at Coastal's that day, and he got locked up. He had been trying to reach out to her, but nothing worked so he figured coming to her house was the best thing to do. He also thought that since he and Rayshon handled a situation for NiNi, it might have put him in good graces with her.

"What do you want, Gutta? I thought you was locked up." Onyae's face had attitude written all over it.

"Here." He handed her a piece of paper.

"What's this?" she asked.

"Look at it," he told her.

Onyae rolled her eyes, but she still looked at the paper. It was Gutta's results from blood work he'd recently gotten done. All the blood work came back negative indicating that he didn't have a STD. All Onyae could do was smirk knowing that he went out of his way to prove to her that he didn't have anything.

"I appreciate you doin' this," she told him.

"Yea, I put you through enough. I felt like that was the least I could do. Plus, it's always good to know ya status especially comin' across dirty bitches like Krystal," he said.

"Yea, I feel you. I was really thinkin' bout killin' that bitch the next time I saw her," Onyae stated seriously.

Gutta shook his head no.

"Nah, leave that killin' shit to me, shawty, but anyway wassup wit' ya cous, tho? Rayshon had to shoot that nigga Damon's shit up. Muthafucka got a serious problem," Gutta said.

Onyae looked confused. She had heard about the shooting, but she never knew who did it. It was weird to her because her aunt lived on a quiet street, so there wasn't any drama on that end, nor did she have any enemies.

"Yawl did that shit?" she asked in shock.

"Where ya cousin' at?" He switched the subject.

"She in the house," Onyae told him.

"Go get her right quick. Rayshon had to handle some business, so he wanted me to deliver a message to her personally," Gutta stated.

Onyae gave Gutta a concerned looked but turned to run in the house to get NiNi. When she returned outside, Gutta was standing outside of his truck leaning on the hood.

"Wassup? Onyae said you had somethin' to tell me. Is Rayshon okay?" NiNi was concerned.

"He good, shawty. He just wanted me to tell you to let him know if that nigga ever puts his hands on you again. A bullet gon' be more than he needs to worry about," he replied.

It didn't take much for NiNi to put two and two together; she realized that they were the ones behind Damon almost getting shot and killed.

"Gutta! Rayshon did that?" she asked in disbelief.

"I don't know why the shit is a surprise to yawl. We don't play that shit, and don't bring up me beatin' Krystal's ass cas' that whore ass bitch had it comin'."

NiNi was lost for words. She couldn't believe that Rayshon had tried to take Damon out all because she told him that he'd hit her a few times.

I wonder what he would do if I told him the full truth about what Damon really does to me, she thought.

Chapter 20

On Thursday afternoon Yoshi, Onyae, and NiNi had just gotten back to the house from a long day of shopping. This was one of the few times that NiNi actually got to have fun and be happy without regretting it.

"Thanks, so much yawl. I really don't know where I would be without you two," NiNi said when she removed all of the designer clothes and shoes from the shopping bags.

Yoshi was an on-call nurse for personal house visits, group and nursing homes and the money she made helped upgrade her and her daughter's life completely.

"Awwwwwww boo! You know we got you!" Onyae hugged her.

Onyae was glad to be able to help her cousin. She didn't work but she had a mean bank account which consisted of the back child support from her no-good daddy. Her mother had to take him to court several times in the past in order to get the money; Onyae had the savings account her mother put it in when she was younger. All Yoshi wanted Onyae to do was graduate high school. Still, Onyae worked at fast food joints the entire time she was in high -school; she had stacked a nice lump sum, so she didn't have to work as much once she graduated high - school. She wanted to be carefree before she decided to go off to college.

"No need to thank us, baby. You practically gave up ya entire teenage life just to take care of ya mother. It's my obligation to make sure you good at all times," Yoshi told her.

Unexpectedly, NiNi began to cry. Onyae had a feeling as to why she was crying so she hugged her tighter. Yoshi, on the other hand, assumed she was crying because of her mother.

"Hey, it's been a long few weeks. How about yawl call yawl lil' friends over, and I call mine over and we have ourselves a game night on Friday? I'll order food, and we can sip a lil somethin', what yawl think?" Yoshi suggested.

"That sounds like a plan, Mom. NiNi what you think?"

Onyae wiped the tears from NiNi's eyes. She knew that her mother was trying to lighten up the mood with her suggestion.

"Yea, it's cool. I don't even drink, but the way Mommy been actin' towards me, I damn sure need one," she responded.

"Baby, it's gon' be okay. Don't stress yaself out. My sister got a lot goin' on, and I'm sure her mind stays on overload. You continue to go by and check on her every day to make sure she takes her meds, but you come straight back here afterwards. I don't want them jumpin' on you cas' they mad at me and ya uncle," Yoshi said while rubbing her niece's shoulder.

"Yea, cous, I love Auntie, but she'll catch these hands over you, and you already know I don't like that nigga so it's nothin' to get him touched," Onyae stated seriously.

"I can't just stay away. I don't trust him around my mother by himself all the time. I think he takes advantage of her, especially when she's on her meds," NiNi told them.

Yoshi shook her head. She knew the love NiNi had for her mother was unconditional, and she knew that NiNi knew it was best to no longer pry in her mother's life. She was a grown woman, and she made the decisions she thought were most suitable for her life.

"NiNi, ya mother is livin' her life, and now it's time for you to live yours. You can't keep babysitting Neosha no matter what. She has to see shit for what it really is on her own, and none of us can make her see it. Understand?"

As bad as NiNi wanted to disagree with her aunt, she couldn't.

"Yea, Auntie I hear you," she replied in a dry tone.

Chapter 21

Kick Down pulled up to Neosha's house at exactly 5:15pm Friday evening, and he parked in the back of Neosha's van. He hadn't spoken to his sister in a few weeks, and it bothered him that she'd stopped talking to him. All he wanted was for her to be smart about the decisions she was making. He didn't see Damon's pickup truck which was a good thing because now he would probably have a good chance at getting some sense into her.

Kick Down got out of his girlfriend's car and walked up to Neosha's house.

Knock. Knock. Knock.

"Neosha! Open up, girl, it's ya big bro!" he yelled from the other side.

Kick Down had just caught Neosha before she went back to the living room to lay down. She was tired and had just taken her meds, and all she wanted to do was sip on her freshly brewed coffee and watch her soap operas until she drifted off the sleep.

Neosha sighed loudly as she walked to the door and unlocked it. She slung it open with a look that let Kick Down know she was not in the mood for any of his bullshit.

"Sis, I ain't come over here to start no shit." He made his intentions clear.

Neosha waved her hand to stop him from talking. She was so over him and Yoshi trying to control her life.

"Kick Down, all I want is for yawl to leave me alone. I can't take this anymore. Yawl goin' too hard for no reason, and I'm tired of it."

"Come on, sis. I ain't have no intentions to make you cry or storm out that day. I just wanted to talk some sense into you that's all," he assured her.

"Talk some sense into me about what? About Damon? A man that loves me and my daughter unconditionally!"

"NiNi don't even like that nigga!" Kick Down shouted.

Neosha rolled her eyes.

"NiNi thinks her father is just goin' to magically appear one day and the shit is not goin' to happen. Damon ain't did a damn thing to that girl. They don't have a relationship cas' NiNi don't want one wit' him, and at this point I just don't give a good fuck about it. Damon has been in my life for ten years now, and I don't see or want him leavin' anytime soon. So, yawl just gon' have to suck it up and deal wit' it," she explained unapologetically.

Kick Down placed his hands on his head, sighed, and looked up at the sky.

"I don't wanna lose you, sis, but it seems like you got ya mind made up. So, wit' that bein' said, what can I do to make our relationship better?" he asked.

It didn't take Neosha long to think of a solution because she had been feeling this way for a while now.

"Respect my man, my household, and my decisions. If you can't do that then you can kiss my ass and stay the hell outta my life, and that's real shit."

There was nothing Kick Down could do or say to change his sister's mind. He loved and respected her too much to lose her again and knowing that she could be taken off this earth at any given time, made his decision less selfish.

"Okay sis. Whatever you want," he told her.

The words hurt him to speak, but he had to do whatever he could to keep his sister in his life. He didn't even say goodbye before he walked off the porch and down the sidewalk. When he got back into the car, he wondered just how much it was going to take for his sister to see what they'd been seeing in just a matter of months.

Chapter 22

"Nah, yawl niggas cheatin'. I'm up outta here." Gutta laughed.

"Hell yea. Man, ain't no way we done lost four fuckin' games in a row," Khalif said while taking a sip of his Heineken.

"Awwwwww, yawl salty or nah?" Onyae laughed.

"They real salty. Cholesterol high as fuck over there. They clearly don't know how we get down over here. We fucks it up in some spades. Yawl better tell 'em!" Yoshi laughed while giving Onyae and NiNi high fives.

"You ain't gon' back ya friends up?" NiNi asked.

Rayshon threw his hands up.

"Shit, ain't nothin' I can say. I ain't never got my ass beat in spades like this. Yawl got me in here lookin' like Meek Mill and shit."

They all burst into laughter.

"You funny as fuck," Onyae said.

"Get ready to take another ass whoopin'." Yoshi shuffled the cards and dealt another hand.

Khalif got up to grab another beer.

"Yo bruh, can you pass me one of those," Gutta said to Khalif.

"No problem," Khalif said before grabbing another Heineken beer.

"Thanks, bruh," Gutta said and then cracked it open and took a long swig.

The game had started, and NiNi got up to use the bathroom. She wasn't aware that Rayshon had been watching her every move. He could sense that her mind was somewhere else despite all the fun they were having. He got up and waited outside the bathroom until she came out.

"Oh! You scared me," NiNi said as she grabbed her chest.

"My bad." He laughed.

"Why are you just standin' there?" she asked, still holding her chest.

"It seemed like somethin' was botherin' you. You know I had to come see if you was good," he said.

"Thanks, but I'm good," NiNi told him, and proceeded to walk away.

Rayshon gently grabbed her and wasted no time getting straight to the point.

"Look ma, we been dealin' for a couple months now. Regardless, of the little time we've spent together. I'm feelin' you and you clearly feelin' me. Let's stop all this bullshit, ma, fareal," he told her.

"What you talkin' about?" she asked knowingly.

Rayshon looked at her with a 'you know what I'm talking about' look as he stuck his hands in his pockets.

"I'm tryna make you mine, ma. I done already said it many times before, and I meant it. I'm just waitin' for you to be ready to accept the fact that I ain't goin' anywhere."

"Rayshon, I don't know…"

"You wanna come to my crib tonight? You never got the chance to cas' you said you was goin' through a lot at the time." He cut her off.

NiNi thought long and hard on it. She didn't know the first thing about being with a man, but she couldn't deny the fact that she was in love with Rayshon. She didn't know how it happened, but she didn't want the feeling to go away.

"Thank you for doin' what you did. I didn't expect you to do somethin' like that. Especially for somebody like me," she said to him.

"What you mean somebody like you? Ma, when I said I got you I meant that. As long as you wit' me ain't no nigga or female gon' ever harm you. Now, you ain't answer my question, you gon' come chill wit' a nigga tonight?" he asked her.

"How about tomorrow? We can spend the weekend together," NiNi blurted without really thinking about the decision she made.

"That's ya word, ma? No holdin' back cas' you good for that," he told her.

NiNi stood on her tippy toes and pulled him close to her so that she could kiss him on the lips.

"That's my word, Rayshon."

Rayshon looked down at her, and he knew for a fact that NiNi felt his dick getting hard, but he couldn't help it. It was something about her that had him feeling some sort of way. It wasn't that he thought she was different, he knew she was different, and he wanted her in his life permanently.

Chapter 23

NiNi tossed and turned all night. It was 6:00am when Onyae heard a bunch of noise in her room. She cracked open one eye and saw NiNi in the closet, and a bunch of clothes on the floor. Onyae felt for her phone beside her and when she finally got it, she checked the time. She jolted up in the bed and gave NiNi the look of death.

"Bitch, it is six in the fuckin' mornin'! You better be up gettin' ready for some dick, shit!" Onyae spat.

NiNi laughed.

"Girl, I can't sleep at fuckin' all. I'm seein' Rayshon tonight, and I just don't know what the fuck to wear."

Onyae rubbed the remaining sleep from her eyes and yawned.

"Bitch, don't wear anything. Just go naked and fuck the shit outta him," she suggested.

NiNi looked at her like she was crazy.

"See, you bad for my life, hoe!" She laughed.

Onyae shrugged her shoulders.

"Hey, it is what it is, but text him and tell him to come pick you up since you can't sleep."

"Onyae, it's 6:05am. He's probably sleepin'," she said.

"Okay and? Shit, I was sleepin' and you still woke my ass up. You better call him and wake him the fuck up. Tell him that's your dick and you want it now!" Onyae said and then burst out laughing.

"Ugh, I can't stannnndddd you!" NiNi laughed before picking up her cellphone and taking it off the charger.

She scrolled through her contacts until she came across Rayshon's name. She pressed the call button and put the phone to her ear.

Ring. Ring. Ring.
Ring. Ring. Ring.
Ring. Ring.

"Yo?" He cleared his throat.

"Um, hey, were you sleepin'?" she asked as if she didn't know the answer to her own question.

Rayshon pulled the phone away from his ear to glance at the time. When he saw what time it was, he plopped his head back down on the bed.

"Ma, it's six in the mornin' of course I was sleep, but wassup?" he asked.

NiNi looked over at Onyae for assistance. Onyae turned around on the bed and started humping it. NiNi rolled her eyes and laughed.

"Uh, well, I couldn't sleep, and I know we supposed to see each other later, but I was wonderin' if you could come and pick me up now," she told him.

Rayshon didn't want to get out of his warm bed but spending time with NiNi was rare. It was hard for him to finally get her to let him in, so he was going to take every opportunity he had with her.

"Ard ma. Give me a few to get myself together," he told her.

A big smile spread across NiNi's face, and Onyae stuck her tongue out and started dancing in the bed to the imaginary music.

"Okay, I'll see you in a few."

"Ard."

Click.

"He said give him a few and he'll be here!" NiNi squealed.

"Yassssssss bitch! You bouta throw that ass in a circle, ayeeee, throw that ass in a circle!" Onyae sang.

"Shhhh! Before Auntie wakes up and cuss both our asses out," she said.

"Oh shit. You right, but bitch don't dress all extra. Just throw on somethin' simple, but cute. I'm tellin' you that shit will have a nigga goin' crazy," Onyae said, getting out of the bed.

"You sure?" NiNi asked.

"I'm positive. Now, let's get you somethin' cute out, chick!" she said and began to go through all the clothes that NiNi had thrown on her floor.

Chapter 24

After Rayshon picked NiNi up, he took her right back to his house, and they slept for hours. When they finally woke up, he ordered food, and they explored his bedroom which was amazing to NiNi.

"This all ya jewelry?" she asked.

"It's on my dresser, right?" he responded in a smart tone.

NiNi glanced back at him sitting on the bed.

"Don't get smart, nigga. It was just a question," she snapped.

"I ain't gettin' smart, ma. But everything in here is mine regardless if you think so or not. What type of niggas you done dealt wit' before? You don't believe shit I say," he said while getting off the bed.

"I don't be fuckin' around like that, but I'm aware that niggas be lyin'," she stated.

"You got a lot to learn about me, ma. I'ma change ya life, just watch."

"Yea, how so?" she asked.

"You'll see, but in order for that to happen we gotta spend more time together, and you gotta stop blockin' me out. I don't care how much you goin' through. You gotta let me be there for you through it all, ard?" he told her.

NiNi didn't respond just yet. She picked her phone up off his dresser and texted Onyae.

NiNi: *Hey, so I'm stayin' here wit' Rayshon tonight. I know auntie won't mind that I'm wit' him if she ask you where I am, but just in case my mother reaches out to you being that she's not really too fond of me right now just cover for me tonight and tomorrow, okay?*

Onyae: *Yassssss bitch! You know I got you. I love you boo, and text me if anything. Xoxo.*

NiNi giggled. She loved how she was never judged by Onyae, and how much she wanted her to finally live.

NiNi: *I love you too hunnie. Oxox.*

She placed her phone down on the dresser when she was finished texting Onyae. Rayshon was still towering over her which made her a little nervous even though this wasn't their first time being around one another.

"What?" she asked in a schoolgirl like tone.

"Why you so nervous? You can't be nervous dealin' wit' a nigga like me. My whole persona reads gangsta," he told her.

"Who said I was nervous? What if I like that gangsta in you? Hell, I might even love it, shit you just never know." NiNi looked up at him and poked out her lips with a hint of attitude.

She was always surprised by the confidence that came out of her. She never thought she'd have that much spunk talking to Rayshon or any other man.

"So, whatchu sayin' you in love wit' my gangsta?" Rayshon asked.

He bit down on his bottom lip and looked down at her through low eyes. The passion that burned between them was as strong as the root that connected to a tree. NiNi became bashful; she looked down at the floor as chills caught her body. She could feel Rayshon's strong gaze.

"Nah, lil mama, pick ya head up. You no longer have to hide or feel the way you do. Show me that girl that I met at the store that day. I know I took ya breath away, but you made it obvious that you was feelin' a nigga," he said. He put his hand under her chin and lifted it so that she was looking up at him.

NiNi looked at him and smiled. She removed his hand from her face and poked her lips out. "Yeah."

"Yeah, what?" he asked with a raised eyebrow.

"I'm in love wit' ya gangsta."

Rayshon couldn't help but to show his pearly whites from her response.

"So, you gon' ride out wit' a warrior like myself?"

"I'ma ride wit' you until I can't ride no more. I'll be ya Keedy, and you can be my Mayhem." She laughed.

He leaned down and kissed her passionately. NiNi didn't hesitate to let him devour her with his lip lock. She gently placed her hand on the side of his face. He picked her up and walked over to the bed and laid her down.

"I love you, NiNi."

They breathed heavily as they kissed each other.

"I love you too, Rayshon." She managed to get out between their brief pause.

NiNi didn't know what it was about her that made him love her, but she knew exactly what it was that made her love him. Rayshon was her superman and had been since the day she first laid eyes on him and he wasn't even aware of it.

She removed his shirt, and he removed hers. He gave her sweet pecks on her forehead and her nose.

"Silly." She giggled.

Rayshon stuck out his tongue and glided it across her lips. NiNi's body shivered as if the wind was blowing, and her nipples got hard. She wasn't sure if it was because she was nervous or actually turned on by what he was doing to her. Her heart fluttered as his hands caressed every curve of her bodacious love handles.

"Wa—wait," she panted.

Silencing her with another signal of love, he lifted her up just enough so that he could unsnap her bra. Rayshon traced his tongue down the middle of her chest and around each nipple, handling them both with proper care. He motioned towards her tummy and she grabbed the sides of his head, stopping him in his tracks. NiNi never had the pleasure of enjoying sex; she'd never even had consensual sex. The way he was treating her body felt so unreal and she wasn't sure if she could handle it any longer. Rayshon hadn't even entered her yet and a fire had already started to burn between her legs.

"I—I don't know if I can do this."

She looked at him with sincerity in her eyes causing him to crawl up so that he was now face to face with her. "The day I said I got you, I meant it. I'm not gon' hurt you. All you gotta do is take that wall down so you can see for yourself."

Rayshon didn't need an answer because her actions spoke for her. She brought his face close to hers and they shared their love with one another. He removed her hands from the sides of his face and went down and planted delicate pecks all over her tummy. He wasn't fazed by the extra love that she carried or the stretch marks tattooed on her body in the shape of thunder bolts.

He got up on his knees and pulled off her pajama pants, exposing her red boy shorts. He looked at her and smiled.

"My favorite color." NiNi blushed by the simple words that came out of his mouth.

He cupped her breasts and went down further until his face was buried deep in her love cave. He licked, sucked, and nibbled as her sweet nectar flowed out and onto his lips.

"Ooooo, ooooo, Ray—Rayshon," she moaned.

The way she called his name was music to his ears and it made him go wild. He removed his hands off her breasts and placed each of them between her inner thighs. He pushed her legs up to her chest, sticking two fingers inside her, and eating her until her clit thickened and her legs began to shake uncontrollably.

NiNi's mouth opened but nothing came out. She had a death grip on the sheets. Her body jerked and caught a chill which was followed by a gush of her sweet liquid flowing into Rayshon mouth. He swallowed all of her and flicked his tongue back and forth at a fast pace.

NiNi tried to scoot back, but he had such a tight hold on her that she was unable to move or go anywhere. Rayshon could feel his dick begging to be released from his grey sweatpants. He released NiNi out of the pinned position, got off the bed, and pulled his boxers and sweats down in one swift motion. The look on NiNi's face told Rayshon exactly what she was thinking.

He's going to kill me, she thought.

"I'ma take my time wit' you."

He answered as if he could read her mind. She wasn't sure how he was going to be gentle with something as big as what he was working with.

Taking his time with her, he kissed her succulently and climbed between her legs. He licked her ear in a circular motion and without warning he glided himself inside of her cupcake. NiNi dug what nails she had into his back as she gasped.

"Oooo."

Rayshon bit his bottom lip, closed his eyes, and paused to prevent himself from bustin' before he should have. Her tightness latched on to the girth of his manhood and her warmth made his toes curl.

Finally able to take control, Rayshon moved in and out of her love tunnel at a steady pace. He didn't rush, but instead he gave her deep, slow, and meaningful strokes. NiNi winced each time he gave her more and more of him. It was a mixture of pleasure and pain, but nothing could have prepared her for the ten-and a half inch love muscle he introduced her to. On top of her being so inexperienced, Rayshon was thick and he filled her up completely.

With each stroke NiNi's juices soaked the sheets beneath them. Rayshon's lips met hers once again and the only sounds that could be heard were the smacking of their kisses and the squishy sounds of her juices when their bodies connected time and time again. As the hours went on, Rayshon made sure to explore each part of NiNi's body. His shoulders jerked forward and NiNi looked him in the eyes.

"What's wrong?"

She waited for an answer, but he gave none. The expression on his face went from a scowl to a relaxed look. He placed his right arm on the bed and sat up just a bit as he reached back with his left hand pulling the covers over them. NiNi thought that she had disappointed him because she didn't know how to have sex. She thought going with the flow would be okay. Not knowing what to say at that very moment, NiNi allowed Rayshon to rest on her. She caressed his head until she heard a light snore coming from him. A smile crept across her face as she felt his heartbeat. NiNi closed her eyes and drifted off to sleep along with the man she thought was capable of saving her from such a brutal life. She was in love and had been since the day she first laid eyes on him. What she didn't know was that being in love with Rayshon was going to bring her more than she bargained for.

Chapter 25

The next morning NiNi cracked open her eyes as the sun managed to creep through the white blinds on the windows. She yawned, and then rubbed her eyes as she got out of the bed and walked over to the dresser to get her phone. It was going on 11:15am.

"Aw, damn. I gotta get home," she said out loud, instantly thinking about her mother.

She was about to get herself together when she realized that her mother had been doing fine for the last week perhaps and she didn't need to rush to her aid.

Relax, NiNi, she thought.

After taking a couple of deep breaths, NiNi looked over and saw that Rayshon was gone which made her panic a little. She jumped up and quickly put on her clothes before rushing down the stairs; she ran directly into Rayshon.

"What's wrong, ma?" he asked with concern written all over his face.

NiNi grabbed her chest.

"You weren't in the bed. I thought you left me."

Rayshon didn't know whether to smile, frown or even how to take what she said in. It was clear that she had a fear of being alone; no matter how much NiNi tried to hide it, he was beginning to unravel just how damaged she was.

"Nah, never that." He gave a quick response. "So did me not being in the bed wake you or did somethin' else wake you?"

NiNi was still trying to shake off the panic she had.

"I thought I had to get home to my mother because she takes her medicine at one o'clock, but then I realized she's been doing good for the past week without me so there's no need for me to rush home. Besides, I don't even live there anymore really," she explained.

"A'ight, so call her just to make sure she took her medicine. I'm only suggestin' that because you still seem jumpy and concerned. Ya moms is important so call her; and why don't you live there anymore? Did they put you out or you left by choice?" Rayshon was curious.

"Yea, you're right. I could call her, but we really haven't been talking like that. I don't even know if she'll pick up because she'll probably think I'm tryna start some mess. Oh, and no they didn't put me out, well not really. My aunt just thought it would be best if I stayed wit' them for a while."

Rayshon didn't know the ins and outs of everything that was going on, but he agreed. He knew for a fact that NiNi was safer living with her aunt and cousin.

"That's wassup ma, I agree wit' ya aunt, and as far as ya moms, I don't think she would not answer for you, but if you feel that way just send her a text. I just want ya mind to be put at ease for our remaining time together."

NiNi smiled at his concern.

She unlocked her phone and did exactly what Rayshon suggested and texted her mother.

NiNi: *Hey Mommy. Good morning. I just wanted to make sure you knew to take your meds on time. If you need me, you know how to reach me. I love you.*

NiNi was still standing on the last step while Rayshon stood in front of her leaned on the banister. She was waiting patiently for her mother to text her back, but she grew impatient, so she called her.

Ring. Ring. Ring.

Ring. Ring. Rin…

After six rings NiNi was sent to voicemail. She pulled the phone away from her ear and looked at it as if she was hearing things. It wasn't like her mother to not answer for her unless she was sleeping, but she knew for a fact her mother was up and watching her soap operas.

Ring. Ring. Ring.

Rin…

NiNi was sent to voicemail once more. It really hurt her to know that her mother didn't want to speak with her and for what reason she didn't know.

Neosha: *NiNi, I'm fine. Stop calling me back to back.*

When NiNi read the text, she was even more hurt.

"You good, ma?" Rayshon asked once he saw her expression sadden and her energy shift.

"She sent me to voicemail twice and practically told me to stop callin' her. I don't know what I did wrong," she said.

Rayshon could tell that NiNi truly cared about her mother, but something was blocking their relationship and he figured that something was NiNi's stepfather. He stood up from leaning on the banister and gently pulled her close and gave her a peck on the lips.

"Don't even trip, ma. You didn't do nothin' wrong. Just look at it as she don't want to be bothered by anyone. Not just you. It could be the mood swings from the medicine she takes, ard?"

NiNi appreciated the fact that Rayshon tried to lighten the mood to a more positive one, but she was well aware that it wasn't the medicine. She responded to him by wrapping her arms around him and burying her head in his chest. She loved the feeling he gave her and right now his love and affection was something she needed.

"You hungry?" He broke the silence.

NiNi lifted her head up.

"I don't really know. I mean, I'm really not a morning eater," she replied.

"Baby girl, you gotta live a lil. Breakfast is the best part of the day, and the most important meal," he told her.

"Oh, shut up." She playfully pushed him. "If breakfast is so important then why don't you cook me somethin'?"

"A nigga can throw down, ma," Rayshon told her.

NiNi eyed him up and down. Rayshon was literally the man of her dreams; she wondered was there anything he couldn't do. He was the total package and she still wasn't convinced that he was really her man.

I really have a boyfriend, she thought.

She was so preoccupied with how much of a man he was that she didn't realize she was staring at him in a flirtation manner.

"Damn, we gon' continue to stand here or you gon' come in the kitchen so I can start cookin' for you? I know I look good, but no need to drool ma, you gon' eat in a minute." He laughed.

NiNi snapped out of her mini trance and rolled her eyes at him.

"I can't stand you!" She laughed.

"Yea, yea." He waved her off and turned to head into the kitchen.

NiNi eyed him as he walked in front of her and she wondered how a man could look so sexy in something so simple.

Rayshon was dressed in a pair of all red basketball shorts, a black T-shirt, and his black Adidas slippers. NiNi sat down at the table while she watched him prepare to cook her a meal, and she couldn't deny the fact that she was eager to taste his cooking being that he was such a hood dude. She was pleased to see how clean he was, although he told her the other night that he didn't play about that. Still, seeing him wash his hands and wipe everything down after he handled raw meat really impressed her.

"Ya mother taught you well," she blurted out.

Rayshon glanced back at her. "Hell yea she did. I learned from the best."

"Oh, don't get too cocky now. I still gotta taste it to see if it's on point like you say it is. All I was sayin' is ya mother taught you well," NiNi said.

Rayshon waved her off and without looking back he said. "Believe me, ma, ain't nobody getting' cocky. I just know what I can do so it's confidence more than anything. And trust me, once you taste my cookin' I guarantee we gon' head back upstairs and you gon' let me break that thing down again somethin' proper."

NiNi couldn't do anything but laugh.

She had all intentions on spending time with Rayshon when she first came there the other day, but after she spoke to Onyae, they had sex all day and night and she was sure that Rayshon had explored every part of her body. She was sore, but not sore in a way that she'd felt before. The soreness between her legs was strictly from the size of Rayshon's dick and the fact that he was between her legs for what seemed like hours. It wasn't from being violated like she'd experienced time and time again. Rayshon took care of her; it shocked NiNi that he didn't want her to do anything to him; Rayshon's main focus was pleasing her.

"So, did I do it right last night?" she asked.

The question caught Rayshon off guard. He remembered NiNi telling him she wasn't a virgin, and he could tell that she was a bit inexperienced but to ask him such a thing had him a little mind boggled.

"Do what right?" he asked.

He already knew what she was referring to, but he wanted her to say it.

"Um, us doing it. Like did I do it right?"

Doing it? He thought.

He brushed it off and made a mental note to just teach her and mold her instead of judging her.

"If ya pussy was whack I would've told you. You good ma, relax."

"You sure? Like, I know you've probably been wit' a lot of girls that can do more stuff than I did, and I don't want that to make us break up or anything."

No matter how many times Damon took what he wanted when he sexually abused her, she was still inexperienced. NiNi knew that the things Damon did to her weren't things a man should do to a woman, but all she knew was what he had done because he was the only guy she'd had any sort of sexual relations with.

"I have been wit' a lot of bitches, but that don't mean anything. Whatever you don't know how to do, I'll teach you. Again, relax," he told her.

NiNi wasn't so sure about what Rayshon was telling her because from what she'd witnessed, guys normally told females how good it was. Well, at least that's what she's heard guys tell Onyae time and time again.

"Just be honest. You didn't like it, did you? It's okay if you didn't."

Rayshon was just about done cooking when he turned the stove off allowing the remaining heat from the burner to cook the eggs.

"How many niggas you been wit'?" he asked while fixing her plate.

NiNi was ashamed to tell him because it had only been one and it was by force.

"Why?"

Rayshon turned around and sat her plate on the table in front of her.

"It's just a question. You ain't gotta answer if you don't want to," he assured her.

"Sexually or boyfriend wise?" she asked.

"Both."

Rayshon was finished fixing his plate and after he placed it on the table, he got two cups out and filled them with orange juice.

NiNi was embarrassed to even tell him but she did anyway.

"I've never had a boyfriend before, and I only been wit' one person sexually and I would rather not talk about it."

"You ain't never had a boyfriend before? I can't even believe that," Rayshon said while sitting down. He gave NiNi her cup before taking a sip of his.

"Well believe it," NiNi said and then began to eat her food.

Her taste buds were dancing after each bite. She didn't even realize Rayshon was staring at her; when she finally noticed it, she stopped mid-bite.

"That shit good ain't it? I told you."

NiNi rolled her eyes.

"It's a'ight." She chuckled.

"Yea a'ight. A nigga throw down in the kitchen, so give me my credit."

NiNi took another forkful of eggs and nodded her head.

"Okay, okay, it is good. But so what?"

"Damn, you a hater but it's cool though."

"Awww babe, I'm just playin'. This food is bomb fareal though."

"I know you was playin'," Rayshon responded with a mouth full of turkey bacon. "So is it ard if I take you home tomorrow mornin'? I wanna spend some actual time wit' you today bein' that I long dicked ya head off yesterday."

"That's fine, but speakin' of yesterday. You still didn't answer my question," NiNi said.

Rayshon finished chewing and then took a sip of his orange juice before responding.

"What question?"

"Was it good?" she asked again.

"Why you keep askin' that? You insecure or somethin', ma?" Rayshon asked.

He managed to bypass it the first couple of times she asked, but now he could tell that it was a real issue for her, and she wasn't going to stop asking until he answered.

"I just wanna know, that's all. But the way you're actin' confirms that you didn't enjoy it." NiNi lowered her head a bit and lost her appetite.

Rayshon frowned.

"So me knockin' the bottom out ya shit all day yesterday and even eatin' ya pussy and ass aint't enough to let you know that it was good? Damn ma, you delusional."

NiNi didn't know whether to take what he said as a compliment or an insult, so she just looked at him and excused herself from the table.

"I'm gonna go shower and get some clean clothes on."

NiNi didn't like the fact that he said she was delusional and being that she didn't want to ruin her last day with him, she decided to just remove herself before things got out of hand.

"Fareal ma?" he asked.

"Fareal what?" NiNi stopped in mid-step.

"You just gon' get up like that and not finish eatin' or our conversation?"

"Rayshon, I would like to shower. I don't wanna just sit around knowing we've been sexing one another all night. I just don't like the feeling. Now, is it okay for me to take a shower?"

NiNi knew she was overreacting a bit, but she had to get used to being with Rayshon. Although he made her feel comfortable, she still had to mentally instill the fact that he wasn't Damon in her head. Whenever Damon violated her, she would sit in the shower and scrub herself until her skin wrinkled.

"Stop playin' wit' me, yea it's okay for you to take a shower. Everything is in the bathroom, extra towels, washcloths, all that if you need it," he told her.

NiNi nodded and made her way upstairs.

She looked in her overnight bag and got out some clean panties, socks and a bra and then searched her overnight bag high and low for her body wash.

"How the hell did I forget that out of all things." NiNi was annoyed with herself.

She threw her stuff on the bed and left out of the bedroom.

"Rayshon, I forgot my body wash. Do you have anything I can use that don't smell like a whole nigga!" she yelled.

"I got Dove soap in the bathroom closet!" he yelled back.

NiNi walked into the bathroom and turned on the shower. Rayshon's entire house felt so at home. The color scheme in his bathroom was chocolate and soft yellow which made it feel so warm and cozy, and he even had a light switch that dimmed the lights if she wanted to. NiNi removed her clothes and stepped into the hot shower; allowing the water to ease the tension in her neck as she closed her eyes.

NiNi jumped when she felt someone grab her causing her to almost slip and fall.

"Rayshon!" *Whap!* She smacked him. "What are you doin'? Why would you do that?"

"I'm sorry, babe." He tried to kiss her, but she stopped him.

"No, Rayshon. You can't do stuff like that."
NiNi was shaking.

Rayshon was apologetic for scaring her, but her actions concerned him. The fact that she was shaking, and she barely wanted him to touch her bothered him.

"NiNi, I'm sorry, ma. I didn't mean to scare you. Relax, I'm not tryna hurt you," he assured her.

He pulled her close to him and wrapped his arms around her allowing her to calm down and feel his energy so she could know he meant no harm at all. Eventually, NiNi got herself together.

"Why the hell you in here anyway?" she finally spoke.

"Damn, a nigga can't wash his ass too?" he joked.

"Nope, you could've waited until I was finished. You just tryna be nasty." She smirked.

Rayshon kissed her on her neck.

"Yea I am."

He gently pushed her against the wall and slid inside of her from the back. NiNi winced a little. Regardless if they had been fucking all night or not, she wasn't used to his size. Rayshon thrusted his hips and slid in and out of her slowly while giving her passion marks all over her neck.

"Oooo, Ra—Rayshon," she moaned.

Sex with him made her body quiver. He applied pressure to her with the intent to please her pussy and not hurt it. He cupped her titties, gripped her thighs and played with her precious pearl while the hot water ran down on them. NiNi was in heaven until she felt him pull out and let her go.

A look of confusion spread across her face when she turned around. "Wha—what are you doin'? Why you stop?"

"This dick got you snappin'." He laughed and kissed her.

"You finished? Like, we done?"

"Nah, I was just switchin' positions." Rayshon caught her off guard when he picked her up and wrapped her legs around him while he cupped her ass.

"Oooh!" she gasped.

"Mmm," he moaned.

NiNi clawed at his neck while he stretched her out with each stroke. She was feeling every inch of his dick and she wasn't sure who was soaking him up more, her pussy or the water from the shower.

"Alright, ba—by, I wanna stop," she panted.

The position was a bit much for NiNi and she took as much as she could before getting overwhelmed which only took a couple of strokes. Rayshon didn't nut yet, but he also didn't hesitate to stop when she said she wanted to stop.

"Mmmm, you sure?" he kissed her and then put her down.

NiNi nodded.

"You not mad are you?"

"Nah, babe. I'm not mad."

NiNi placed her hand on his cheek and kissed him. She loved how caring he was to her and for the next fifteen minutes they washed one another up, rinsed off, and dried one another off while sneaking in kisses the entire time.

"What you about to put on?" she asked when they made it back into the bedroom.

Rayshon had grabbed the remote and pressed play on a movie.

"*Streets*. You ain't never seen this? It got Meek Mill in it."

"No, I don't really watch TV, but is it good?"

NiNi had dried off and put on one of Rayshon's T-shirts instead of the clothes she got out.

"Hell yea. It got Meek in it so of course it's good," he boasted.

Rayshon threw on a pair of boxers and basketball shorts before he laid down in the bed. It was as if NiNi was waiting for him to lay down because as soon as he did, she laid down beside him and snuggled up close.

"After the movie go off, what you wanna do today?" he asked.

NiNi didn't mind lying up with Rayshon. She would do it forever if she had to.

"I just wanna be under you. Just hold me and don't let me go. That's all I want," she answered.

Rayshon kissed NiNi on her forehead and wrapped his arms around her making her feel safe and secure once again. He was making NiNi feel safe, and she was making him feel like Superman. The fact that she made him feel like he was the only thing that mattered when they were together was dope to him. Rayshon could feel how genuine she was and that was something that was rare when it came to the females he encountered. He was about to fully give love another chance and block out every negative thing he'd been through with Sharee. It was all about him and NiNi; she had him, he had her and that was all they needed

Chapter 26

NiNi wiped the sleep out of her eyes once again as she yawned continuously.

"I'm so tired. I don't recall ever being this tired before. All I wanna do is get back in your bed and go back to sleep," she said as they walked out the door.

"That's cas' you ain't never had no real nigga dick before," he stated while he locked his door.

"Can you shut up." NiNi was a bit embarrassed.

"For what?" He looked confused. "Ain't nobody out here, and even if I didn't say that I'm sure my neighbors heard me dickin' you down last night by the way you was screamin' and creamin' and don't touch that door either."

NiNi was blushing and smiling from ear to ear as she stood by the passenger's side door waiting for Rayshon to open it for her.

"I never did any of what we did last night," she said as she got inside the truck.

"I could tell, but it's plenty more where that came from cas' I'm a freaky ass nigga. You only saw a little bit of what I got in me."

Rayshon started up his truck and pulled off. The ride was quiet as NiNi sat in deep thought. This past weekend was something she always dreamed of experiencing but never thought she would. Her stepfather had stolen her innocence at such a young age, and he continued to take it. She didn't know what it was like for a man besides him to want her, but Rayshon had showed her what it felt like, and it felt damn good.

NiNi hoped that what they were building was real, but she couldn't help but to think about Damon and Rayshon's loudmouth ex-girlfriend.

"You good?" Rayshon asked, finally breaking the silence.

"Yea," she responded dryly.

"You sure? You in deep thought over there." He could sense that something was bothering her.

"I'm fine." She forced a fake smile.

He didn't pry. He felt like if she wanted him to know what was wrong then she would tell him. Rayshon decided to switch the subject.

"So, when we doin' this again?"

"Doin' what?" she asked.

"Spendin' the weekend together. Shit, or even the week together."

"Um, I don't know. I guess whenever you want to. I mean, I know you got shit to do and you can't just be stuck up under me all the time. I ain't never been wit' no hustla before but I heard how yawl do," she responded.

Rayshon cut his eyes at her.

"I'ma boss, baby. That shit is way different from a hustla. I started out as a hustla and made my way to boss status, so you know what that mean?"

NiNi looked over at him.

"What?"

"It means I make the rules and I can change and break the rules if I want. I got a whole team that move when I say move; not to sound cocky but I'm just bein' real. So, if I wanted to take you to a private island and spend a month wit' you, I could do that wit' no problem and the money would still be rollin' in."

NiNi was completely turned on by everything Rayshon had just said. She had never met a man who had so much confidence and swag. She knew that if she was going to be with him then she needed to get rid of the little abused girl and become a woman, but that was easier said than done.

***

"Biiitttccccchhhhhh! You gotta tell me everything!" Onyae squealed when she ran outside.

She didn't even give Rayshon a chance to open NiNi's door good before she bombarded them both.

"Damn, let me get out the truck good." NiNi laughed.

"Girl, fuck all that. I couldn't wait until you got back. You don't know how hard it was for me not to text you and ask you questions," Onyae said.

"Girl, relax. I'll let you know everything, but before I do, did my mother call you or auntie? I texted her yesterday and she responded as if she didn't want to talk to me. She didn't even answer the phone when I called." NiNi's face saddened.

"No, but, boo, don't let that fuck up your mood! You done went out and got some good dick and when you get some good dick you never let anything fuck that up. Besides, Mom did say that Uncle Kick Down drives by there on his way to work and he hasn't been seeing Damon's truck, so I don't know. Maybe Auntie and him are taking a break or they're done and right now she's just tryna get her thoughts together," Onyae told her.

NiNi's eyes lit up. "His truck ain't been there?"

Onyae shook her head. "Nope!"

"Thank God!" NiNi said out loud and then turned to look at Rayshon. "Babe, can you drop me off at my mother's house? Her boyfriend isn't there so I'ma go check on her and then walk back over here."

"Oooooooo, babe?" Onyae playfully pushed Rayshon. "You done dicked my cous down somethin' good!"

"Yooo, chill." He laughed.

"Onyae, shut upppp!" NiNi said.

Onyae shrugged her shoulders.

"Aye, I'm just sayin' it went from hey to bae real quick and I'm here for it. Now, I'ma let you go over there and check up on Auntie, but as soon as you're finished come back so I can get allll the tea, because I know that shit is hot and ready like Little Caesars."

NiNi and Rayshon burst out in laughter.

"I'm serious. Hurry up and take her to her mom's so she can get back here. I'ma be waitin'!" Onyae turned and ran back into the house.

NiNi laughed again before Rayshon helped her back inside the truck. When they made it to her house, she was so relieved to see that Damon's truck really wasn't there.

Thank you, God, she thought.

Her mood went from uneasy back to happy and she was sure that the remainder of her day would be better.

"You goin' back home?" NiNi asked once Rayshon opened the door for her.

"Nah, I'ma go check Gutta out over in Millville. We got some business to handle so I'll be gone for the rest of the day, but I'll be local so if you need anything just hit me up," he told her.

NiNi wrapped her arms around his neck once she finally stepped out of his truck.

"Be careful, okay?" She kissed him.

Rayshon had his arms wrapped tight around her waist and she felt so safe and secure.

"Always, ma."

NiNi didn't want to let him go, but she had plans on hitting him up later on once she felt like he was done handling business.

"Okay, well I love you."

"I love you too."

They let one another go and Rayshon watched NiNi walk to the door before he got back in his truck. She waved at him and blew him a kiss and he played along and caught it.

Thank you for sending me someone like him, God, she thought before walking into the house.

"Mom!" NiNi called out.

"Shhh, she's sleeping." Damon walked into the dining room and looked at NiNi catching her completely off guard because his truck wasn't parked outside.

"What are you doin' here? Did you give her, her medicine on time?" she asked.

"Who dropped you off?" he asked while ignoring her question.

"Did you give my mother her medicine, Damon?" NiNi asked again.

She didn't have time for his bullshit. NiNi came there in excitement to check on her mother so that she could head back to her cousin's house, and Damon was trying to knock her off her high.

"NiNi, who dropped you off?" His voice was much firmer this time.

"Why the fuck are you worried about who dropped me off? You not my fuckin' father! Don't worry about shit I do!" NiNi snapped as she pushed past him.

Don't let him win, NiNi. Don't let him fuck up your happiness, she coached herself in her head.

NiNi had spunk. Rayshon had her on another level of confidence which had her on cloud nine and she wasn't about to let Damon ruin it. She walked down the hall to her mother's bedroom and pushed the door open. Neosha was sleeping peacefully. NiNi wanted to wake her up so bad, but she didn't. After going against her better judgment, NiNi kissed her mother on the cheek and left out of the bedroom. She closed the door behind her, and headed to her bedroom, and closed her door.

NiNi needed to grab a few things from her bedroom before heading back over to Onyae's house because she was running low on panties and bras. While she was doing so, she could see the shadow of someone standing outside of her bedroom. Fear consumed her when she noticed that she had forgotten to lock the door. As soon as she attempted to reach and lock it, Damon pushed his way in.

"Get out!" she screamed.

"Shut yo fat ass up, bitch!" Damon barked.

He shut the door and turned around. Damon glared at her with anger in his eyes. NiNi's body trembled and the only thing she wanted was for Damon to leave. For years she had dealt with his emotional, physical, and sexual abuse and she was tired of it. She loved her mother to pieces, but she couldn't take it anymore. Her body, mind and spirit were tired and now that she had finally experienced a bit of love and happiness from Rayshon she was not about to let Damon's evil ass take it away from her.

"Get the hell out!" she screamed.

Whap!

Damon backhand smacked her without hesitation.

NiNi grabbed her face. The burning sensation caused her eyes to tear up.

"Some nigga droppin' you off now?"

"Why the fuck do you care? Leave me alone! I'm not going to allow you to continue to ruin my life!" NiNi screamed as she tried to push past him.

Whap!

Another hard smack went across NiNi's face, but this time it was an open handed. He pushed NiNi up against the dressed and forced his hand inside her leggings. He rammed his finger in her pussy and felt her openness. Looking at her with hate and disgust, he sniffed her long and hard.

"Bitch, you must think this a game," Damon said to her. That was the last thing he said before lifting his fist and slamming it down on her jaw.

Smack! Pop!

Whap!

"Ahhhhhh! Ahhhh!" NiNi screamed.

She could taste the flavor of blood in her mouth after the first three punches. He grabbed her hair and slapped her back to back across her face and then rammed her head into the closet door.

"Ooowwww! Please stop," she mumbled through a bloody mouth as tears rolled down her cheeks.

Although she was getting beat up, she held the waistband of her leggings with a death grip. She couldn't take any of it, but she preferred the physical abuse over the sexual abuse. She wanted Damon to give her beatings and nothing else. As a matter of fact, she didn't want to give any man her body ever again; any man but Rayshon.

"You gon' learn to not give another nigga what's mine, bitch!"

Damon still had a handful of her hair as he yelled at her. He yanked her head back and pushed her to the floor. NiNi balled up in the fetal position as he stood on top of her glaring at her like the bully he was.

"Since you wanna go out and fuck anotha nigga, I'ma show yo ass tonight."

NiNi didn't look up. She didn't want to give Damon any eye contact. She laid there with her eyes closed as she covered her face with her left hand and held onto the waistband of her leggings with her right. She knew that Damon was going to teach her a lesson, and that lesson consisted of fucking her until she couldn't take anymore.

"Get up, shower and come straight in ya fuckin' room until I'm ready for you," he ordered before walking out and slamming the door shut.

NiNi started to cry again. She always prayed that one day her mom would catch him in the act, but just like all the other times, she never did. Although she attempted to fight back, she always seemed to feel powerless against Damon.

She laid there feeling hopeless with no will to live like she always did.

***

An hour later NiNi stood in the mirror in her bedroom looking at the black and blue bruises that decorated her face. Her left eye was swollen shut, the left side of her face was swollen and so was her mouth. Tears rolled down NiNi's face, and all she wanted to do was scream to the top of her lungs, hoping to release some of the pain and hurt that consumed her over the years. The only thing NiNi wanted to do was to make sure her mother beat cancer, but the price she had to pay for it was overwhelming. NiNi wasn't sure how much longer she could fight.

NiNi grabbed her cellphone off her bed and texted Onyae to let her know that she wasn't coming back to her house

NiNi: *Hey, I'ma stay here and hang wit' mommy for the day.*

Onyae: *Hey chick! I was just about to text you and ask you what the hell was takin' you so long, and okay is she good?*

NiNi: *Yea, she's fine.*

Onyae read the text from her cousin and could tell that something had happened. NiNi's response was dry and she only did that when something was bothering her. She hoped that it wasn't what she thought it was. Their uncle mentioned he hadn't seen Damon's truck there the whole weekend, so she encouraged NiNi to go see her mother. Before she assumed anything, she decided to ask her.

Onyae: *NiNi is everything okay boo? You was so happy before you went to see auntie. Did yawl argue? Is she upset wit' you? Do you need my mom to call her??*

When NiNi didn't respond right away, Onyae tried to call her but she didn't answer and just seconds after that she attempted to Facetime her but NiNi rejected the call. She tried to call again just in case it was NiNi's service messing up, but sure enough she rejected that one too.

NiNi: *I can text, but not facetime right now.*

Onyae: *NiNi, what the hell is going on? Did Rayshon do something to you when he dropped you off? I'll kill that*

muthafucka if he did something to you baby. Tell me what he did to you.

Tears were rolling down NiNi's eyes as she read Onyae's text. The love her cousin had for her was unconditional. She wanted to take her life right then and there, but Onyae's concern for her wouldn't allow it.

NiNi: *It wasn't Rayshon. It was that bastard! I had no idea he was here Onyae because like you said his truck isn't here. I guess he saw Rayshon and it almost happened again, but he noticed that I had been with someone else and he hit me. Onyae he beat me so bad. I've been in pain for the last hour. I screamed. I cried. I yelled and I even tried to fight back! Onyae I did it all and she didn't hear me. My mother didn't hear me. He makes sure she's either not here or not coherent when he bothers me.*

NiNi cried hard when she finished sending the text off.

Onyae: *I'ma kill him! I swear I'm on my way over there now. I'ma kill him!*

Onyae was in tears. She was so tired of her cousin hurting, and him hitting her was the last straw. He turned a peaceful dream into a nightmare and there was no way that Onyae was going to sit back any longer; especially after seeing how happy NiNi was before she left. She knew that if Damon kept this up, NiNi would either kill herself or leave Rayshon alone, and she wasn't about to stand by and let either one happen.

NiNi: *No! Onyae please. I don't want anyone to find out. You know what will happen if someone finds out.*

Onyae: *I don't give a fuck. I'm tired of that pussy. I'll chop his fuckin' dick off and feed it to that dirty ass nigga! You about to live wit' us for good! And auntie can come too if she wants but if not fuck her and fuck that bitch made nigga. On God!*

NiNi: *Please, just let me handle this. Promise me you won't say anything. I'll figure out a way to tell my mother what's been going on, but please.*

Onyae shook her head as she read NiNi's text. She wanted to say fuck a promise, and run down on Damon's bitch ass, but she decided against it for now. She was going to give NiNi an ultimatum, and her response would determine her next move.

Onyae: *You got until tomorrow to tell Auntie or I will.*

NiNi: *I promise I will. But please don't say anything until then.*

Onyae: *Smh, I got you boo, and I love you. Always remember that. Xoxo.*

NiNi: *I love you too. Oxox.*

As soon as Onyae was finished texting NiNi, she did what she said she was going to do and that was call her aunt to cover for NiNi. She went into her favorite contacts, came across her aunt's number and pressed the call button.

Ring. Ring. Ring.
Ring. Ring. Ring.

"Hello?" Neosha picked up on the sixth ring.

Her voice cracked as she spoke, and she had a bit of a slur too.

"Hey Auntie. Sorry to wake you. I just wanted to call you right quick to let you know that NiNi came to check on you but you were sleepin' so she came back over here. She couldn't call cas' her phone died and she in the shower right now. I know how she is about you, so I told her that I'd call and let you know that she did come over there to check on you being that yawl haven't been on the best terms. And of course I wanted to check on you too," Onyae said, playing it off.

"Oh, baby, I'm fine, and thank you for calling. Tell NiNi I love her and to stop worrying so much about me. I was upset at first, but I'm not anymore. She needs to get herself some fresh air. I'll be fine," Neosha said.

"Yeah, she just be worried about you that's all. But I'll tell her, Auntie. You finish getting some rest. I love you."

"I love you too, baby."

Click.

Onyae felt so guilty. She wanted to tell her aunt everything right then and there, but she made her cousin a promise. Sometimes she hated how close they were, because when it came to serious situations, she wanted to be the first one to tell so the problem could be resolved. But her loyalty to NiNi prohibited it.

***

"Hey baby," Yoshi purred into the phone.

"Wassup beautiful. How you doin' tonight?" Khalif asked.

"I'm good. Especially now that I'm talkin' to you," she said flirtatiously.

"Hmmm, is that right. You need anything? You good?" he asked.

"Yeah, I'm good. Will I see you tonight?" she asked, already knowing the answer to her question.

"Why you askin' a question you already know the answer to?" he said, reading her mind.

Yoshi laughed.

"I just wanted to see what you was gonna say, big head."

"Yeah, you love this big head tho'," Khalif shot back.

Yoshi's got hot and bothered by his response. She loved how thorough he was.

"Shut up. What time you coming over?" she wanted to know.

"Actually, I wanted to take you and the girls out tonight. Surprise them so they could get to know me a little more, ya know? Then tomorrow I can take yawl shopping. You think Onyae will actually accept my offer this time? It's been awhile so I'm hopin' so."

"I think that's a great idea, and I'll call my niece as soon as I get off the phone cas' she'll help me talk Onyae into giving in." Yoshi laughed.

"A'ight cool, I don't want her to be uncomfortable so if she ain't wit' it, let me know. I just want to show her I'ma real stand up dude."

"I know, baby, but let me get on the phone with my niece, and I'll call you back in a few."

"A'ight bae. I love you."

"Mmm, I love you too, baby."

Yoshi ended the call and selected NiNi's name in her contacts. When she didn't answer on the second call, she quickly scrolled to Neosha's name and called her. She had a feeling Neosha was probably in bed, but she still called her because she wanted to get the message to NiNi and to see how Neosha was doing being that Onyae said NiNi had stopped over there to see her earlier.

Ring. Ring. Ring.

Ring. Ring.

"Hello?" Neosha answered as she cleared her voice.

"Hey baby. How you doing?" Yoshi asked.

Neosha took a moment to register the voice on the other end. She was still very tired from her medicine and the last thing she wanted to do was talk on the phone, but realizing it was her sister she tried her best to remain coherent for a few.

"Oh, I'm doing just fine. How you doing? How is my niece?" Neosha asked her baby sister not quite remembering that she had just talked to Onyae.

"I'm good, and she's good too just getting on my damn nerves. I called to see how you were doing, and to see if NiNi wanted to come by for dinner tonight. Khalif wants to spend time with the girls considering Onyae ain't been too open towards him. He suggested dinner and a shopping spree, and I know NiNi can use some fresh air," Yoshi said as she stood in her walk-in closet. She pushed clothes to the side searching for an outfit for the night.

Neosha rubbed her right temple and then rubbed her hand over her forehead to try to gather her thoughts.

"That's good, but I thought NiNi was already there. I haven't seen her all day, and Onyae called and said that she stopped by here and then headed back over there so I didn't question it," Neosha replied.

"Sis, NiNi ain't been here all day which is why I called. You sure Onyae called you and said that?" Yoshi asked. Because if Onyae had called her, why did she ask Yoshi about her as if they hadn't talked.

"I'm more than sure. I was a little groggy when you called but when you mentioned NiNi I remembered that Onyae called me earlier. She said that NiNi would be over there. What's going on?" Neosha started to get worried.

She sat up on the bed and attempted to get up but stopped when her sister assured her that everything was ok.

"Nothing at all. You know how those girls is. Always up to no good but let me call you back cas' I'm about to shower." Yoshi played it off.

She was pissed because Onyae had lied, and that was something she never did so she knew something was up, and she was about to get to the bottom of it.

"Okay, well let me know what's going on. You know I don't play when it comes to my baby."

"I will, sis. Don't worry."

Click.

Yoshi didn't waste any time getting to the bottom of things.

"Onyae, get yo ass in here!" Yoshi called out as soon as she ended the call.

Onyae was in her room texting Gutta when she heard her mother scream her name from her bedroom. She had to do something to keep her mind off NiNi, and she knew texting her boo would keep her occupied. The firmness in Yoshi's voice let Onyae know that she was in trouble, and that was rare for her.

"Yes, Mom," she answered. She hopped off the bed, ran out of her bedroom and into her mother's.

"What the fuck are you and NiNi up to and don't fuckin' lie to me or I'ma punch you dead in yo shit," Yoshi warned.

Onyae swallowed hard.

She wasn't afraid of no male or female, but her mother was a different story.

"What you talkin' about?" She tried to act confused, but Yoshi wasn't buying it.

"Don't fuckin' play with me. I called Neosha to see where NiNi was because you said she went over there earlier, and I wanted to see if she wanted to come back over tonight to go out to dinner with us. Neosha said that you called her and told her that NiNi was gonna be over here for the day, but NiNi isn't here. Now, I'ma ask you again what the fuck is yawl up to? Is she out with Rayshon? She's grown so why are yawl lying about that? Didn't she just come back from spending the weekend with him?" Yoshi questioned.

"No, Mom she not wit' Rayshon. Damn, why you trippin'?" Onyae was getting annoyed.

"Girl, who the hell you talkin' to? Don't try me, Onyae. Tell me where NiNi is now!"

Yoshi barely raised her voice so by that and her flared nostrils, Onyae knew her mother wasn't playing.

"She's home! She been there all day since she left here. In her room with the door locked! You happy now, damn?" Onyae pouted with her arms folded.

"Who the fuck do you think you talkin' to, Onyae? Don't fuckin' play with me! Why the hell did you lie to your aunt if NiNi has been home all day? Why didn't she come back over here?"

Onyae was never one to get emotional, but she couldn't control the tears that had welled up in her eyes. For years she kept NiNi's secret, and she felt fucked up for doing so. Her loyalty ran so deep for NiNi that she allowed it to cause her to standby while NiNi got sexually and physically abused.

"It's hard to explain, Mom. Just chill. NiNi is good okay?" She wiped her face.

"Why are you crying, Onyae? What's going on with NiNi?"

Yoshi grew to be more concerned because her daughter never cried. Being emotional just wasn't Onyae's thing. Something had to truly be bothering her.

"Nothing, Mom. It ain't nothin'."

Onyae tried to turn and walk away, but Yoshi grabbed her. Her mother's intuition had kicked in and demanded that she get to the bottom of whatever it was that was going on.

"Don't walk away from me. Tell me what's going on? Is NiNi pregnant? Did she get hurt by Rayshon? What is going on?"

"Mom, leave it alone." Onyae tried to pull away, but Yoshi yanked her back.

"You ain't leaving this damn room until you tell me what's going on!"

Onyae blew out a frustrated sigh and shook her head. She had just given NiNi an ultimatum and here she was caught between a rock and a hard place.

"She not pregnant, Mom, and no, Rayshon didn't do anything to her. She just not in the mood to be dealin' wit' anybody. She good tho'. Trust me." Onyae tried to convince her mother.

She turned her head in the other direction so Yoshi wouldn't see the tears that appeared again. Her mother grabbed her face and turned it towards hers. She looked at her with the sincerest and most caring look a mother could give. Yoshi was no longer upset with Onyae. She was concerned and not knowing what was going on was eating at her.

"Baby, please tell me what's wrong. Did NiNi do something that she's afraid for Neosha to find out?"

Onyae shook her head from side to side.

"Then why are you crying, Onyae? I can't help if you don't talk to me."

"You can't help wit' this, Mom. That's why I'm tellin' you to just let it go." Onyae's voice cracked.

"I promise you I'll fix whatever the issue is. I put that on my life, baby, just tell me what it is," Yoshi said.

There was no more holding back. Onyae no longer felt the need to keep this secret. It had been going on far too long and to continue to sweep it under the rug was a threat to NiNi's life. NiNi was an emotional wreck and Onyae knew that sooner or later she wasn't going to be able to save her from suicide. She had to put a stop to it before it was too little too late.

"He's touching her, Mom," Onyae blurted.

She allowed the tears to flow down her face freely after she spoke. Yoshi was looking confused.

"Who's touching her?"

"Damon. He's having sex with NiNi, and he threatened to stop payin' Auntie's medical bills if NiNi said anything. He beat her up today. She said he beat her up bad. That's why I lied and said that she was over here because she didn't want to come by here and risk you seein' her face. She told me to lie for her and I did, so that her mother wouldn't see what happened to her and start to ask questions. She's been in her room since Damon beat her up. Auntie must've taken her meds because that's the only time he's able to do anything to NiNi," Onyae explained.

Yoshi couldn't believe what she was hearing; her heart was hurting for her niece. She now understood why NiNi hated Damon, and she couldn't blame her. She understood why NiNi had stopped her life completely and spent the majority of her time at their house. She also put two and two together when it came to the unexplained bruises NiNi carried. All of the unanswered questions that had once come across Yoshi's mind, were now answered.

"How long has it been going on?"

Yoshi wanted to know every little detail, and Onyae felt like now that she had confessed what was going on telling the full truth wouldn't hurt too much more.

"It started when she was nine. Just a few months before her tenth birthday. I didn't find out until she was twelve, but even then, I couldn't stop it. She told me to promise her that I wouldn't tell anyone. I did, Mom. I promised her. I'm sorry." Onyae cried.

It was now Yoshi's time to cry. Her niece's life was ruined at such an early age, and she was disgusted because it was going on right under everyone's noses. She prayed and hoped that her sister wasn't a part of what happened to NiNi. Because if so, she was going to beat every inch of her sick ass because no child deserved to endure the things that NiNi did.

Yoshi let go of Onyae and grabbed her chest as if she was in physical pain, but she wasn't. She was emotionally broken from what she'd just heard. A mother's job was to protect their children, and an aunt was the next best thing to a child's mother. Yoshi and Neosha both failed at protecting NiNi. She couldn't do anything about it then, but she damn sure was going to do something about it now.

She looked through her cellphone until she came across her brother's contact. Yoshi pressed the green call button and put the phone to her ear.

Ring. Ring.

Ring.

Her heart was beating a mile a minute because she knew exactly what was going to happen when she revealed what had been going on with his niece.

Ring. Ring.

"Yo, baby sis. What's goin' on?" he finally answered.

"I need you to get over to Neosha's house right now and kill that nigga! He's been raping NiNi, Kick Down! Damon's nasty ass, he's been raping that baby!" Yoshi tried to be strong while she told her brother what was going on, but the mention of what happened to NiNi broke her.

Uncle Kick Down didn't say a word in response. His cellphone dropped to the floor of his girlfriend's apartment. Without saying a word, he grabbed his keys off the kitchen table.

"Baby, where you going?" she called out.

Kick Down hopped off the porch and ran to the driver's side of his work van. He barely closed the door before he started it up and peeled off.

Bang! Bang!

Bang!

"I'ma kill that nigga! I swear I'ma kill him!" Kick Down screamed as he punched the steering wheel.

***

When Onyae heard her mother say her uncle's name she knew all hell was about to break loose. She watched as her mother walked out of the walk-in closet and hurried to put on some sneakers. Yoshi grabbed her metal bat just like the one Onyae had in her bedroom.

"Let's go!" she yelled.

Onyae ran behind her mother. She had no time to put on any shoes, but she did have enough time to grab the bat that sat behind her bedroom door. Onyae ran out of the house behind her mother and they hopped in her car. Yoshi pulled out of the driveway so violently that Onyae's head jerked back. The drive from Yoshi's house to her sister's house was about three minutes away, and Kick Down lived about the same distance. Just as she suspected, by the time she pulled up, Kick Down was hopping out of his work van.

Yoshi put her car in park and hopped out with Onyae right on her tail. Onyae was scared because the look in Kick Down's eyes looked like a lost soul. No words were spoken as they watched Kick Down run up the walkway and do what gave him his name back in the day.

Bang! Bang!

Bang!

Kick Down reared back and gave the door to Neosha's house three hard kicks before it flew off the hinges. The way NiNi's house was set up, the basement was right there as soon as one opened the main door to the house. Kick Down slung the basement door open and ran down the stairs looking for Damon because, from the looks of his last visit, that was his favorite spot.

NiNi heard the bang and ran to hide inside her closet. She just knew that Damon had gotten angry again and was coming at her. Fear seeped through her pores as tears rolled down her face, and her bladder grew weak. NiNi was now sitting in a puddle of piss, but she didn't care; her heart was thumping and jumping damn near out her chest. She covered her ears with her hands and closed her eyes as she rocked back and forth like a scared child.

***

Damon jumped out of the bed and ran out of the bedroom he shared with Neosha. He didn't even make it down the hall before Kick Down was coming around the corner into the hallway. Damon saw the glare, the anger, and the look of a madman in Kick Down's eyes. Damon didn't get a word out before Kick Down attacked him.

Whap! Whap!

Smack!

"You son of a bitch! You touched my niece, muthafucka, I'ma kill you!" Kick Down yelled as he threw a combination of punches at Damon's face.

The first punch dropped him, and Kick Down continued to pound on his face. He took his head and slammed it into the floor causing blood to gush out. The commotion caused Neosha to jump up. At first, she thought she was dreaming, but hearing all the noise right outside of her bedroom told her she wasn't. She hurried out of bed, tying her housecoat as she exited the room. The moment she stepped around the corner, she saw her brother damn near killing her husband.

"You're gonna kill him, stop!" she yelled.

Yoshi hurried and hopped over Kick Down, as he was on top of Damon punching his head into the floor and grabbed her sister. Neosha tried to fight her way through, but Yoshi wasn't letting her go.

"Get his ass, Unc, kill that nigga!" Onyae cheered him on with her bat still in her hand.

"Yoshi, let me go! Kick Down, get off him!" Neosha screamed with tears running down her face.

Neosha had no clue what was going on. All she knew was that her brother was about to kill her husband and her sister and niece were standing back allowing it to happen.

"Yoshi, what the hell is wrong with you? Get him the fuck off him!" Neosha screamed.

"Fuck no! That dirty ass nigga deserves what he's getting! Kill him, Kick Down, kill him!" Yoshi screamed.

Neosha couldn't stand back and watch Kick Down do such a thing. She wasn't as strong as she was before the cancer attacked her body, but she didn't allow that to stop her from trying to fight Yoshi.

"Neosha, stop!" Yoshi said as she struggled to not hit her sister but to restrain her.

Tears rolled down Neosha's face as she scratched, punched, and kicked Yoshi. Damon was lying there lifelessly, and her heart broke into pieces seeing Kick Down still punching on him.

"Why won't you stop him!" Neosha asked.

"Auntie, he deserves this!" Onyae yelled at her.

Seeing the fight in her aunt as she tried to get to Damon made her angry. She wondered where her fight for NiNi was all those years. Although Neosha didn't know, Onyae still hated how blind her aunt was.

"No one deserves that! Kick Down, stop it!"

Kick Down had finally stopped. He was breathing heavily as he stood up; sweat dripped down his face and blood covered his knuckles and shirt. His chest was heaving up and down, and he mustered up a mouth full of saliva and spit on Damon.

"Rest in hell you rapist muthafucka!"

Kick Down snarled as he looked at his sister who looked as if she was watching a horror movie.

"Where the fuck was you at when this nigga was raping my niece? Huh? Where the fuck was you?" he asked with a look of disgust spread across his face.

Neosha didn't want to believe what she had just heard. Her mouth fell wide open, but no words came out. She suddenly became weak. The hallway walls seemed to be closing in on her as her mouth watered and the taste of vomit filled her mouth. She didn't want to believe that the man she had fallen madly in love with, and that took care of her and her daughter would do such a thing. But in that moment, she realized that all the years of NiNi having a strong dislike for Damon, giving him attitude, and never wanting to be around him was for a reason. Her mind quickly went back to the day of her doctor's appointment. She was blind to the fact that her daughter was trying to tell her what was going on in her own way.

"What you over there thinkin' about?" Neosha asked.

"Just this girl me and Onyae know. She's goin' through a lot, Mom. I wish I could help her, but I don't know how." NiNi's voice became babylike.

"Well, what's going on with her?" Neosha grew concerned.

NiNi sighed and shook her head.

"Her stepfather is touching her and her baby sister. She threatened to tell her mother, but she told me and Onyae that he don't care cas' he knows for a fact that she won't believe a word they say. It hurts me, Mom, cas' she comes to us all beat up, crying, and just don't know what to do."

It all made sense to her now. The many bruises she saw on NiNi's face and body, the distance she kept from the house unless NiNi was checking on her, making sure she took her meds, ate, had the right amount of fluids in her, and got her proper rest. NiNi was trying her best to tell her, but Neosha had failed her in so many ways.

Neosha couldn't take it anymore. She began to get dizzy, and her vision doubled. Her chest started to hurt, and she grabbed it hoping it would ease the pain. She fell against the wall reaching out for help as her vision became blurry; it seemed as if no one was helping her. She couldn't blame them because in so little words NiNi was reaching out for help and she never bothered to listen to her daughter's silent cries. Neosha collapsed to the floor, and everything went black. The pain in her chest got worse as she took what felt like her last breath.

"Oh my god! Onyae, call 9-1-1!" Yoshi shouted.

She dropped to the floor and shook Neosha with fervor. Kick Down hopped over Damon's body and kneeled down to pick his sister up.

"Fuck that, I'll take her myself," he said. He stepped over Damon's body once more to exit the house.

"Onyae, get NiNi and come to the hospital in my car. Get her now, and don't waste any time!" Yoshi yelled.

Onyae had her hand over her mouth with tears running down her face. She never intended for her auntie to be so affected over what happened. Knowing that the situation might've cost her aunt her life, broke her.

"Onyae, I need you to be strong. You hear me? I need you to be strong!" Yoshi said firmly before leaving out.

NiNi who was afraid the entire time finally came out of the room once she heard all of the commotion stop. She opened the door and ran right into Onyae, and Onyae hugged her as soon as she opened the door.

"We gotta go, sis," she cried.

"Where?" NiNi asked.

She didn't see Damon's body on the hallway floor because she hadn't come all the way out of the bedroom.

"It's Auntie. She passed out, and…and I don't know what's wrong with her. We gotta go, we gotta go now." Onyae finally stopped hugging her.

She grabbed NiNi's hand and pulled her out the bedroom; when she did, NiNi finally saw Damon's lifeless body lying there. She didn't ask any questions, nor did she care why he was lying there bloody. Her only concern was her mother; she'd get the full story on what went down later.

Chapter 27

NiNi sat in the emergency room of Vineland Hospital crying her eyes out as she waited to hear how her mother was doing. Although she was beaten and battered, her mother was still her main concern. A nurse came out and asked her if she wanted to be checked out, but she declined. NiNi's face was swollen, and the few people that were in the waiting area gawked at her.

"What the fuck is yawl lookin' at?" Onyae scoffed.

They quickly turned their heads and tended to their own business like they should have been doing from the beginning.

"NiNi, can you please talk to me? I'm sorry for puttin' so much stress on ya mother, but when I found out what that muthafucka was doin' to you, I couldn't sit back and let it go down," Kick Down explained.

He was hurting for his niece and his sister. He never meant for things to go down the way they did, but his natural instincts told him to protect his niece; something they all should've done.

"I'm not mad at you, Uncle Kick Down. Thank you if anything. I just want my mother to be okay. She's suffered so much, and without her I'm nothing." She cried.

Both Yoshi and Onyae rushed to hug NiNi. The situation was worse than what they thought. NiNi had been through a lot and they feared that losing her mother would be the thing that finally broke her.

"You got us, NiNi, you got us." Onyae whimpered.

"I know, I know."

Yoshi pulled away from NiNi and pulled Kick Down to the side. There was a lot that needed to be said; the car ride to the hospital had her mind roaming. She felt like now was the best time to get things out instead of waiting for things to simmer down before she touched basis on NiNi's situation.

"Wassup, sis?" he asked.

He could see that more than this situation was bothering her, and he wanted to know what was up just in case he had to put hands on another nigga or bitch.

"Whatever the outcome is with Neosha, I want NiNi to come live with me," she told him.

"Sis, that nigga ain't gon' be there. My niece is gon' be A-OK. All I'm worried about right now is makin' sure Neosha is good."

Yoshi pursed her lips, shook her head, and waved Kick Down off.

"It ain't as simple as you think, Kick Down. This shit has been goin' on for years, and my niece is damaged. I can't let her go back to that house. Now, if Neosha makes it out of this, then she can come too, but I refuse to let my niece live in that hell hole for another day. I knew I didn't like that nigga for a reason."

"What do you mean this has been goin' on for years?" he asked, as he cocked his head to the side.

"KD, Damon has been raping her since she was nine. She didn't say anything because he was supporting her and her mother, and then on top of that he started paying Neosha's medical bills once she was diagnosed with cancer."

Yoshi looked up at the ceiling and fanned her eyes to keep the tears in; she got emotional just speaking on the situation.

"Are you fuckin' serious? How you know this, man?" he asked.

"Onyae told me a little, but I know there's way more that I don't know. But I don't want to go at her asking her all types of questions. I know she can't handle that right now; however, I do want to get her checked because that nigga was a scandalous ass nigga."

Kick Down's nostrils were flared as he listened to what his sister told him. All he wanted to do was go back and stomp Damon's ass into his grave. Killing Damon just wasn't enough in his eyes. He felt like he should've tortured him for what he did to his niece because he was sure that NiNi was tortured for years. No one deserved to go through all the heartache NiNi encountered.

"She not gon' wanna do that, Yosh. I mean that girl been through enough, and I doubt if gettin' checked is on her mind."

"I don't care what's on her mind. I want her to get checked. Just in case. This has been going on for years, and

I know that NiNi ain't been to the doctors for anything serious cas' if she did then Neosha would've found out," Yoshi said to him.

"But what if she did find out? Man, what if she knew about this shit all along? I swear, I don't wanna think like that, but, Yosh, this shit is crazy. How she ain't know that this was goin' on wit' her daughter? Like, how the fuck she ain't know? I get that she had cancer and that she was on a lot of meds, but that's bullshit bein' that this shit has been goin' on since NiNi was nine. How the fuck she ain't know?" Kick Down got mad all over again.

Yoshi allowed a fresh batch of tears to fall from her eyes because that was also something she wondered, but she realized a long time ago that her and her sister didn't share the same strength. Granted, NiNi and Neosha had a beautiful bond like Yoshi and Onyae, but Yoshi could tell that since NiNi looked so much like her father there was a lot that Neosha blocked out when it came to NiNi. It wasn't an excuse, but Damon had Neosha mentally gone after she was already mentally abused by NiNi's father.

A nurse approached them again and suggested that NiNi get checked. She couldn't force her, but she was highly concerned for the young girl and knew that she needed to be checked out.

"NiNi, you need to go get checked, boo. I know you don't want to, but please do it for us. We just wanna make sure you're good, okay?" Onyae said.

Being that NiNi was beaten and also raped, they needed to run tests to make sure she was okay internally. She finally agreed; Onyae wanted to go back with her, but NiNi declined her as well as her aunt and uncle. She was already embarrassed enough, and she didn't want to be questioned if the doctor said anything out of the way. While she was in the back getting checked, Kick Down questioned Onyae more about what was going on and she told them all that she knew, and she no longer regretted it. It was a relief to Onyae to finally let the truth out knowing that NiNi would never have to go through any pain again. She prayed to God that Damon was dead and if he wasn't, she knew her uncle was going to make sure he was the next time he saw him.

An hour had passed as they sat in the waiting room, talking and trying to get to the bottom of things. NiNi came out of the room bawling as tears gushed down her face. Onyae stood up and rushed to her side before Yoshi or Kick Down could get out of their chairs to see what the problem was.

"What's wrong, NiNi?" she asked.

NiNi was snotting and snorkeling everywhere. She was shaking and crying uncontrollably.

"NiNi, please tell me what's wrong?" Onyae asked again.

"Baby, let us know what's going on," Yoshi spoke softly.

"NiNi, what happened back there?" Kick Down chimed in.

"I-I-I'm pregnant." She dropped down to the floor and screamed in horror. "I'm pregnant!"

Everyone looked towards them wondering what was going on. Nurses and a few doctors even ran out to see if everything was okay, but the look Kick Down gave them let them know not to come any farther.

"NiNi, it's okay, baby. We will get through this. We will get through this together," Yoshi proclaimed as she consoled her niece.

"Fuck no! I don't want this baby! I don't want this fuckin' baby! I want to get rid of it like I did with all the rest!" she screamed.

Yoshi, Onyae, and Kick Down had no words. It was at that moment, they realized just how much NiNi had gone through. They didn't need for her to explain to them what she was talking about. It was clear that she meant that she had been pregnant plenty of times before and she had aborted them all. They wondered just how many more secrets she kept within.

To Be Continued. . .

Connect with Author Reds Johnson

Facebook:

Anne Marie Johnson

Facebook Like Page:

Author Reds Johnson

Facebook Readers Group:

Booked & Bossy

Promo Group

The Queen & Her Crew Promos

Twitter:

@ISlayBooks

Instagram:

Reds Johnson

Fashion Line Instagram:

Tilted__Crowns

Website:

www.iamredsjohnson.com

Amazon Author Page:

Reds Johnson

AUTHOR BIO

Reds Johnson, is twenty-six-years-old. She was born and raised in New Jersey. She started writing at the age of nine years old, and ever since then, writing has been her passion. Her inspirations were Danielle Santiago, and Wahida Clark.

Not only is she an indie author, but she's also an author under Wahida Clark Presents. She's known for her Silver Platter Hoe series, and after five years in the literary industry she's 40 plus books in the game.

She writes with such passion, and originality. The stories she writes hit so close to home for many. You can find Reds writing in the following genres: urban, romance, erotica, bbw, and teen stories and each book she's penned is based on true events; whether she's been through it or witnessed it.

CPSIA information can be obtained
at www.ICGtesting.com
Printed in the USA
LVHW031503241220
675096LV00002B/202